The Fighting Chance

Book Two of
The Human Race

Tahnee Fritz

For Mom

Part One

"And another one bites the dust!" I exclaim as the blast from the gunshot fills my ears.

The zombie falls to the ground in a puddle of its blood. The brown stuff sprays out from the wound on his head and is currently painting the green grass. It's the fourth one I've killed today and the sixth counting the two my partner took down. Yet another good day as we sit perched about five feet above the ground in our little watch tower outside the city.

Yes, I still live in Des Moines. It's been a little over a year now and I don't see things changing. This place is pretty awesome, especially when you're quick to make a name for yourself. Which is exactly what I did. Living a monotonous life, doing the same thing day after day just isn't my cup of tea. So, I did what I do best and made sure zombie killing stays in my repertoire. Good thing there was plenty of room on the security force and even more room for ideas on how to keep this place safe.

"Nice shot, Bridget." My partner, Keith, states with a hint of admiration to his voice, "You always hit them right above the eyes."

Keith is an older man I met before I joined the security. He used to be a veterinarian and chose to kill zombies and vamps instead of picking up where he left off when he got here. He's just one member of my little team out here on the exciting side of the wall. There are twelve other towers, each with a team of their own. There are three towers to each half mile surrounding the city and two people to a tower. The project isn't complete yet, but the city is hard at work on getting it there.

The towers weren't my idea, but I am in charge of my team. Dwayne is the mastermind behind it all. He came up with this idea about six months ago when a horde of over a hundred zombies charged the wall. They never got through, but the government in the city has been afraid of that happening ever since. Dwayne proposed the idea and within minutes it was approved. Naturally, he came to me to head up a team and we take the first shift of the day and another team comes out in the afternoon and stays till dusk. We don't keep people out here when the vamps are hunting. The patrolmen on top of the wall take care of those things.

I take a drink of my water and stare out to the woods in front of our tower. Not a day goes by that we don't see at least one zombie. It might take a little while for them to show their ugly faces, but we always get a shot in. I get to share the fun of killing these things with five others who take just as much pride in doing this job as I do. That is the main reason I picked them to be part of my group. Since the towers aren't finished, there are only three other teams during this shift and, yes, we do have a little contest each week to see which group kills the most zombies. The winners get the weekend off.

The trees in front of us are quiet right now. That last zombie was the first one we've seen in a couple hours. There is not much time left in our shift, then we'll be walking back to the gate and heading home. Vehicles and ATVs aren't allowed on this side of the wall. Someone learned the hard way that the noise from the engine attracts zombies and it's harder to aim when you're trying to steer.

"Got big plans for the night?" Keith asks as he checks how much ammo is left in his shotgun.

I shrug and put the cap on my bottle of water, "Don't know yet. Other than dinner and hanging out with Ryder."

"My wife is making her famous chicken casserole tonight. I say famous because this is the fourth time in the last two weeks that she's cooked it." Keith jokes.

He's been married since before the zombies and vampires took over. His whole family, wife and two kids, survived the journey to get here. They've even managed to keep their dog the entire time. Ryder and I have been invited over for dinner with his family on a few occasions and they are great. The kind of family I used to have. One filled with love and laughter and other amazing feelings only a family can give. I met Keith a few days after his family made it here. When the horde came to the wall, he was one of the first people to jump in line when I asked who'd be willing to step outside the gate and take the zombies down. He's a pretty good shot and isn't afraid of much anymore. *Just like me.*

Carter is another member of my team. I didn't really choose him, he sort of told me that he was doing this to make sure I don't get myself killed. He became one of Ryder's closest friends over the last year and has promised him to keep an eye on me while we're out here. That and it's really nice to have an old friend on my team.

Speaking of old friends, I have to pay a visit to my dear friend, Sherry. I see her all the time, but she insists on me coming over at least every night. She lives in the house next door to mine, sharing it with her father, her cousin Dillon, and Seth. Oh, and I can't leave out the newest addition to her little family, her son Isaac. Ever since we left Hatfeld, she and Seth really hit it off and got *busy* when they got comfortable. One thing lead to another and baby Isaac was born. He's a cute kid with his daddy's looks and his mother's personality. I can't wait to see what that'll be like when he gets older.

Ryder and I share our small house with Carter who made up the basement as his own so we could have the entire second floor of the house to ourselves. There's a black cat who made a home with us as well. She comes and goes whenever she pleases because Ryder doesn't have the heart to turn an animal aside. At least he let me name it. Vambie seems to suit the little demon just fine. Other than the mice and birds she brings home, I'm sure she would love to make a meal out of my hands and legs sometimes. She bites me every day, so naming her a mixture of the two monsters I hate the most seemed right.

A slight breeze blows through the area sending chills up my spine. It's that time of year when the temperature starts to drop. The days are getting shorter and snow will cover the ground soon. Compared to what I've gone through in the past, winter here is nothing. I get to stay indoors with heat and hot soup instead of fighting the cold and walking through it. I will have to do my job out here in the towers, but I'm sure we'll have snow days every once in a while.

I take a deep breath through my nose, smelling anything that could be coming near us. This gift of mine is another reason I'm so popular amongst the security force. It has saved quite a few lives and others have started looking to me when things don't seem right. It still has yet to fail me.

"Smell anything?" Keith asks.

I shake my head and say, "Other than the few lying out there, not a thing. Zombies must be getting scarce today."

Keith smiles, "Good. Making it home in one piece is always a blessing."

I shrug, "Yeah, but it's much more exciting when we see more than a few."

"Of course the magnificent Bridget would say that." He jokes.

I shrug, "I am known to be a bit crazy. If you ask Ryder, he'll tell you all about it."

"I have before." Keith replies. "It is quite amazing listening to your story of survival. Other than the crappy parts, I mean."

"I know. I do enjoy reliving some parts of my journey to this point in my life. Mainly after I met Ryder and saved his ass a few times. Life got even better from that point on." I reply.

Keith nodded, "Life got better when I got to Des Moines. No more fighting for food or killing off zombies and vamps. We still do, but this is easier. I don't have to worry about my kids getting attacked or eaten or starving to death anymore. That and I have a home here. It's great knowing I'll have a place to sleep from now on."

I shrug, "I didn't mind sleeping under the stars or in a random building somewhere. I'm just glad I get to make a difference in this place."

Other than Ryder and my few friends being here, that's my favorite part about the city. I can live with the rules and put up with the people that annoy me. As long as I still get to make a difference in the outcome of the human race, I don't care where I am. Having humans survive what's left of the world is the most important thing. Being part of the reason why we're surviving adds icing to the cake.

* * *

I get home around dinnertime and the sky is slowly getting dark. It takes a little while to walk from the gate, even longer when I talk with some of the others on the security force. We had to tally up our zombie death toll and I'm proud to say that my team is ahead by three zombies. One more day to go and I'll be relaxing this weekend. If things go right, it'll be the third week in a row where my teams wins. We're just that good.

I walk through the front door of the two-story house and smell meat cooking on the stove in the kitchen. Ryder works for one of the construction crews in the city, building houses and expanding the living quarters here. He normally gets home after I do, but sometimes he gets here early and starts cooking. Thanks to Carter for giving him some lessons, he's gotten quite good at it. I've had many great dinners here due to their cooking.

Our house isn't very impressive. It's just like most of the small houses in the city. Two bedrooms on the second floor with a full bathroom. In the living room, there is a flat screen TV hanging on the wall. We don't have cable, no one does, but we have plenty of movies to choose from. Most of the time we lounge around and talk about things. It's rare for us to turn the *boob tube* on. The kitchen is small as well, with the normal appliances you'd see in a kitchen. There's another full bathroom right before turning to get to the basement stairs on the other side of the kitchen. Carter fixed the basement up as his own little apartment and we never venture down there.

I shut the front door and walk through the living room, "That smells amazing." I say as I make my way to the kitchen.

Ryder glances over his shoulder and tosses me a smile, "Thanks, babe. How was your day?"

I shrug as I sit at the table set for three and say, "Eh, same as always. Killed some zombies, bullshit with Keith, then walked home. How was yours?"

"Kind of boring. The house we're working on is having issues so we all got off early. I went to the store and picked up a few things, then went to Seth's. Isaac started bawling, figured that was my cue to leave."

I let out a slight chuckle, "That kid has quite the voice on him. He'll be just like his mom."

He flips a piece of chicken over in the frying pan and it simmers, letting steam rise to the ceiling. I used to feel bad about having Ryder cook our meals all the time. That is until I tried making supper one night and it turned out very badly. I'm not even sure how I messed this meal up, seeing as how it was soup and all, but I did and I've never cooked since. Not that anyone's complaining about it.

The front door to the house opens and I recognize Carter's heavy footsteps. I can hear him kicking his boots off before walking through the living room and into the kitchen. I've noticed over the last year that he's kind of a neat freak. He likes to have a clean house and hates when things get left lying around. You'd think for a big guy like him, he'd be a lot less into cleaning and more into kicking some ass, but he's just different.

Carter walks to the fridge and takes out a few bottles of water. He sets each one on the table then sits in the chair across from me. After taking a big swig of the cool liquid, he shakes his head in disgust.

"God, I miss beer." He says.

Des Moines is a dry city. Alcohol and tobacco are *very* strictly forbidden. People don't need to be contributing to the problems of the world. Also, those two things can really affect your judgment if you're face to face with one of the monsters.

"You'll get over it." Ryder says.

"I don't know, man. Before all this, I could drink a six pack like it was nothing." Carter replies.

"Never had the opportunity to touch the stuff and I probably never will." Ryder adds in. "Although, my foster parents probably bled beer and whiskey."

Carter laughs, taking another drink of water.

Just like Ryder, I've never had a taste of alcohol. My

parents only drank when they went out for dinner on date night. Dad never wanted that sort of thing in the house in case one of us kids decided to try a sip. He hated getting mad at us whenever we did something wrong, I could only imagine how much that would tear him apart if one of us got drunk.

The familiar click of the dial on the stove catches my attention. Ryder is taking the frying pan off the burner and heads for the table. He dishes us each a decent sized chicken breast, then goes back to the stove. From the oven, he takes out a tray of bread then comes back and dishes us each a slice. Finally, he sits down next to me and takes my hand.

Another thing that I've had to get used to about Carter, is that he is a *really* religious man. He goes to church service every Sunday morning, refusing to go to work until he's done. He tries not to shove it in our faces about going with him or forcing us to see things his way. As long as we do one thing for him each night, he leaves us alone about it.

He takes Ryder's free hand and reaches for mine. I reluctantly reach across the table and let him wrap his fingers around my hand, then he bows his head and closes his eyes.

"Dear lord, we thank you for another day on this planet. Another day of getting to survive when hell is on our door-step. We thank you for this meal we are about to eat and for the opportunity of having food at our disposal. We pray that you help more humans find this city so they can have the same blessings we have been given. Thank you, lord, amen." Carter lets go of our hands and lifts his head.

I might not be very religious or keen on the whole *God* idea, but Carter sure is good at saying grace. Ryder's done it a few times and I was made to try it once. I failed and things got a little tense at the table, but at least I tried. It's just too hard to thank a mythical man in the sky who's responsible for all the bad things happening to the humans. I probably shouldn't have said my grace sarcastically that night, but I never have to do it again.

I count that as a plus in my book.

I take a bite of chicken, letting the flavor caress my taste-buds. I still can't get used to eating this good every night. Having a home-cooked meal was rare for me before we came to Des Moines and I'm really trying not to take it for granted. I know things could go to hell at any minute. Vamps could find a way in or zombies could break through and this will all be a distant memory. I don't really want to go back to search-ing or begging for food each and every day. Hoping I'll find some tiny morsel to fulfill my stomach's demands. I spent five years living like that and it's one of the few things I don't miss.

"Oh, Bridge," Ryder says, after swallowing the food in his mouth, "Sherry wants you to come over tonight."

I nod, "I know. She's been hassling me to come over for a while."

"Why don't you?" Carter asks.

I shrug, "I don't know. She has too many other girls hang-ing out with her all the time."

"Yeah, they're called friends. You should try it some-time." Ryder says.

"I have friends." I retort.

Carter shakes his head, taking Ryder's side in the argu-ment I know I'm going to lose, "The others on our zombie task force don't count. You need actual friends to hang out with *outside* of work."

"I'm sure those other girls Sherry has over aren't so bad." Ryder adds.

I don't know about all that. I used to be great at making friends with anybody. As long as they were nice to me, it didn't matter who they were or what their social status was. The girls in *this* city aren't like the ones I went to school with. Most of them have lived here their whole lives and have never set foot outside the wall since it was built. They talk about having a great life and starting a family and having babies. They're happy living an old-fashioned life where they stay home and the man goes out and does things.

I don't fit in with that type of lifestyle. I live for the adventure of life outside the wall. I look forward to waking up in the morning to go to work and do what I'm best at. They don't understand me and none of them care to. It's much easier keeping my friendship circle to those who share a similar interest as I do. The men and women on the security force and the other teams out in the towers defending the wall, are great friends in my opinion. They know exactly what I've gone through in life and many, if not all, of them can relate to my story.

I take another bite of chicken. Their stares are starting to get distracting and a little awkward. It has been a few minutes since any of us has said anything and I know they want me to say the next thing. It wouldn't be so bad to hang out with Sherry for a little bit tonight. I can't lie, I hope it will just be the two of us. I know I'm wrong because she normally has her other two best friends with her all the time. They live across the street from us so it's easy for them to come over whenever they want.

"I guess I'll go over there after supper. I'm not promising I'll stay forever, but if it'll get you two off my back about having friends." I finally say.

Ryder smiles with food in his mouth and says, "Good."

"Yeah, you can't lose the only girl friend you have in this place." Carter adds.

I roll my eyes and rip off a small piece of my bread. I never thought living with two guys would be this annoying. The world didn't prepare me for this sort of thing.

* * *

A little over an hour after supper and I find myself sitting on a recliner in Sherry's living room. Ryder and Carter came along with me and are currently playing pool in the basement with Seth and Jim. Us girls are left alone in the living room to gab about whatever goes on in this city. I wish I could say it was just the two of us. I mean I *really* wish I could say that. There are just three other girls sitting on the couch beside Sherry and Isaac talking their lives away.

I know the girls Sherry has chosen to surround herself with. The red head, Jessica, she's pretty nice. She's the only person I can relate to in the slightest. Her family came here right after the wall was built and haven't left. The girl sitting next to her is stockier with a chubby face and long, black hair. Her name in Claire and likes to eat *way* too much. I'm not saying that to be mean or anything, but it's true. Every time I see her, she's got some form of food in her mouth. Right now, she's the only one eating a pretty big slice of apple pie while the rest of us haven't touch the stuff. The third girl, sitting on the other side of Sherry, is someone I absolutely cannot stand.

Every time I run into this girl, she gives me the dirtiest looks and keeps walking. Her name is Mandy. She never has anything nice to say to me, but really tries to be nice when we're with Sherry. She'll say hello to me in a snotty tone of voice and avoid me for the rest of the time. But, when Ryder comes around, I'm completely nonexistent. I've seen her check him out on many occasions. She'll eyeball him like he's a piece of candy and loves doing it while I'm around. I know he's handsome and I know other girls probably check him out. Mandy is just the only one who does it to piss me off and she loves doing that.

Right now, Mandy hasn't paid me any attention. She's too busy ogling baby Isaac and listening to Sherry go on and on about how hard it is to sleep at night. The same boring things I've heard about a million times. I haven't really been paying too much attention to what those girls are talking about. I find that if it doesn't have anything to do with something exciting or newsworthy, I kind of don't listen. I smile and nod at whatever they say, but adding to the conversation is definitely not something I'm going to do. These girls never talk about zombies or vamps or adventures, so I'm pretty quiet on these little get-togethers.

"I just can't believe how much he cries overnight. I figured he would for the first couple weeks, but he's two months old and he still won't stop." Sherry says and I twirl my bangs around my finger.

"My mom said that most babies cry at night until their potty trained, if not longer." Claire adds in and I toss a lose strand of hair to the floor.

"My little sister never cried at night. Mom and dad had to go in and check on her every once in a while to make sure she was still breathing." Jessica states and I let out a yawn.

Sherry smiles, "Yeah, I'll just have to get used to it. Seth can sleep right through the crying, but I wake up every time. I'll feed him and change his diaper and he falls right back to sleep, but then the crying starts again in an hour."

"Okay, so enough about babies." Mandy speaks up and they all look her way. "Let's change the subject. Jess, I hear you have a new boyfriend."

Jessica's cheeks instantly blush, matching the color of her hair, "Yeah, his name is Luke. He's pretty amazing. We met at my dad's café."

"Oh, that is so great!" Sherry says with a smile.

"Yeah, I wish I had a great guy." Claire states.

"Is he hot?" Mandy asks.

Jessica runs her fingers through her hair and says, "He is pretty good looking. A little nerdy with his big glasses, but I like that."

"Boring." Mandy says, "I hate nerds or guys with glasses. I'm more into the hot, shy ones with the messy brown hair. A guy who could really take care of his girl." She sort of gives me a sly smile and I know who she's talking about.

"Well, every girl on the planet wants that kind of guy. We just have to find the one we know we don't want to live without and make him ours." Sherry states. "I found mine."

Mandy runs her fingers through her bleach-blonde hair and says, "I found one. I'm just trying to work on making him mine. He just has a girlfriend right now and I need to eliminate that problem." Definitely a snide look being passed my way.

Girls can be so petty and mean when they're jealous. Mandy would never have a chance with Ryder, even if they were the last two people on the planet. I know him and I know he doesn't go for girls who are demanding or whiny when they don't get their way. He likes the girls who can do things for themselves and save his ass on more than one occasion. That's why he loves me and I love him right back.

So, it's a little natural for me to laugh at her attempt at making me feel threatened. I can't help but let the smile cross my lips and shake my head at her. I've gone through too much in my life to let this girl get on my nerves.

"What are you so smiley about?" Mandy snarls at me.

I shrug, "Oh, I'm just having a *great* night. I love hearing about how much you want a guy in your life. Makes me so glad I have Ryder and I'm never letting him go."

"Bridget without Ryder," Sherry sighs, "I think the world would come to a screeching halt if that ever happens."

I nod, "Heads would probably roll at that point."

Sherry knows there's an odd amount of tension between Mandy and I. She's pretty good at handling it and always takes my side. I don't even know what happened to get that girl to hate me so much. I don't care to find out, but it's just weird how people can be like that.

"Oh, I doubt it." Mandy states.

It's very rare for me to ever want someone to be a zombie or a vampire. I'm not supposed to wish that sort of thing on humans. Mandy is an exception. If she were a zombie, I'd get to have the pleasure of shooting her in the head and feeling great about it. If she were a vamp, I could torture her and let her boil to death in the sunlight. Either way would be a win in my corner. I know that's horrible to think about. She just brings that part out in me.

Sherry is quick to change the subject again. Isaac squirms a bit in her arms and she lets the other two girls help make him smile. They enjoy it and go about tickling his tummy and making baby sounds at him. It's easier for me to sit back, relax with my feet dangling over the arm of the recliner and secretly wish Mandy would be lying on the floor in agony right now. She's staring daggers at me so I deserve the right to think horrible thoughts about her.

I'm still a little crazy and demented when it comes to certain things. Living on the outside of the wall for five years will do that to ya.

* * *

I guess the night could have gone worse. Spending time with Sherry wasn't too horrible, even though they talked about Isaac and passed him around the room the whole night. I've never held a baby before Sherry had him, so it was quite awkward to hold that little boy. I had no idea what to do and he screamed at the top of his lungs the second my hands touched him. That's why it's best not to have those little things. It's easier to give them back when they belong to someone else.

The sun set about two hours ago. This city has a strict nine o'clock curfew so we had to head home about that time. Sherry gave me one of her infamous bear hugs before we walked the short distance to our house, then up the short flight of stairs to our bedroom. Carter disappeared into the basement and closed the door behind him.

There's one thing I love most about this house and that would have to be our bedroom. It's nothing too spectacular, just a king sized bed and a dresser Ryder and I have to share. There is a walk-in closet, which is nice, and the bathroom connects to this room as well. The reason I love this room the most, is that it's part of a normal life I thought I'd never have again. I got so used to sleeping under the stars or in the back of some random vehicle or in a building somewhere. This room and the bed I sleep in every night is probably one of the best things there is to a person like me.

Other than Ryder, of course.

I kick my boots off at the foot of the bed and change into my shorts and tank top pajamas. Ryder sleeps with only a pair of black sweatpants on, which I have no complaint about *at all*. I love seeing him without a shirt on. It's hard not to stare sometimes and he laughs every time he catches me making googly eyes at him. I can't help that I love seeing his stomach and chest and even that annoying little scar on his shoulder. It might be a reminder of something horrible, but to me, it's a reminder of the night I fell for him. If he hadn't shown me that scar, we might not be here today, so yes, I enjoy seeing it with the added bonus of everything else he hides under his shirt.

Ryder climbs into bed first as I flip the light switch off and get under the covers. The only light comes from the moon shining through the crack in the curtains on the window facing the backyard. I forgot how nice it was to sleep without a light on until we started staying at this house. I got so used to always having a fire going that it became natural. I even fell asleep with the overhead light on the first few nights after we got here. It just took a little while to get used to things in the city.

I still find myself trying to get used to some things.

"Looking forward to work tomorrow, Bridge?" Ryder asks, covering himself up with the blanket.

I nod, "I don't think you can call what I do work when I enjoy it so much."

He smiles and says, "Wish I could say the same."

"I thought you liked doing that construction stuff." I question.

He shrugs, "I do, it was just never my dream job."

"Yeah, I get that, but you are doing something that contributes to the community here and that's pretty important." I reply.

"You are right about that." He says, I can hear bitterness to his voice.

"There's something else though, isn't there?"

Ryder sighs as he turns to face me, "Do you ever miss the way things used to be? Like before we got to the city, not before the vamps and zombies?"

"Well, yeah, I think you'd be a little crazy not to miss *some* things out there." I reply. "Why?

"No reason."

I roll onto my side and stare at him. He's not normally the one who starts talking about things outside the wall or our life as travelers. This life in the city was something he's always dreamed of having and he couldn't stop talking about it for weeks after we got here. It has been slightly over a year now, but he shouldn't be changing his mind about this place already.

"Ryder, what's wrong?" I ask. "You aren't normally this down in the dumps."

He tries to pass me a meaningful smile, but I can see right through it, "I don't know what's wrong. I love it here, I really do, but I just wish it was more than this. I wish it was more than just waking up in the morning and going to work every day. I miss the changes that came with being on the outside and I guess I thought that after a year of living here, I would start to see that again. I was wrong."

I shake my head, "You're not wrong. You do different things all the time. You build houses and give people the opportunity to start a new life here."

"I guess I do." He says with a smile.

"See, there's no reason to try searching for a different calling in this place. You found something that really makes a difference in peoples' lives and that matters to the world." I say, hoping anything that's coming from my mouth helps. "Unless you really want to change things up a bit. Keith and I would *love* to have you help us outside the wall. I know how much you *enjoy* doing that."

He shakes his head and quickly says, "No. Carter tells me all the horror stories that goes on out there and I'd rather not be a witness to that. It's bad enough that I have to worry about you being out there when those things show up. I'm not that good with a gun, so it's best I stay on this side of the wall."

I give him a playful punch to the arm and say, "You don't have to worry about me. I know what I'm doing out there no matter what Carter likes to tell you."

He leans over and kisses me, "I know I never have to worry about you. It's one of the things I love the most. Other than your craziness. Nothing tops that."

I smile and give him a little kiss right back. I put my hand on the back of his neck and he scoots closer to me on the bed. Our bodies touch and he drapes one of his legs over mine and rubs my back with his hand. This is another thing I love the most about this bedroom of ours. I get to have as many intimate moments with Ryder as I possibly want.

Those moments never get old.

* * *

Ryder and I slept like rocks throughout the night and woke up refreshed in the morning. We ate a nice breakfast of bacon and eggs, then we were off to work. He walked with Seth to the job site, while Carter and I piled in the truck that takes us to the gate. That was a couple hours ago.

It's been quiet out here so far. The birds aren't even chirping this morning. That might have something to do with how drizzly and dreary it is. The clouds threaten rain, which I really hope it holds back. We have a roof over our heads in the tower, but it does leak in a few places. On days I wear my hair down, like today, I'd rather not get soaked to the bone.

Keith sits on the stool beside me and snacks on bread for lunch. The whole morning dragged by ever so slowly. No zombies, no vamps wanting to be brave, and no humans looking for a new home. If it weren't for the people in the other towers, I'd feel completely alone out here. Good thing I have Keith to talk to in order to drown out the constant quiet of the woods.

"How was your evening?" he asks as I sit on my stool and look out to the trees.

I shrug, "Not too bad. Went to a friends, got to piss some girl off, then chilled with Ryder until we fell asleep."

"More productive than my night. The wife had me help her clean the house and I hate doing that." He says.

I smile, "You can borrow Carter for a day or two. He's really good at cleaning our house and I'm sure he'd love to help with yours."

Keith laughs and takes a drink of water, "You think today's going to have any excitement?"

"Doubt it. Haven't had much of that all week." I reply.

We could go a few days without seeing a single zombie out here. I guess that's a good thing. Zombies are running thin around the wall allowing us the opportunity to be safe for a while. Until we see the next horde coming our way. We're prepared for it this time. We have the manpower, the gun power, and the mind strength to do what we need to get those things away from our home. Humans live here, zombies and vampires can find a new place to bother.

I guess they don't want to leave us alone today. The faint sound of a gunshot shoots through my ears and I turn my head toward the sound. It's coming from a different team. Hopefully that's the only zombie they see so I won't have to worry about anything today. Keith and I stay quiet for a few minutes, our guns clenched tight in our grip. I keep my eyes peeled for any movement in the trees while he searches the area around us. That single gunshot is all we hear while we wait, so we can relax again.

Keith takes a deep breath, "Wonder who got that one."

I shrug, "We'll find out when we get back."

He nods then drinks more of his water. It still feels too quiet and uncomfortable to be out here. I hate when it's like this. The world is practically begging for something bad to happen to us while we are out here, almost helpless, in a world with undead creatures waiting to eat us. That's not exactly fair if you ask me.

I sit on my stool and rest the gun on my lap. I stare down at the metal in my hands. This thing has saved my life on so many occasions and is my favorite reminder of my dad. This gun was the last thing he was able to get for me and I'm really surprised I've been able to keep it in such good condition. It has yet to fail me, meaning I have yet to fail my family.

I'm still alive after all this time without them. My heart

still beats in my chest, I can feel it right now. The lump still forms in my throat when I think about them and picture them in my head. I would love to have them here in Des Moines with me. That would complete my dream life. Having Ryder *and* my family all together so we can be happy. My mom would hate me for coming out here and doing this every day, but she'd get over it. I think Charlie and dad would even join me and we could take down zombies as one big, happy family.

"Bridget," Keith's calm voice interrupts my thoughts, "you alright over there?"

I nod, "Just thinking."

"I've been told that thinking is bad for you." He says and I finally look up.

"You need to quit listening to what Ryder says. He's not always right, ya know." I say.

He shakes his head, "He's been right about things before."

I roll my eyes and take a deep breath through my nose. The cool air fills my lungs as something else warns my mind, erasing my family from my thoughts. I get up from the stool and stare out to the trees. There's something out there. That smell has never proven me wrong and I'll be damned if I start getting it wrong now. That horrid, dead stench is the only gift I've ever been thankful for in this world.

"You smell them, don't ya?" Keith asks, standing from his stool as well.

"Help! Somebody help us!" both of us hear the calls coming from the woods and I'm the first to jump out of the tower.

That was a human voice we heard and they are probably being chased by the dead thing I'm smelling. Keith follows me and gets out of the tower as well. I hear the voice again, this time it's closer and I can tell it's coming from a man. There's sheer panic to his voice as he calls for help and I'm hoping we are able to give that to him. This is the first human we've seen in a few weeks and the first we've had to save from zombies since we started this tower thing.

"Keith, radio the others and tell them to be on alert." I order and head for the sound of the voice.

He nods and goes about with his task. A set of heavy footsteps rushes up behind me and I feel a hand on my shoulder. I turn, only to catch eyes with Carter and his gun.

"You heard that man too?" he asks.

I nod and sniff the air again. The dead smell is stronger than before and more intense. There's more than just one of those things heading our way and we might actually have a problem. I keep my gun clenched in my grip and walk a few more steps toward the sound of the voice. He calls out again and I hear a female voice along with his. Their running footsteps come next as they trod over dead leaves in their path.

"There!" Carter shouts and points.

Through the trees, I can see them. A family with two very young children. A baby in the mother's arms and a toddler in the father's. They are running as fast as they can, trying not to look back at the group of zombies chasing after them. Carter shouts at them to come our way and the father spots him and obeys.

The rest of my team joins us, readying their guns and weapons. I run my fingers through my hair and prepare myself for this mini war we are about to rage upon the oncoming zombies. I can't tell how many there are, but by the sounds of the groans, there's more than just a few. They stammer through the woods, some bumping against the trees and tripping over their feet. They move fast, catching up with the family they're after.

"Oh thank god, help us, please." The father pleads as he approaches us.

"Get behind us and stay down." Carter orders.

The family gets as close to the wall as possible and crouches low to the ground. The baby and the little girl are sobbing loudly, blending in with the moans coming from the zombies. My team lines up in a row and we wait for the monsters to get out of the tree line. We'd be wasting our bullets by firing randomly, hoping to land in the skull of a zombie. The five other people with me are the best I could have chosen and they know exactly what to do.

There's Carla, another badass much like myself. Before she came here, she actually used to hunt the vampires at night just for the thrill of it. Then there's Dennis and Pete. They're best friends who lost everything together a few days before they found this place. They've known each other forever and were ready to die until they stumbled upon the giant wall of the city. And of course we already know Carter and Keith. They just add to this awesome team of mine.

My heart pounds a little faster in my chest. I'm not afraid of how many zombies are coming at us. This sounds crazy, but I'm excited about encountering this many. I can see about fifteen of those stumbling bastards and it's been awhile since we've seen a group like this.

The first one comes lumbering out of the tree line, twenty feet to go and he'd be right on top of us. I step out in front of my group and aim the gun in my hand. I let my index finger squeeze the trigger and the bullet shoots out, making a crater in the skull of the zombie. His brown blood sprays through the air, adding to the misty rain coming from the sky. His friends walk all over him as they keep coming at us. None of these zombies are hesitating. All of them have hunger burning in their eyes.

Two more shots are fired and two more zombies go down. They look like strings of spaghetti as their arms fly over their heads and go crashing to the grass at their feet. I take another shot, sending the bullet through the brain of a female with a scratch down the length of her face. She falls face first on top of another zombie.

"Is this the excitement you've been waiting for?" I hear Carter's voice ask me over the sound of gunshots.

I let the smile cross my lips and say, "A little bit. You gotta admit, you've been wanting something like this to come along too. You just don't show it like I do."

"No one shows anything like you do." He replies.

Three more go down, adding to the heap on the grass. Blood oozes from the wounds on their bodies, staining the grass a dark brown. The group of zombies is thinning and we're down to the last two standing. Well, one of them is climbing over her dead friends to get to us while the other one is standing. The woman doesn't bother me. I let Carla take her out. The bullet rips off a chunk of her skull and hair goes flying through the air. The one left standing, stares at me with a look in his eyes causing me to lower my gun.

"Don't shoot, guys." I order to my group and they lower their weapons.

I step away from my team, getting closer to the hesitant zombie. He's the first one like this that we've seen since we put up the watch towers. He's a younger man, probably my age, with black hair and a dark green t-shirt with blood around the collar. His eyes look sad as he stares at me. I can tell he's longing for something, a life he'll never have again. I don't know if his human self is in there somewhere, I'm kind of hoping it isn't. I couldn't imagine what that life would be like, knowing that you've killed dozens of humans by ripping them apart. I'd rather put the bullet in my own head if it came down to that.

I move closer to him, stopping just before the pile of dead zombies. He takes a step back and I raise an eyebrow out of confusion. I've seen the hesitant ones before. The ones that will stare at us, contemplating a nice meal or not. I've seen these creatures destroy themselves just to save a few humans who were faced with death by vampire. I've never seen a zombie look so sad, so depressed that he's actually stepping away from me.

"Can you understand me?" I ask, feeling like a fool for talking to a dead thing.

I stare at his lifeless black eyes, hoping for some hint that he can. His hands dangle at his sides, blood and grit caked under his fingernails. His jeans are ripped in one of the knees and various holes are scattered through the fabric. He blinks his eyes at me and takes another step backward.

I don't pay too close attention to zombies when I'm face to face with them like this. But, I swear to the man in the sky that I have never once seen one of them blink like that. I didn't think they even could do that anymore. Here this one is, slowly backing away from me, blinking his eyes like he understood what I said. If I wouldn't get shot for just thinking this, I would love to bring this zombie back with me and figure this whole thing out. There has to be a reason why they hesitate like this and someone needs to find out.

Why not me?

"Bridget," Keith calls from behind me, "you alright?"

I let this young zombie walk away from me and he disappears amongst the trees. He displayed something I can't comprehend and I'm not going to kill him for that. I run my fingers through my damp hair and turn around to face my team. Carla and Pete are busy tending to the family while Keith, Carter, and Dennis stare at me with awe on their faces.

I smile at them and say, "I'm great, never been better." I walk toward them, "Let's get these folks inside and checked over. I think I'm gonna call it for the day."

"You sure?" Dennis asks, "We still have a couple hours left."

I nod, "You guys can stay out if you want. I'm gonna go in with the family and make sure they're alright."

I join Carla and Pete as they help the mother in the family get to her feet. She's clutching her baby against her chest and refuses to let go of him. The father holds the little girl and follows me to the gate. They seem alright to me. No bite marks or scratches that I can see right off the bat. They are really shaken up and tense and afraid, but that'll pass.

This day might have started off a bore, but saving this

family really puts it over the top. Even if, by some random chance, my team didn't get the most zombies this week, we deserve the weekend off just for saving these few people. We don't get this very often.

* * *

I showed the family to a small doctor's office about a block from the gate. They were scanned and deemed free of infection of the undead kind. They've been given plenty of water and food to eat while they're being looked over. The baby even got fresh formula in a nice bottle and the little girl got a new dolly to play with. Dwayne is in the room with them, talking to the father about what happened and how they found this city. He says it's important for humans to know the way here. More will come that way.

My hands are shaking as I stand in the middle of the street and stare at the wall in front of me. I don't know why I feel nervous all of a sudden and I don't like it. This feeling doesn't mix well with me. Maybe it has something to do with killing all those zombies out there. I've run into plenty of monsters on my own, so being nervous about it seems a bit redundant to me. Maybe my mind is still wrapped around the hesitant one. I just can't figure out why he reacted after I asked him a question no zombie should be able to understand.

Those beasts are so frustrating anymore. Every time I think I have them figured out, they go and confuse me even more. This is already a tough life to live *without* the confusion of the vamps and zombies. I don't need anything else to drive me crazy.

A door opens to my right and I hear footsteps walking toward me. I quickly tuck my gun in my jeans behind my back and cover it up with my hoodie. I don't need to hide it, it's just a little awkward having it out when we aren't in danger.

"Excuse me?" I hear a man's voice and I turn my head to see the father of that family walking toward me.

I raise an eyebrow and say, "Yeah?"

He smiles as he stands next to me in the street, "What's your name?"

"Bridget."

"I'm Martin, my wife in there is Judy and our two kids, Abby and Taylor." He says with a smile.

"Nice to meet ya." I state.

He takes a deep breath, "You saved us out there. I thought for sure we were goners until we ran into your team."

I shrug, "That's why we're out there. We make sure people find this place and no zombies or vamps get through."

"We thought this place was just a rumor, but chose to check it out anyway. We want a new, safe life where those demons can't get to us." Martin says.

"Des Moines can give you that and more." I say.

"I can see that." He shoves his hands in his pants' pockets nervously, then continues, "I really came out here to thank you for helping us. I don't want to think of what could have happened if your group wasn't out there watching."

Another shrug, "You don't need to thank me. I enjoy what I do and saving you is an added benefit."

"You *enjoy* killing those things?"

"I know it's weird." I reply with a nod.

"How old are you?"

"Just turned twenty one, why?" I ask.

He shakes his head in disappointment, "You're too young to be enjoying this. You should be having fun with your friends and not killing those things out there."

Martin walks away from me before I can retort leaving me to feel even more confused about everything. I know I'm young and I know what I *should* be doing with my life. The world and the amazing cure kind of changed how things should be. Teenagers are out there roaming the streets, shooting whatever creature, human or not, that gets in their way of survival. Little children are forced to grow up wondering if they'll have a future or not. I was forced to watch my entire family die in front of me which took away a good majority of my future.

I can't have a normal life with normal friends anymore. My life didn't turn out the way it should have and I'm okay with that. I have all that I need right now. The love of the best man in the world, a friend who never wants to leave me alone sometimes, and the perfect job someone like me could ask for. Who cares if this isn't what I *should* be doing. This is what I *want* to be doing.

Dwayne walks through the door as Martin goes back inside to his family. I save him the trip of walking all the way to the middle of the street and meet him on the sidewalk outside the brick building. He has a gun tucked safely in a holster on his belt, one which he rarely uses. He never comes with us to the other side of the wall and enjoys sitting behind a desk with some of the other officers on the security force.

"Good job out there today." He says with a stern look on his face.

"Thanks."

"Tell me about this zombie that got away from you. That doesn't sound like the Bridget I know." He states.

I shake my head, "He didn't want to hurt any of us so I didn't want to kill him. No sense in wasting bullets on the hesitant ones."

"Sure," he says, unconvinced at what I said, "Martin and his wife told me where they came from and how they got here."

"Took them awhile. I've been standing out here for like an hour." I say, snidely.

He chuckles, "There's a village about a two day walk from here. Other humans are there trying to survive. They said there's not a lot of people, but they do have firepower and resources like food and water."

"Okay, that's good for them." I say.

"It's great others are surviving out there. They are travelers just like us, Bridget. They deserve a chance at getting a better life here in the city." Dwayne states.

"Yeah, what are you getting at?"

"I was talking to Carter in there. He thinks it might prove beneficial if we take a trip to this village and see how they're really living. Maybe try talking them into coming back with us. Tell them how they won't have to worry about zombies or vampires or anything." Dwayne says, "Des Moines will be good for them and they'll be good for this place."

I raise an eyebrow, "I guess that would be a smart thing to do. Anyone with a functioning brain would be all over the idea of living safely behind a fortified wall. Especially when I'm out there defending it every day."

Dwayne smiles and says, "That brings me to something I need to ask you. I want you on this expedition with me. You, Carter, Keith, the rest of your team. You guys are the best at what you do and we know you can keep us all safe. I trust you with my life and so does every other soul in this place. You're the best person to be right by my side, running the show out there."

Excuse me while I allow the small version of myself to jump up and down, screaming for joy in my head. I might not admit this to too many people, but I would *love* to spend a few nights on the road again. Reliving the life I used to have and getting to do things I love doing in the real world. Being a traveler was one of the most exciting things I've ever done in my life. Getting to do that again, even just for a few days, would be a dream come true.

There's just one thing that holds me back.

And I have no idea how I would explain this to him.

"Bridget?" Dwayne says, getting my attention again, "What do you say?"

I swallow hard, trying not to jump the gun on this decision, "You know I want to more than anything, I just can't say 'yes' without talking to Ryder first. If I do something like this and not let him know, that could destroy us."

Dwayne nods, "I understand that, but we kind of need an answer now."

"Why? When would we be leaving?" I ask.

"Sunday." A simple answer.

"That's soon."

He nods, "I know, but Mayor Whitmore is already being informed of this news. You know how he is when he knows other humans are out there. He'd want us to leave now if he knew that was possible."

I nod and take a deep breath. That Mayor is by far one of the most humane people I've ever met. He cares so much for humans and animals. If the zombies and vamps weren't trying to kill and eat us, he'd care about them as well.

Still, this is a big thing that I'd be doing. Risking my life for the off chance at convincing a few people to come back with us. That would be amazing and totally worth it if they chose to, but it's a long shot at getting travelers to do anything they aren't used to doing. One reason why I'm a little crazy at times.

I stare at Dwayne. He's patiently waiting for my answer.

"Ryder might kill me for this, but I'll do it. I'll come up with some way to explain to him why this needs to be done and I'm sure he'll understand." I say.

"He won't have anything to worry about. You're the bravest person I've ever met and you'll have myself and Carter to keep an eye out on ya as well." Dwayne says with a smile. "Just talk it over with him and we'll discuss this again tomorrow."

I sigh and nod my head. Dwayne goes back to the doctor's office and disappears inside. He's so good with people now. Encouraging them to do all they can to survive is sort of his thing. I guess my little speech in Hatfeld really stuck with him.

* * *

Ryder's home by the time I get there. I can see his shadow moving by one of the living room windows. I walk up the few, short steps to the porch and stare at the grey front door. The gold doorknob is old and faded and the lock is scratched up pretty bad. The window was spray painted black before the house was given to us. I assume the original owners did that when the cure's side effects took over. People were always doing strange things thinking it would help their chances. Maybe this worked, maybe it didn't. I'll never know.

I'm a little nervous to go inside. Ryder and I haven't really been apart, other than when we're working. We haven't gone an entire day without each other since we met. I don't really know how I'm going to explain to him that Dwayne wants me to leave for a few days that could possibly end up being forever. I know he'll be upset and probably not want me to go. *Hell*, I wouldn't want him to go if he were in my shoes. Then again, I'd probably go with him.

I let a sigh escape me as I grip the cold doorknob and turn it. There's a tiny squeak when the door swings open and again when I close it. I run my fingers through my hair, catching on a few snags. Ryder is busy trying to get the DVD player to work. He's not the greatest when it comes to that ancient machine. Half the time it doesn't want to turn on or the movie decides it doesn't want to play for us. It is getting pretty old and the movies are all used and worn out.

I smile when our eyes meet. He's banging the remote against the palm of his hand, cursing under his breath. How could I possibly leave this man? He's so funny and does all the right things. I know it will only be for a few days, but that's long enough for me to miss him already.

He stares at me for a moment, then says, "What are you thinking about?"

I shrug, "Nothing too much."

"Liar." He's great at detecting that. "What's up, babe?"

I inch my way over to him and take the remote from his hands. I toss it on the recliner in the corner of the room and wrap my arms around him. I close my eyes and lean my head against his shoulder. He enfolds me in his arms, letting me feel safe against his warm body. This is always the best place to be when I don't want to be in the real world.

"Did you have a bad day?" he asks.

I shake my head against him and say, "No, I just wanted to hug you."

He strokes my hair with one hand and rubs my back with the other. What is it about being in the arms of the only person on the planet you would die for that makes everything worthwhile? How can this small hug make what I have to tell him so much harder?

I'll never be done asking myself unanswerable questions, no matter how irritating they are.

"Bridget, you know I can tell when something's bothering you." He states, "You might as well tell me."

I open my eyes and pull myself away from him, "I do have something really important to tell you."

"Okay."

"We rescued a family today. A mom, dad, and their two really young children. They were being chased by a bunch of zombies and we were there to help." I say.

"That's great." He says.

I nod, "Yeah, it is. They said they came from some village out there. A day or two walk from here."

"That means there's more humans surviving on their own."

"Exactly," I run my fingers through my hair again, "Dwayne wants to find this village and convince the people there to come here. He thinks it'll be beneficial to both them and us, which I agree. They'd have a better chance at living a good life here instead of hoping to make it another night in some random village. He's getting a group together and plans on leaving Sunday morning."

Ryder's face goes from happy to confused in the short few seconds after I said that. His eyes look sad. They're practically begging me not to tell him what he probably has figured out.

"He wants me and my team to go with him. I'll be leading the group with him and we'll find those people out there and come back with or without them." I finally manage to say. "We'd probably be gone for about a week."

He nods, "A week?"

"I think so."

Ryder takes a deep breath and starts pacing around the room. At least he's not begging me to stay or change my mind about going. He's not arguing with me about wanting to do something as dangerous as this.

"You told Dwayne you'd go?" he asks, not looking at me as he continues to pace.

I nod, "Carter would be going too."

He keeps pacing, rubbing his hands on top of his head. I've never actually seen him like this before. I can't tell if this is a good reaction or something I should be worried about. He's nervous, his pale face and frightened eyes give that away. His hands are shaking and he's breathing faster now. Maybe this wasn't the best idea in the first place. I knew going beyond the wall and actually being gone for a few days would be a huge risk.

"Ryder," I speak his name quietly, "You okay?"

He nods his head at first then switches to shaking it in denial, "I don't know what I'm thinking." He stops pacing and faces the doorway to the kitchen.

"I don't have to go if you really don't want me to. I'm fine staying here with you." I say.

"No, I can't be the reason for holding you back. I know this is something you want to do."

"Yeah, but I don't care. I'm not going to leave if you think it's a bad idea."

Finally he turns his eyes to me, "That's not what I'm thinking. Like you, my mind is on something far crazier than that."

I raise an eyebrow, "Okay?"

"I think I want to go with you."

I can honestly say I did not expect those words to come out of his mouth. He's not real keen on the idea of ever going back to the other side of the wall. Living in the city, being safe for the rest of his life, that's his dream.

"You do?" I ask, quite confused.

He nods, "Yeah, I do. Something about that seems like a great idea."

I move toward him and press my palm to his forehead like I'm checking for a fever, "Hmm, you don't feel warm, but you're saying things you wouldn't normally say. Have you been replaced with a different version of my Ryder?"

He smiles and takes my hand to hold it, "It's still me."

"This doesn't sound like you."

"I know, but I think it would be good to go out there. After this last year of having a perfect life with you and not worrying about things anymore, a part of me misses the excitement that's out there. A *very* small part. Besides that, if you're going out there, so am I. We do this together."

I smile and nod my head, "Together."

He puts his hand on the back of my neck and presses his lips against mine. I squeeze his hand tight and close my eyes. In a way, I'm really glad he wants to do this with me. It wouldn't be the same on the road without him. I'd be bored and lonely, saving people who are completely capable of saving themselves. Then again, I'm worried something horrible will happen because of this. Things can always go wrong, no matter how much you try planning and preparing for it. There are two things out there that can make things go really bad, really fast.

Chances are, we'll run into both of them.

* * *

It's Saturday afternoon already. Last night flew by so fast. We ate dinner without Carter because he stayed at the gate talking with Dwayne about things. Ryder finally got the DVD player to work and we watched an old comedy. Seeing those actors on the screen makes me wonder what happened to them. If they're out there wandering as zombies or vampires, or if they managed to survive and are safe somewhere. Not like it matters what happened to them. They were merely in my life as entertainment.

I have a new form of that now.

Right now, I find myself sitting in a large room with Ryder in the chair next to me. We're in an old elementary school that has been converted to the headquarters for the security force. It still feels like a school, though. The room we're in still has old drawings and paintings hanging on the walls. The paper is old and yellow and the crayon marks have faded, but they remain. Someone told me it would be too much like throwing away the past if they took them down and no one wants that.

Dwayne is busy at the front of the classroom, leaning against the white board with the head of security right next to him. That man, Gary Nugget, *yes his name makes me laugh every time I think of it*, is shorter than Dwayne but just as buff. He's older with greying hair and stubble on his chin. He's always wearing camo pants with black combat boots and a brown t-shirt that's so tight, his arm muscles bulge through the sleeves.

Both of them stand in front of the room with about ten of us sitting in small chairs. I knew there wouldn't be too many volunteers for this mission. It has the potential to be extremely dangerous and possibly deadly. I am glad to see that most of my team is here though. Carter, Carla, and Dennis sit in the row behind us. Keith stayed behind to be with his family and I had no intention of asking him to come with us anyway. The man sitting beside Ryder is another army veteran, Tom is his name. The other four in the row behind Carter, are people I don't know much about. Two of them served in the navy and have seen their share of death out there. The last two are volunteers from one of the other tower teams. They go out in the afternoon, so I don't talk to them too much.

We are currently getting an idea of what we'll be doing when we leave tomorrow. We'll be walking in order to keep the noise at a minimum and not attract the wrong kind of creatures. Each of us is responsible for bringing a pack with plenty of ammo and food. Gary has instructed us not to bring anything sentimental or a change of clothes. Things like that will weigh us down and I know all about that.

"I trust that you all know how to ration what food you bring with you. If there's any possibility of this group getting lost, you'll need all the food and water you can carry." Gary states. "As much as I would love to join you on this mission, my place is here with the rest of the security team. You'll be in good hands with Dwayne here. Next to him, you answer to Bridget and listen to what they tell you. Do not step out of line. That is how things go wrong."

I nod as I stare at him. He would be a great asset to this group. I feel we'd have a better chance at surviving out there with his expertise and knowledge about killing. But, he's right. This city needs him more than we do and if things go wrong, this place will be missing out.

"Dwayne will explain when you'll be leaving tomorrow and when he expects to return." Gary takes a step backward and Dwayne moves away from the wall.

"Be ready to go by ten in the morning. There will be a truck going to each of your homes to pick you up. If you are not ready to go, you will be either left behind or you'll be going unprepared. If that happens, you can't be upset when you piss off the others who are prepared and have brought food of their own and are forced to share with you." Dwayne says in the most demanding voice he has. "After we pick you up, we'll be coming to the gate and walking from there. According to the family that arrived yesterday, it's a two day hike to that village. I expect to get there, stay overnight if they'll allow it, and head back with or without them the next day.

"Our goal with this is to try to convince those people to come here. They know it's unsafe out there and I'm positive all of them want to live in peace instead of boarding their lives up day in and day out."

"What if they don't want to come back with us?" I hear Carla's voice ask from behind me. "How can we just leave them out there?"

"We can't force them to come here. That's not what this

place is about. We want to save the human race, but we aren't going to *make* someone live here against their will. If they want to face the world out there on their own, then so be it." Dwayne replies. "We're just going to do our best."

When Dwayne really wants to do something, he sure can sound convincing. He takes his job very seriously and would do anything to keep our race alive. He's a completely different man than when I first met him. Back then, he'd rather hide away in a basement than try to make a difference. I love this improvement.

Despite him telling us what our mission is out there, he's not getting to the important details. He's omitting the dangers that we will come across. I guess that is my job in the group. Dwayne is here to convince them, while I'm here to kill whatever zombie or vamp we come across. The others going with us are just as capable of doing my job as I am. They are all good with guns and killing things. It's the mere thought of *who* I am and *what* I've done in my short life that gives me the opportunity to help lead this thing. Also, people really like someone who isn't afraid of much anymore and that makes me just about perfect for this job.

"Do you have any more questions before I dismiss you all?" Dwayne asks.

It takes a minute before the boy in the last row to speak up, "What happens when we run into those things out there?"

There's the question I knew someone would ask.

Dwayne turns to me and says, "Well, if we run into anything and you find yourself unable to pull the trigger, Bridget will be happy to help you out."

I nod and smile at him, "Damn right."

The group behind me chuckles and Ryder squeezes my hand. He's still nervous about this whole thing, but he hasn't changed his mind about going through with it. I guess I'm a little nervous too. This last year of living a somewhat normal life makes it seem like it's been forever since I was a simple traveler outside that wall. There aren't any run ins with vamps or looking over my shoulder here. I'm completely safe and I know once we're on our way, that safety is gone.

"Before you head out and get ready for tomorrow," Dwayne continues, "I want you to think about what we're doing. Don't think about the people we're hoping to find or the thrill of being outside the wall for a few days. Really think about what we're risking out there. While you're doing this, if you get any second thoughts about volunteering for this mission, maybe you should reconsider. This isn't something we want you to go on if you are unsure about anything."

The group is quiet.

Uncomfortably quiet.

I can hear everyone breathing and wonder which one of them is having second thoughts right now. You'd be crazy not to have at least one voice in your head telling you this is a horrible idea. There are monsters out there that *want* to destroy us. They want to rip us to shreds and take our very lives without even thinking about it. I guess the voice in my head isn't the *right* voice I should be hearing. The sane Bridget, the one who wouldn't go through with this even for all the money and gold in the world, never speaks up or gives her opinion anymore. I know she's there, she's just really good at hiding.

"Alright, remember we'll be picking you up at ten tomorrow so be ready. Dismissed." Dwayne says.

The others behind me get out of their chairs, letting the wooden legs scrape against the floor as they move. I take a deep breath before standing up. Ryder follows me and Dwayne stops us before we are able to leave. He waits for everyone else to disappear down the hallway, including Gary, before talking privately with us.

"Ryder, I didn't think you'd be willing to go with us." Dwayne says.

"I can't imagine letting Bridget go without me." Ryder says with a smile.

"You know you don't have to, right? I mean, you know what the possibilities are out there and the chances of us getting back in one piece." Dwayne says, killing the nice buzz he had going.

"It'll be fine. I know whatever problems we run into, there's plenty of us to stop it. There's not a doubt in my mind about getting back to the city." Ryder replies.

Dwayne smiles, "Good. I'm glad you'll be going along with us."

"Me too." I add in.

"You two should head home and prepare for tomorrow. Get plenty of sleep tonight and eat a good breakfast." Dwayne turns around and walks down the hallway.

Ryder keeps his hand clasped in mine as we follow him down the hall. A few of the locker doors have been left open and a few still have school bags and books inside. It's like the day never ended here and this place is waiting for the kids to return. There's a million places in the world much like this building. I don't know if it will ever get back to the way it used to be, but the more humans that survive, the more we have a chance at getting some of that back.

* * *

We ate a quiet dinner with Carter. It was excruciatingly awkward. None of us wanted to start a conversation that didn't involve complimenting the meal. Carter said grace before we ate, omitting anything that had to do with our mission. I guess asking god for help and support in that particular area was off limits.

After dinner, we each got a bag ready to go for the morning. I retired my old backpack and opted for something a little easier to carry. I got a dark blue shoulder bag, similar to Ryder's dinghy old satchel, and realized how much easier it is to move around without something big and bulky on my shoulders. It's easier to get into if I need something, like more ammo, which has its own compartment on the front of the bag. I grab a couple bottles of water and some food that won't weigh me down. Things like crackers and bread and stuff that won't go bad too fast. The guys packed the heavy, canned foods and a few dishes in case we need them. We set our bags by the front door before bed, then Ryder and I went upstairs.

The black cat, Vambie, is lying at the foot of the bed, wagging his tail and purring. Ryder pats his head and the cat adores it. If I try to touch him, he hisses at me and bats my hand away. To think that I let this cat sleep on my bed and eat some of my food and he still treats me like garbage. No wonder I'm not an animal person.

Ryder sits on his side of the bed with a lamp on next to him. Both of us are hoping we'll get some sleep tonight. I can't speak for Ryder, but I know I'm more than excited. Not that it's going to be super fun or amazing, but it's just going to be so different than what we've been doing. Terrifying and life threatening, but still exciting.

I pull the covers over my legs and sit close to Ryder. The heat from his body warms mine and gets rid of my goose bumps. It can get a little chilly in these old houses.

"Are you nervous about leaving?" Ryder asks.

I nod my head as I scoot a little closer to him, "Of course I am."

"No second thoughts?"

"Are you having some?" I ask in reply.

He shrugs, "I guess so. I'm just afraid of running into something out there and not being ready for it. I'm worried we won't find those people or, if we do, they'll try to kill us for wanting to help them."

"I don't think they'll try to kill us. The family we saved told us the people out there are good. They're just trying to survive like everyone else." I say.

"You're probably right." He says, then glances down at the cat.

He still has that worried look on his face. A look I don't see too often anymore. He's thinking too much about something and I might have a gut feeling of what that *something* is.

"You're thinking about what happened in Hatfeld, aren't you?" I ask.

He licks his lips and nods. The people in that town were supposed to be nice and friendly and look how wrong we were. We were so close to death after the few days we stayed in that place all because of the humans who chose to reside there. There's no saying if the people in this village are as caring as what Martin's family said they are. For all I know, they could be doing the same thing Nick was doing in Hatfeld. If that is the case, at least we're more prepared this time around.

"Ryder, you shouldn't think about that place. Just think of it as a horrible nightmare and push it out of your mind." I say.

He takes a deep breath, "I try, I really do. I just hate how a place so evil is also filled with so many great memories. I fell in love with you in Hatfeld and almost died that very same night."

"I know, but that's not going to happen this time. There are still good people out there and we're bound to run into some of them. We might as well try saving them before their time runs out." I say.

He turns his eyes to me, "Since when are you the super caring type of girl? I thought I was the only one you wanted to save?"

I shrug, "Well, I've already saved you so many times, I think it's time to find another stranger to help out."

He rolls his eyes, playfully, then brings his lips to mine. I close my eyes and let the wonderful sensation of his kiss fill my body. Even in the darkness behind my eyes, I can still see Ryder standing there with a sexy smile on his face. I love how he's always on my mind.

I put my hand on the back of his neck and move even closer to him until our stomachs are touching. He puts his hand on my waist, holding me tight against him. The feel of his touch on my skin as he slides his fingers under my shirt, sends tingles up and down my spine. The butterflies are dancing around in my stomach the same as they do every time we have our intense moments.

I run my fingers through his messy hair as our kiss gets deeper. There's something about being this close to Ryder that makes me fall in love with him all over again. He is still capable of forcing the bad thoughts from my mind. He pulls his lips away from mine and moves them across my face and down my neck. I hold him close, feeling myself breathe faster and I'm loving every second of it.

He moves his mouth to my ear and stops with the kissing, "Bridget?" he whispers.

"Yeah."

"Promise me you won't let anything bad happen to either of us while we're gone." He demands.

I plant my lips on his forehead for a long second, then say, "I'll die before I'd ever let anything bad happen."

He closes his eyes and his lips meet mine once more.

* * *

The truck was there to pick us up exactly at ten o'clock in the morning. Dwayne wasn't kidding when he said to be ready on time, which we were. When am I *not* prepared for things? If there's the possibility of killing zombies and vamps, I'm always on my toes. I was the first one out of bed, in and out of the shower, dressed and standing by the door before the other two had even opened their eyes. I practically had to jump on Ryder to get him out of bed.

I guess I'm a little more excited about this little voyage than I thought. I should probably tone it down a bit.

It's a good thing I always like to wear my hair in pony tail when I do things like this. It would be incredibly annoying right now since I'm sitting in the bed of the truck with the others. There's no room in the cab for everyone to fit. The cool morning air kind of sucks too, even with my favorite hoodie on. Yes, I got it out of retirement for this specific occasion. The fur around the hood might be a little matted in places and it's a little faded. At least I washed it. I just felt the need to wear this little memento of my days as a traveler. It also goes great with my skinny blue jeans and black, leather boots.

Ryder looks the same as always. Black hoodie with a red shirt underneath and jeans and tennis shoes to complete the mix. His hair is a mess, but I like that. Everyone else in the truck with us is dressed and look ready for a battle. A couple of the guys are decked out in camo with rifles strapped to the their backs and a utility belt around their waist. Carla has on a baggy sweatshirt and loose fitting black pants. Her combat boots and shotgun make her look like a total soldier.

We were the last of the group to be picked up before heading for the gate. It's a short drive and my heart pounds the whole way there. My gun shakes in my hand as my knees bounce up and down. I have my bag sitting next to me, filled with everything I'm positive I'll need out there. Ryder has his as well and his gun is tucked safely inside. His hands are clasped together in his lap as he stares at the houses as we pass them.

He's nervous. Every few seconds I can hear him breathing quickly and the second that gate comes into view, I swear he stops breathing entirely. His eyes get wide with fear and the color fades from his face.

I lean close to his ear and whisper, "You still up for this? We don't have to go if you don't want to."

He shakes his head from side to side and says, "I'm good. Just nervous."

"Okay." I say and lean away from him.

Dwayne pulls the truck to a small building right by the gate. There are a few men standing there waiting for us. They are just here to help with the gate and see us off. Once the truck is parked and the engine is shut off, the tailgate gets dropped and we start unloading onto the street. I hop down first and the others follow. Carla and Dennis join me and we wait for Dwayne to climb out of the drivers' seat. There's eleven of us total who are going to the other side in search of that village. As long as there are at least eleven of us who return, I'll be alright.

Gary Nugget is at the gate with a stern look on his face. He stands with three of his men and greet us. His arms are folded across his chest and a pistol is holstered on a belt around his waist.

"Good morning, guys." He says, taking a few steps closer.

"Morning, sir." Dwayne responds.

"Glad to see everyone's prepared and ready to go. I trust all of you have your bags packed with only things you'll need out there. Food, water, ammo, and medicine." Gary states.

Everyone nods their heads and says some form of "yes" in reply.

Gary takes a deep breath and lets his arms fall to his side, "What I'm about to tell you is not something any of you want to hear, but it has to be said. The world out there is a dangerous one. Zombies and vamps hide in the shadows day in and day out. You all know this. You need to be prepared for anything. Have your gun loaded and with you at all times. If you get caught in a bind, do what you can to get out of there and use your best instinct to determine the right thing to do. Under no circumstances should you allow yourself to come into close contact with a zombie or a vampire. Don't hoard your ammo when you see one, but remember to use it wisely.

"We are giving you five days to find the village out there and convince as many people as you can to come back with you. If those five days are up and you are not back here, we will assume the worst and will not send a search party." Gary lets out a solemn sigh, then goes on, "I know this sounds harsh, but you know the consequences of what you're doing. Risking the lives of our men to search for this group is not worth it. What you're doing is trying to get as many humans to survive this world as possible. Survival is the reason we cannot send people to look for you. If the five days pass and you find yourself still alive, do what you can to make it home."

I take this moment of silence to glance at the others in the group. Dwayne and Carter stand like bricks as the words are thrown at them. Carla nervously shifts from one leg to the other. Her partner, Dennis, runs his shaking hands through his hair. The rest of them are frightened as well, but no one turns around. No one takes the easy way out and heads home.

I turn to Ryder as he grabs my hand and squeezes it tight. He smiles at me when our eyes meet and I smile right back. He seems confident and ready to go.

"I do hope all of you return and bring more humans back with you. I believe in this mission and trust each and every one of you." Gary motions to a man behind him who takes the order and begins opening the gate. "Be careful out there and God bless you all."

The familiar sound of the gate squeals open and Gary steps aside so we can walk by him. Dwayne leads the way and Carter follows close behind. I keep my fingers entwined with Ryder's and we walk along with them. The footsteps of the rest of them stomp behind me and we walk through the gate, going to the other side of the wall.

This is something I'm used to. If it were a normal day, I'd be heading to my left and to the tower I call my office. This isn't a normal day and we walk straight, down the same highway that brought all of us to this city. Something Ryder hasn't seen in over a year and he's more than tense as his eyes pass over the trees on each side of the road. He whips his head around when we hear the gate being shut and locked behind us.

"Hey," I say, "it's going to be okay."

He turns to me and nods his head, "I know. This is just so weird being out here again. I mean, not for you, but for me it is. It seems like a whole lifetime has passed since I've been out here."

"Yeah, I get that." I say.

The group fans out so we take up the whole street. We walk in pairs, keeping our eyes peeled for anything that could jump out at us, human or non. Dwayne leads the group, walking with the two army men by his side. Carla walks with Dennis and they keep their chatter quiet. Carter walks with Tom and the other two kids who volunteered.

"I have to admit, I thought for sure we'd run into zombies the second that gate was opened." Ryder says.

I smile, "No, it's actually really quiet out here most days. Kind of peaceful."

"I try to forget that you come out here every day and kill those things for a living. Don't get me wrong, I love having a badass for a girlfriend, I just worry a lot." Ryder says.

"You don't need to worry, Ryder. I know how to protect myself *and* the rest of my team are just as awesome as I am." I say.

He smiles, "I'm grateful you have a team like that who looks out for each other. I'd hate to go day after day thinking you're out here all alone."

"Me too." I reply.

We walk onward, our hands clasped together. This is just like old times. The days I remember so fondly and hope to never forget. Our lives started out here on this very stretch of road. We're heading away from safety this time, but at least we have a good mission on our minds.

* * *

It has now been two hours since we left the city and started on this journey of finding more humans. Dwayne figured it was a good time to stop for lunch and take a break for a few minutes. We found an old house on the side of the highway in the middle of nowhere. It's a tall, two-story farm house with a barn not far away. I was voted to go inside and scope the place out before settling down. I didn't go alone. Ryder came along with me and checked the main floor while I took the upstairs. We came up empty handed and the rest of the group came inside and found a nice place to eat our lunches.

Ryder and I chose a spot on the front porch instead of sitting inside with the others. We sit on an old, rickety swing-set hanging from the ceiling. The chains might be a bit rusty, but the swing holds up and doesn't break when we sit down. Ryder digs in his bag for a bottle of water and a small pack of the bread he brought with us. Not a whole lot to eat considering how we can't really bring anything cold or a dessert of any kind. I wish I could have something sweet to snack on. Despite what you might think, chocolate is still very hard to come by in the city. It's like the food died out.

Breaks my heart a little.

Ryder pushes on the porch with his foot, making the swing sway a bit. I take a bite of bread and stare out at the yard. I imagine what this place was like when the world was alive. An old farmer out riding his tractor while a yellow lab chased after him, barking the whole way. Grandkids played on the front lawn as their grandmother sat on this very swing to watch them. Family reunions were probably held in this very house. A place perfect for get-togethers that is now an abandoned dump slowly withering away.

It's really sad thinking about things like that. Picturing how the world used to be and how it *should* be is devastating at times. There's nothing to bring the world back to normal. No new cure to change the undead back to the living. Nothing that can bring the people I care about back to life and nothing to take the bad memories of my life away. The world is a complete wasteland and it's good that I'm used to it.

"What are you thinking about over there?" Ryder asks.

I snap out of my mind and smile at him, "Nothing, just wondering about things."

"What kinds of things?" he asks.

I shrug and say, "I don't know, just trying to picture what this place was like before things went to shit."

He smiles, "I'm sure it was great."

I nod, "Probably."

Ryder sighs after taking a bite of bread, "I do miss this."

"Miss what?" I ask.

He motions to the world beyond the porch and says, "This. Traveling, being out here in the middle of nowhere, not knowing what we'll find the next day."

I think for a moment, then say, "Yeah, I miss it too."

"I even miss the zombies and vamps sometimes. Killing them, of course. I'm not that crazy to actually miss those nasty things."

The smile widens on my face and I say, "You know, I'm actually a little surprised we haven't run into anything yet. I figured I'd get the chance to kill one of those bastards by now."

"We still have a long ways to go, Bridge. We'll run into some zombies and you'll be able to show this whole group how much of a badass you are at killing them. Just like the day we met."

That was such a great day. It might have started out horrible with thoughts of not wanting to live on my mind. Then running into those zombies in that little town made things worse and I really thought I was going to die. I can't forget about the vamp I killed at the gas station before that.

I let out a quiet laugh as I think of that day and say, "You know the day I met you, I stopped at a gas station outside that town. I ran into a vampire there and killed her. And I never told you this, but I found a bag of stale potato chips and had the best lunch that day."

"You found food that day and didn't save any to share with me? What the hell?" he jokes.

"Yeah and I almost didn't turn toward that town. I was about to get on the highway until I saw a building and thought there could be something there." I say. "Best choice I ever made."

He nods, "You know, that same night I think I already knew I wanted to be with you. Not just because you were company and the only human I'd been in contact with in days, but I could tell there was something about you that I wanted to have. I knew you were going to be the one I could trust with anything and I'm glad to know I was right."

"Me too." I say, "and for the record, it didn't take me long to realize the same thing."

He smiles and kisses my forehead. I'm not sure when I turned into such a softy. Before Ryder, this romance stuff was something I never thought I'd have. Now that I have him, I like this part of me. I like thinking about the amazing times we've had and not just remember the zombies I killed over the years. That is a big part of my life, don't get me wrong, but Ryder is a better part of my life. A part I know I can't live without.

I take a drink of water, listening to the sounds coming from the house. We left the door open and can hear everything going on inside. Carla is busy telling a funny story about one of the times in the towers. Something about what one of the zombies looked like and the others were eating up her words. She does have some of the best stories, either about zombies or just about life in general. Their laughter is loud and echoes outside into the empty air around us.

A slight gust of wind blows through my hair as I continue listening. Out of habit, I take a deep breath in through my nose and happen to catch the tiniest hint of something familiar floating in the breeze. Enough of a hint that could completely ruin this day altogether. I set the bottle of water on the swing next to Ryder and reach for my gun. I get to my feet and take the few steps to the stairs and look around.

"What's up, Bridge?" Ryder asks.

"I smell something." I reply.

I didn't realize I spoke loud enough for the people inside to hear me. Their laughter and talking stops and I can feel their eyes on me as I search for the cause of the stench. I take another inhale through my nose and the smell is steadily getting stronger. That horrid stench practically burns my nostrils and leaves a bad taste in the back of my throat. It happens every time those things get close to the city wall. You'd think I'd be used to that smell by now, but I'm really not. There's something about the putrid stench of death that is impossible to get used to. I am stuck with this little gift of mine, so I really can't complain about it.

I jump down the three steps and land on the sidewalk below. The yard is empty as I step foot on the grass. I turn my head to the left, the way back to the city. I look to my right, where the odor gets stronger. I'm sure that has something to do with the zombie lumbering my way. It's moving slowly, tripping over something in its path. I glance back to the porch. Ryder is now standing, staring at the lone zombie while the others pile out of the front door.

"Damn zombies ruin everything." I hear Dennis complaining.

I shrug, "Don't worry about it. You guys can go back inside. I got this."

Carla chuckles as she takes a drink of water. Dwayne disappears back into the house along with the other, older men. I turn back to the zombie and take a few steps closer to it and can get a good look at this thing now.

It's a man, well, it used to be anyway. My guess, he was the farmer of this little plot of land. His clothes sort of give off that country man appearance. He's wearing muddy bib overalls and a shirt that, at one point, I'm sure used to be white. It's too stained for me to really tell. Dried blood is caked on his arms and in his hair. He grits his teeth, lets out a bellowing groan, and moves a little faster toward me. I raise my gun and tilt my head to the side. For some reason, I find myself thinking of my dad right now. He'd be standing right next to me, watching my technique on killing this poor sole. I wish he was here with me. I'd let him take this one.

Ugh! I can't stand this sadness or the lump that's now in my throat. I steady my aim with the gun and wait a few more seconds, until I can see the pitch blackness of his eyes. I let out the breath I've been holding and squeeze my finger around the trigger. The blast echoes and a few birds fly out of their hiding places. The zombie thuds to the ground and his feet bounce off the grass. I nod at my accomplishment and lower my weapon.

I tuck the gun in my jeans behind my back and turn to the house. Ryder stands in front of the swing with his bag on and ready to go. Dwayne has returned to the porch, ready to go as well, and the others are heading inside to get their things. Carla tosses me a silly smile before disappearing through the door.

"We leaving already?" I ask, walking to the porch.

Dwayne nods, "With that thing lurking around, I'm sure there are others close by that heard the gunshot. It's best we get moving again and hope we don't run into anything else around here."

I sigh and say, "Yeah, good idea."

I hear the others inside the house. This time they're quiet, packing their bags and getting ready to hit the road again. I look to Ryder and he hands my bag to me. I put the strap over my shoulder, crossing over my body, and lean against the railing next to him. He runs his fingers through his hair and gives me a fake smile.

"You alright?" he asks.

"Yeah, why wouldn't I be?"

He shrugs, "I saw the look on your face right before you shot that zombie. You seemed kinda sad."

I lower my head and stare at my feet, "Oh."

"What were you thinking about?"

"My dad again. I just wish he was here with us." I reply.

Ryder nods, "I know you do. You always want him around and I wish you could have that. I hate seeing you sad whenever you think about him."

"I'll be alright, though. I got you with me and that's what's important."

The group comes outside with their things and climbs down the porch. Carter lags behind and walks with Ryder and I as we follow them. Once again, Dwayne leads the group with the other guys his age and we head away from the house.

* * *

A few more hours ease by and we haven't run into anything else since the zombie at the farm house. Maybe a few squirrels here and there, but no other living thing is on the road with us. It's really quiet out here, even with all of us having our own little conversations. Carla and Dennis are talking about hunting something for dinner while Dwayne is trying to figure out if we should start looking for a place to camp soon. That wouldn't be the worst idea in the world. I know my legs are getting tired of walking and I'm starting to get hungry again. Not to mention, the sun will go down real soon and the vamps are sure to come out to play.

"You know," I say to Carter and Ryder, "despite the fact that we're doomed to run into more zombies and vampires out here, I'm really glad that it's not raining. I always *hated* that."

Ryder shakes his head and smiles, "That's a little odd coming from a girl who once took a shower in the rain."

"What's this?" Carter chimes in. "I don't think I ever heard this story."

"And you're not going to. That stays at the hotel in Hatfeld." I say.

Thinking of that night, with the cold rain water pouring down upon us, always brings a smile to my face. I don't even have to close my eyes to see the details of what happened between me and Ryder. How could I ever forget the night I found myself falling in love with the perfect guy? I think I'd have to be pretty dead in order for that to happen.

We pass an overturned pickup truck, the windows are completely smashed and glass surrounds the cab. The small sedan crashed into the other side of it is clearly the cause of this accident. It looks like the two vehicles hit pretty hard and the driver of the truck probably didn't see it coming. I can see what's left of him hanging in the drivers' seat with the belt still attached.

Poor guy.

"I'm so glad I was never in that situation." Ryder states, putting some distance between him and the wreckage.

"You wouldn't believe how many accidents and deaths I saw right when the 'cure' took effect. People died in some of the stupidest ways you could possibly imagine." Carter says. "My least favorite ones were the suicides. I hated seeing how people would just give up, even if they weren't bitten or scratched."

I take a deep breath, "I found this family once, before my dad died. We were scavenging an old rest stop in the middle of nowhere. This family was just lying on the floor in the ladies' room, with a bullet wound in each of their heads. I always liked to hope they didn't have any other option. Like they ran out of food and couldn't go on anymore. I don't like to think they just gave up on their lives and decided to end it all."

Carter fell silent after my little story. I know he believes suicide is a straight path to hell, even in the world we're living in. Seeing as how I don't believe in that sort of thing, I just like to assume they go someplace better than this. Maybe when we die, we don't necessarily go to heaven, but we go to the place our minds find peaceful. Our own personal heaven, filled with the people and things we've always loved and cherished. I know it's a longshot to think a better place exists beyond this life. Once we die, I'm sure that's it. There's nothing else after that, other than darkness.

Ryder takes my hand and squeezes it. I turn to him and he smiles at me. That amazing smile gets me to fall in love with him every time I see it.

"Quit thinking so much." He says, quietly.

I roll my eyes and smile as I look ahead. We pass a few more cars and trees along each side of the highway. The woods are starting to thin out and empty corn fields replace them. There's a tractor stuck in the field to my right as though it's waiting for the harvest. At the front of the group, Dwayne stops walking and the rest of us do the same.

"The sun will be going down soon and I don't want to risk walking anymore when this becomes vamp territory. We're going to make camp out here and each of us will take turns keeping watch. We'll gather firewood and keep it small. I know it's cold, but the light will let the vampires know humans are around. In the morning, we'll head out again and find that village."

Everyone nods and Dwayne starts walking down the road. I see him scanning the area, searching for the best place to make camp. There's a building in the middle of the field. It's a long walk to that building and I think he wants to keep close to the highway. No sense in getting lost or in a bind we can't get out of. Some of the guys start looking for firewood and Carter steps off the concrete and gathers a few sticks for himself. Ryder stays with me, his hand still in my own. I don't expect him to wander off with the others. With all of his encounters with the vamps, he's better off staying behind.

"I don't think I'll be getting any sleep tonight." He says.

"I don't think any of us will. It's been awhile since we've been on the road and it's a hard thing to get used to again." I say.

"Just can't wait to find this village and be done with all this zombie and vampire shit. I know I said I missed parts of life out here, but the less we see of those things, the better this trip will be."

I smile and nod my head in agreement, "These few days will be over and done with before you know it. Then, when we're back in Des Moines, you'll miss it again."

He shakes his head, "Probably not for a while, though. We can't all be crazy like the fantabulous Bridget who misses the weird stuff."

I smile and say, "No. The world isn't big enough for more people like me."

* * *

We found a place to camp not far from the highway under two oak trees. The leaves have already changed to their Fall colors and many have started falling to the ground. They were a nice addition to our small fire, making it much easier to get it going. For our dinner, we ate crackers and bread and enjoyed the *wonderful* taste of water to wash it all down with. This sort of thing takes me right back to all those small dinners I ate with my family. We didn't eat the best on the road to Florida and we still didn't eat too great when we got there.

The dinners in the city are much better. Hardly a day goes by where any one person doesn't overfeed themselves. There are many options to choose from, like meat and dairy products and breads of all kinds. Someone even managed to make homemade vanilla ice cream. That was probably my favorite discovery after we got settled in Des Moines. I think my family would have loved that find as well.

The sun went down a few hours ago and the stars came out to play. Two of us are responsible for keeping watch for about an hour while the others sleep. One on each side of the camp, staring out into the vast emptiness around us. I take this shift with Carter. He found a nice spot to sit on the ground while I lean against one of the trees. We haven't seen any vamps nor heard any sign of an oncoming zombie. The night is pretty quiet and it's not even the eerie type of quiet either. It's the perfect-kind-of-night quiet.

I glance over my shoulder, checking on the sleeping members of my group. Most of them are huddled under a blanket or lying on top of each other to keep warm. Even with the fire still dimly lit, the night air is just too cold to not be covered by something. I'm doing alright with just my hoodie on and my arms tightly crossed over my chest. It's cold, but I've been through worse.

The field in front of me is still empty when I turn back to it. The tall grass flows gently in the breeze and nothing is lurking in the darkness. This is the kind of night I always hoped for when my dad and I were camping in the middle of nowhere. If we ever had to sleep outside, it was rare for our night to go uninterrupted. Nights like this one, are cherished in the eyes of travelers.

I glance to the sky. The stars shine bright and twinkle overhead. This is something I don't see too often in the city. The lights are too bright and the stars are diminished because of it. I miss seeing the stars and finding the constellations. It's an entirely different world up there. A world that isn't pure evil and filled with death behind every corner. What's left of the humans will never see a world like that. We're doomed to face each day knowing it could be our last.

I hate thinking like that. I need to shake those thoughts out of my mind and go on with my job. Keeping the group safe and surviving our first night out here is priority number one. I can't let my thoughts cross over to the dark side and get me in trouble.

There are footsteps coming up behind me and I quickly snap my head around to see who it is. Dwayne approaches me, zipping his jacket along the way. He has a great way of scaring people in the middle of the night.

"Why are you awake?" I ask in a hushed voice.

He shrugs, "I can't sleep very well."

"That sucks."

"Yeah, I figured it'd be easier to sleep out here. You

know, in a world with the demons that could eat us." He states, sarcastically.

I smile, "The others are doing fine knowing that."

"I guess it's just been awhile and I'm a bit nervous about this." Dwayne says, looking out to the field.

"What's there to be nervous about? You have a great team here and we all know what we're doing. If anything, the zombies and vamps should be nervous about running into us." I say, hoping that changes his mood a bit.

He shakes his head, "That's not what I'm nervous about. I'm worried we won't find that village or, if we do, it'll be too late. This mission would be all for nothing and I'd go back to the city feeling like a failure."

He and I have a completely different definition of what a failure is. I don't think finding the village in shambles and going back empty handed, constitutes as a failure. If we get there and we can't convince them, maybe that counts. I consider failing at something to lose in the face of a zombie or a vamp. Things just changed a lot after the world died and changed my whole idea of failing and not.

"You won't be going back a failure, Dwayne. If there's nothing out there, we'll be going back as the same people who left. Maybe a bit disheveled and tired, but the same nonetheless." I say.

"No, this is different, Bridget." Dwayne argues. "This is big. We are responsible for finding people out here. If we find that village, there's hope of finding more humans beyond that. There's hope of expanding the city walls and building new homes for the people we find. This wouldn't be our only mission. This would just be the beginning of something that could help us defeat those *things* altogether."

I raise an eyebrow and pass him an odd glare, "I don't think that's how we will end the threat of zombies and vampires. They'll always be out there and always be threatening us. Just because we save a bunch of people and expand the city, that doesn't mean anything."

Again, he shakes his head, "That's not true. There *is* a future for this planet. One without zombies and vampires eating our race. I can see a life where we don't have to fight for scraps and kill just to save our own skins. A life that's not constantly being devoured by things that used to be a part of us. You can't say the world will never be safe again, because I know that's not true. We will have what we used to have and get this planet back in order. Regardless what you believe, Bridget, there is a future here."

He turns away from me, unhappy about what I said to him. I follow him with my eyes and watch him sit on the ground next to the fire. He picks up a stick from the ground and starts poking the flames. I shake my head and turn back to the empty field.

I know every last human on this planet has their own beliefs about things. Some believe there's a god up there somewhere controlling things down here. Others think there will be another cure to end this thing once and for all. More logical people, the ones like me, know better than that. It's been six years now and the world hasn't made progress. Zombies still knock on our doors each day and vampires are waiting for us each night. I know we have the city walls to keep up safe, but they won't last forever. There will come a time where that place is overrun or something gets inside and the whole thing will be over.

I run my fingers through my hair and take a deep breath. The field is dark and empty, still no sight or sound of anything lurking in the shadows. This *was* a peaceful night and one I was actually happy to be awake during. Dwayne and his ideas of a better future sort of ruined it. He never used to be this way. When I met him, he was more than determined to spend the rest of his life in that basement, hiding from the rest of the world until he died down there. After finding sanctuary in the city, he changed and now sees things through different eyes. He wants to believe there's a better world waiting for us. He wants to believe the zombies and vamps will be cured or killed off.

I want to believe he'll wise up and think straight again. There's no room on this planet for meaningless longing of a better world. When you've been through hell and back, like I have, you'll learn that it's never going to get any better than this. Zombies will always be here. Vampires will never go away. There will *never* be a cure and the humans will never have the guns or manpower to take them out entirely.

We're stuck in this world till the end of time whether we like it or not.

* * *

Morning's here now. Well, it's been here for about an hour anyway. All of us ate a small breakfast, taking our separate bathroom breaks, and gearing up for another day of walking. I'm still pretty tired after a night of not enough sleep. Ryder slept like a log, but I kept tossing and turning when my shift was up. My little chat with Dwayne was all I could think about. I never could get to the bottom of why he doesn't think like me.

I yawn as I walk with Ryder and Carter behind the others. Dwayne hasn't said a word to me since we began our trek again. He simply gave us our orders and that was it. I can't help but feel the tension in the air whenever I get near him. He's still upset over our talk and I'm sure he hates me for what I believe in. I guess judgment and drama will never die.

The sun beats down on us as we walk along the highway. We got off on a ramp, heading south a little ways, following the directions Martin's family gave us. We pass car after car and mess after mess of things that went wrong. Houses and shacks were found charred and left in a pile of debris on the foundations. There's no sign of living people or a village that we can see. I know there's still a ways to go, but I half expected to see some kind of sign indicating safety is not far ahead.

Dwayne walks at the front of the group and I notice him glancing over his shoulder. He's checking out what the rest of us are doing and making sure we're not goofing off. He completely ignores me and passes me a snide look instead.

Carter leans close to me and says, "Is it just me or is Dwayne upset with you today?"

I roll my eyes and say, "Well, he's not the happiest person on the planet with me."

"What did you do?" Ryder asks.

I shrug, "Said something wrong. Believe the wrong things about this world. Hell, I don't know. I'm just me and we all know how frustrating that can be."

"That's for sure." Carter says.

"Did you guys talk or something last night?" Ryder says.

I nod, "He was awake during my shift and we spoke for a few minutes. He's worried he'll go back to the city as a failure if we don't find this village and bring other survivors back with us. He says if we find them, we'll be starting something new and can finally bring an end to the monsters of the world."

"And I suppose you told him what you thought about that and he didn't like it." Carter says.

"What else was I supposed to say? I can't lie to him, I'm not like that." I argue. "I just don't understand what could possibly get him to believe there will ever be an end to the zombies and vamps."

Carter shrugs, "Me neither, but I know when to leave

another man's beliefs alone and shut up. You, on the other hand, tend to not do that."

I roll my eyes again and let out an annoyed sigh, "Oh well, he'll be alright."

"I hope so." Ryder adds.

There's a dried up corn field to our left and the leaves crinkle in the wind. A few cars found their way into the ditch before the field and are crashed against one another. I take a moment to close my eyes and let the bad thoughts escape my mind. I can't keep over thinking things and asking myself a million questions that will never have an answer. Thinking gets me in trouble and makes me sad or upset. It's hard to do, but I have to keep my mind clear and get back to work.

The breeze blows through my hair and I take a deep inhale through my nose, letting the scents of the world fill my nostrils. The dried corn smells like dead leaves and dust and I detect a hint of ash coming from one of the charred vehicles. There's something else lingering in the air. It's faint, but strong enough for me to know something's not right. I open my eyes and glance in every direction only to see there's nothing around. I don't find a horde of zombies in the fields as we make our way to an overpass.

"You alright, Bridge?" Ryder asks.

I shrug, "I don't know. Something doesn't seem right."

He takes my hand and holds it tight. I can feel his fingers shaking between mine. He knows whenever I smell something that's not quite right, that it's time to be nervous and prepare for anything.

There is a cluster of cars crashed together on the side of the road. Two of them are completely burnt with fire marks and a few still carry their passengers behind the wheel. They have been dead awhile, but there's still a faint decaying odor to them. This might be what I'm smelling, but I can't think like that. Carla, who's walking with Dennis, glances in the vehicles and grimaces. For a girl who was once a traveler and has seen some pretty messed up stuff, she's still grossed out when she sees dead humans rotting away on the side of the road.

I'm so *lucky* to be used to it and not grossed out anymore.

We move closer to an oncoming overpass. A white van is pressed against one of the cement structural beams and folded together like an accordion. I notice Dwayne whipping his head from left to right, searching for something I cannot see. I sniff the air once more and the odor is quite stronger. Dwayne looks to his left and stares at something for a long moment. He stops walking and holds a fist in the air telling us to stop moving as well. My heart starts beating faster and Ryder squeezes my hand a little tighter.

Everyone in the group is on edge now. Dwayne readies his gun and the guys around him do the same. Carla and Dennis get their guns out and Carter has his rifle ready to shoot when necessary. I wrap my fingers around my gun tighter and I spot Ryder getting his out as well.

I keep my eyes peeled for anything at all. There's nothing under the overpass that I can see. Nothing undead in the cars trying to get at us. But I can smell them. Their stench is growing and I know there's more than what we were hoping to run into. I'm hoping not any more than what we can handle.

"We're not alone here, people." Dwayne says, his deep voice sounding concerned.

The second those words leave his lips, the groaning begins.

* * *

The first zombie comes from behind an over turned minivan. She's short and fat, blood staining the collar of her shirt. Her left arm looks broken and she groans louder when it bangs against the back of the van. I don't know if she felt the pain and I don't really care to find out. Dwayne takes the first shot and gets her right in the head. She falls like a sack of potatoes, hitting the ground with a loud thud.

Two more come from behind what's left of a barn to our left. One only has black pants on, letting his pale, veiny chest reflect the sunlight. The other wears a cowboy hat with part of the brim missing. A bloodlust look in both of their eyes and a groan that is considerably annoying. Another shot is fired and the cowboy goes down first. This draws out five more right behind those two and even more from where the fat woman went down. We have no choice except open fire on these things. Some fall to the cement, never to move again. Others creep closer to their only source of food.

I hear a loud grunt come from behind me. I turn around and see a teenaged zombie rushing at me. I raise my gun and pull the trigger without even thinking. He gets hit in the head and falls face first to the concrete. Once he's down, I notice a small horde of them coming down the highway. Six or seven, I can't really see them close enough to count. The important thing I'm noticing, is that we are surrounded. Our only option is to run as fast as we can and get to the other side of the overpass and pray to whatever god there is, that a safer place lies on the other side. It's a good thing zombies are pretty slow which gives us the advantage here.

I fire a two more rounds, hitting another in the head and a girl in the shoulder. She grunts at me and moves faster. Why can't these be the zombies who hesitate? Those ones are much easier to handle and we waste a lot less ammo on them. These ones here are just really hungry and aren't going to stop coming at us.

"What do we do?" I hear Carla shout.

Ryder has now turned around and starts shooting into the zombies with me. He lets go of my hand and steadies his grip on the gun. I can see it shaking, but he still gets one in the head after he pulls the trigger.

"We've gotta get out of here!" I hear someone shout through the barrage of bullets.

I look around. At least twenty or so zombies are coming at us from all angles, their arms outstretched and their moans only getting louder. If this goes on any longer, there will be a hundred of them coming here just for us and, soon, we won't be alive for them to enjoy.

The group has to stay strong. We have to keep shooting whatever gets within a few feet of us. We still have a clear shot to the overpass and we might find something on the other side. Maybe a building we can board ourselves up in or something up high enough so these monsters can't get us. Anything will be better than sitting out here in the open letting our ammo run low. I'm almost out myself and it's only a matter of time before the rest of the group runs out too. With as many zombies as this, taking the time to reload is practically suicide.

I shoot another in the head. He was just a couple feet from sneaking up on Carter who turns around and nods a thank you.

"We need to get to the other side of the overpass." I shout at him, it's kind of hard to talk over guns going off every second.

He nods and begins urging everyone to move forward as fast as they can. A few break out in a mad dash to get away from the flesh hungry beasts. Ryder and I start walking, him forwards, me backwards. I hear him take a couple more shots, destroying two that were to his left. I get another in the chest, it falls, but is trying to get back up. Three more go down to the right of me from someone else still trying to fight these things off.

I glance over my shoulder. Dwayne and three from the group made it to the overpass and are on the other side. That's not what's catching my eyes. The zombies aren't following them. They aren't going anywhere near the shadowy overpass at all. Their main focus is on those of us who are left trying to get away from them. I shouldn't let it worry me too much, but I can't help but wonder why.

It's darker under the bridge, shielding us completely from the sun. The zombies don't follow us and I stop walking trying to figure out why. All of them are staring at us, devouring us with their eyes. They continue playing their annoying song, yet never pass into the shadows. I run my fingers through my hair and realize something. Probably something I should have figured out a few minutes ago. It's *dark* under this bridge. Dark enough to keep the sun out entirely. What's the one thing on this planet that thrives in the darkness? The one thing that lives in the shadows while we stay away?

"Vampires!" Dwayne shouts, answering my question.

I whip my head around and see three of them jump out from the darkest corner and land on the road. Carter, Ryder, Dennis, and I are the only ones under the bridge and the vamps are blocking the way out. The zombies are keeping us from going back the way we came and we are completely trapped in here.

Dwayne stands on the other side, away from the zombies. I see him raising his gun and taking aim for one of the vamps. He pulls the trigger, but misses its heart. The vamp falls forward and catches himself before hitting the ground. Another one comes out of the shadows and I spot it just in time. It leaps into the air, his main target would have been Ryder if I hadn't got my gun up in time. I pulled the trigger and got the damn thing right in the heart. It's a good thing I don't hesitate with these things anymore.

Ryder didn't even see it coming. He looks down at the

ground, confusion on his face, then passes me a thankful glance. Two more shots are fired and one of the others goes down. I turn and see the other group members standing in the sunlight, doing their best to save us. That actually calms me a bit and I lower my gun. They have a clear shot *and* the benefit of being in the sun where these things can't get them. We're a little stuck and no time to reload our almost empty guns.

Carter takes a shot and gets one in the head. It stumbles backward and trips over a rock before falling on her back in the sun. She screams as loud as she can when the rays begins to boil her skin. It's not long before someone shoots her in the heart to end her misery.

"Bridget, look out!" Ryder shouts and points at something behind me.

He takes aim and pulls the trigger the very second I turn around. One vamp falls to the ground and another comes from a dark corner. I spot the vamp Ryder shot in the heart. She's lying in a growing puddle of her own blood at my feet. She twitches once and I shoot her in the back just to make sure she's really dead. I let out a sigh then look up.

That second vamp is mere inches away from me and I quickly take aim. I pull the trigger, but miss the target. The blast has my ears ringing and the vamp slaps my hand out of his way. He rushes me and I don't have the time to back away. Everything is happening so fast and the only thing I'm noticing anymore is the pain coming from my neck.

The gun slips from my fingers and I don't even hear it hit the ground. The only thing I can comprehend are the teeth sinking into my neck and the pain coursing through my veins. I can feel the blood being sucked from my body, feel his nasty fingers tugging at the collar of my hoody. Two gunshots fill my ears and the vamp gets blown away. He falls to the ground and I stumble backwards, my hand instantly going to my neck. Blood seeps between my fingers and down my arm. My satchel suddenly weighs a ton and is digging further into my neck. I struggle to grab the strap, but I eventually lift it over my head and let it drop to the ground. More blood flows down my arm and I stumble a bit. I can't stop myself from walking back a few paces and don't even realize that I'm back in the sun.

"Bridget!" I hear a voice, but can't tell if it's coming from Ryder or one of the others.

The voice was trying to warn me of the zombie not even a foot away. I feel it's grip on my arm, it's claws digging into my skin sending a new pain shooting through my body. I don't have to look down to know it broke the skin. I can feel the blood soaking the sleeve of my hoody and it's already too late. It latches its jaw to my arm, biting through the fabric. I'm so lost in this whole moment, not even a cry of pain can escape me. I can't move nor can I find the strength to fight the zombie off.

A bullet whizzes through the air and pierces the zombie attached to my arm. I step away from it as two more get taken out nearby. I pull my hand away from my neck and look at the blood in my palm. My hand shakes as I stare at the result of what I thought would never happen. I raise my right arm and see the hole in the fabric, the redness of more blood coming through three small holes in my skin. My jaw drops and I don't know what to do anymore.

I can't believe this happened.

I can't believe I *let* this happen.

In just a few short seconds, I completely failed everybody in my family. I ceased to be able to survive and got bit by not one, but both of the creatures that strike fear in the hearts of whatever humans remain on this planet. This is something I never thought would happen to anybody. Being bit by a vampire *and* a zombie, all in the same short moment, seems like a horror story. A story I'm ashamed to admit that I'm living right now.

What am I supposed to do? There's no stopping the turn my life is going to take. There's no changing back to the normal Bridget I was a minute ago. As much as I really don't want to admit this, I'm dead.

The other zombies aren't coming near me anymore. Either they know something is different or they don't care about me. I look up from my hands and see into the shadows under the overpass. The last remaining vamps fall dead to the ground and the rest of my group stares my way. All of them have fear and worry on their faces. My teary eyes find Ryder and I feel my lips quivering. He's fighting the tight grip Carter has around him. It's the only thing stopping him from running to me.

"Let go of me, Carter!" Ryder screams.

"It's too late, man." Carter's voice sounds calm, but I can hear the sadness. "There's nothing we can do for her."

I feel a pinch in my neck and wince at the pain, letting a slight gasp escape my throat. Whatever is going to happen to me, is starting to. The vamp's venom as well as the zombie's is already in my system and, like he said, it's too late for me. There's nothing they can do. Nothing I can do. I blink my eyes, letting the warm tears hit my cheeks.

"Bridget!" Ryder shouts, still struggling against Carter's grip.

I look him in the eyes. The lump in my throat is choking me and making the pain that much worse. I never thought I'd have to say good-bye to him. I never thought I'd have to leave him like this. I just can't take the risk of staying with this group after getting infected. They'd kill me the second I turn and I won't stop them. If I still had my gun in my hand, I'd end this for them. There's only one thing I can do that makes perfect sense. I have to start walking away from them. To start putting some distance between them and the monster I'm sure to become.

"I'm so sorry, Ryder." I say, fighting through the pain I feel in my heart and everywhere else. "I love you."

I take one more, long look at him. Letting his image burn into my memory. I know I'll forget everything once I'm not me anymore, but I want his face to be the last thing I see. I want to know that I at least thought of the only person I love in this world before I go to hell. Hearing him scream my name, listening to him begging me to stop moving, is killing me inside. Worse than this poison already is. Watching my father die does not compare to knowing that I'll never get to see the man I love ever again.

I can't take looking at him any longer. I quickly turn around and run. His shouting gets more fierce and I'm sure he's really trying to get away from Carter. That guy has a pretty strong grip and I know he'll never let go. I don't want him to. I want Ryder to live a long life without me. I want him to go back to the city and never think of me again.

I get off the road and sprint through an empty field. My legs are being pushed to the limit and my lungs are burning. It's hard to breathe and run as fast as I can with a broken heart and a brick of sadness clogging my throat. Not to mention the extreme amount of pain coursing through every vein in my body.

* * *

I don't know how long I've been running or how far I've gone since I left Ryder at the overpass. I can't bring myself to stop moving, not even for a second to take a breath. The pain of my broken heart hurts worse than the fire burning through my lungs. Even the pain in my neck and arm are no match for what I'm feeling. I know the group will move on without me. I'm not worth running after now that I'm infected.

Everything inside me is completely shattered.

I run through a small line of trees, most likely an old tree farm. All of them are in neat rows and of the same species. The leaves are fading to brown and they crunch under my boots as I run. I hear the wind rustling through the branches above my head and a few birds scattering out of the trees. There's a long, red building with a green roof up ahead. The sign above the door is missing and it left behind a faded spot on the front of the building. It doesn't look like a human has been near this place for a while. The windows are mostly broken out or shattered and debris is strewn all over the place. This might be the perfect place for me to hide and die alone. I just need to make it there.

A sharp pain stabs the inside of my stomach and I have no choice but to stop running. I double over and let out a quiet cry of pain as I clutch my gut. The stabbing hits me again and I fall to my knees next to a tree. I stare at the building ahead of me. It's the only thing to focus on and it's gradually getting blurry. An annoying buzzing sound floods my ears and a pounding comes to the back of my head. Another jolt of pain erupts in my stomach, this time worse than before. I lean forward and hold myself up with my hands on the ground. I clench my fists, squeezing the dirt and leaves as the pain takes over.

The lump in my throat has been replaced with something else. A repulsive taste fills the back of my throat and the buzzing in my ears gets louder with this taste. I feel my stomach begin to convulse which is only making the pain that much worse. There's nothing I can do to stop the bile from escaping me. I vomit all over the leaves on the ground and stare at what's coming out of me. I don't even know what it is. It's black and liquidy and just staring at it makes more come out. I wish it would stop because it is burning the back of my throat like a fire ripping through a house.

My entire body aches and my hands shake intensely. My lips are quivering as my eyes start to water. There's something tugging on my hair, making the forming headache a million times worse. I reach up, feeling the back of my head for the thing that's bugging me. I grab the hair tie and pull it out, letting my hair fall over my shoulders. That seemed to fix the tugging sensation, but my headache remains.

A few minutes pass of me kneeling on the ground, puking next to a tree. The pain in my stomach stops long enough for me to open my eyes and look for the building again. Things start to come back to focus and the buzzing fades a tad. I find the strength I need to get to my feet and lean against the tree as I stand. I feel something dripping from the corner of my mouth and I wipe my chin with the back of my hand. Blood is what I see.

"What is happening to me?" I say through gritted teeth.

At least talking doesn't hurt so much.

I pick up my right foot and start moving away from the tree. I cringe as the pain shoots up my leg and clench a fist before taking another step. My fingernails poking into the palms of my hands helps slightly with the pain. It's not enough to stop it entirely, but it helps.

I move as fast as my body will let me and the building gets closer. The pain isn't going away, not that I was expecting it to. I never thought dying would hurt this much, but I also never thought I'd get bit by a vamp *and* a zombie all in one day.

There are a few trees left before getting to a gravel driveway. There are no cars parked here and the place seems empty and dead. Not like it would stop me from going inside anyway. I'm pretty much dead as it is.

I let go of the last tree and walk over the loose rocks at my feet. It's much harder to move without having something to lean against and it seems like it is taking forever to get to the door. I hold onto my stomach and push through the pain to get there. My head is pounding by the time my bloody hands press against the glass to push the door open. Luckily it's not locked and I walk right in.

There are shelves full of dead plants all over the place and a few bags of seeds cover the floor. One of them has been split open and my feet slide a little when I step on them. The register is at the front of the store and I practically fall against it in order to keep myself upright. I glance up to the ceiling, noticing the windows in it to let sunlight in for the plants. Too bad that didn't save them, but at least it keeps the vamps out.

"Is anyone here?" I manage to say as loud as I can.

I wait a moment but never get an answer. Not a movement, sound, or even breathing. I'm completely alone in this old greenhouse. It's a big relief knowing no one will be here to witness what I'll be changing into. I think that's about the scariest part of it all. Changing into something I cannot control. A creature that feeds on the living in order to survive.

Why was I so stupid? Why didn't I pay more attention to what was happening around me? Why did I have to let everyone in my family down, including Ryder?

These are the worst questions I've ever had to ask myself.

I grip my stomach and walk further into the building. The sharp pains are still there and I feel nauseated. Any minute now and I could be on my knees letting my insides spill out of me again. I grip a nearby shelf to ease in walking and start looking for the bathroom. It's the only place I can think of that will shield me from the world and I can die in a small amount of peace.

At the back of the store is a huge section filled with various types and sizes of pots for planting. Most of them have been knocked over and broken from some kind of struggle and are now in pieces on the floor. Others are still stacked in a neat tower where they'll never move again. I lean against a tall stack of clay pots and look around. Another cash register is at this part of the store and behind that is a room with a restroom sign above it. I force myself to move toward it.

Everything I touch with my right hand leaves behind a

bloody print. The marks from the zombie wound are letting enough blood flow down my arm to my fingertips. I wipe my hand on my jeans hoping that will help, but it doesn't. I touch the wall by the bathroom and a perfectly smeared handprint is left behind on the white paint.

The bathroom isn't anything special. There's a skylight in here as well, which is a little weird if you ask me. The sun shines through the small square in the ceiling to let in just enough light so I can see. There are two stalls and both of the doors are wide open revealing an empty toilet. The garbage can is still upright next to the door. On the wall across from me are two mirrors above two separate sinks. My feet move faster to the mirror closest to the stalls and I let my hands stain the white porcelain of the sink with blood.

I look at my reflection. My face is pale and sickly. My lips are a faded shade of red and my hair looks dull. The bite marks on my neck have turned purple and look infected. I lean forward and stare into my eyes. They are a very dull shade of the same brown they've always been.

A slight jab of pain hits my stomach and I close my eyes for a second. My fingers tighten around the edges of the sink as I fight back this pain. All I can think of is wanting this never-ending struggle to be over with. I know I'm going to die very soon, but I'm not sure I'll survive the pain it will take to get there. This is too much for one person to have to go through and I'd hate to think this what all infected humans had to go through during their own change. If I held onto my gun, I'd be finding it very hard not to pull the trigger to end this suffering.

The pain lets up again and I take a deep, staggering breath. I open my eyes and see my face staring back at me and I lean a little closer to the mirror. My only focus now is the color of my irises.

"Please stay brown." I say to my eyes in the mirror. "*Please* stay brown."

I feel the bile rising in my throat again and I clutch the

sink with my hands. I force the vomit to stay down and keep staring at my eyes. I don't want to see the pitch blackness of a zombie staring back at me. I don't want to see the hazy grey of a vampire in the mirror either. I just want the boring brown eyes I've always had to stay with me, to be the one thing that won't make me a monster.

My nose is about two inches from hitting the glass of the mirror. I stare at my eyes, yelling at them in my head to stay brown as the sickness and pain is constantly rising inside me. As I stare at them, the brown color of the iris begins to change. I shake my head back and forth and grit my teeth.

"Stay brown!" I scream and slam a fist against the mirror.

A crack spiders its way across the glass. It distorts my reflection, but I can still see my eyes. A grey hue has taken over the brown in them. It doesn't cover my entire eye like the zombies black ones nor are they hazy like the vamps. They are just grey and appear lifeless. I close them and lower my head in shame.

At that instant, a pain so sharp hits my entire body and I can't stop myself from collapsing to the floor. I land on my shoulder, the pain from that doesn't even affect me. I grip my stomach and stare at the wall in front of me. There's nothing to keep the pain from coming, nothing to keep myself from changing into a new kind of creature to infect the human population.

I wish I would have held onto my gun. My suffering would have been over by now with one quick pull of the trigger. My life would be over and I wouldn't be dying on the floor in some bathroom in the middle of nowhere. I'd be *forever* dead and get to spend the rest of eternity wherever the dead go. Whether that be in heaven or hell, as long as I'd get to see my family when I got there, I really wouldn't care.

It's cold on this floor which is only making the pain seem *much* worse. My whole body is shivering and my teeth are chattering. The tears coming from my eyes are the warmest part of my being and even they hurt. I don't have the strength to wipe them away. Every movement I make feels like knives stabbing my body. It feels like my insides are on fire while the rest of me freezes on the floor. My heart is beating so fast I can't calm down enough for it to slow its tempo. It's getting hard to breathe without feeling like my lungs are going to explode, but I feel like vomiting if I hold my breath.

I close my eyes, hoping this will all be over soon. I don't know how much more of this I can take.

Through the blackness behind my eyes, I see Ryder's face. The only face I want to be seeing right now. He's upset and tears fill his eyes, but that's still him. I wish I could hear his voice. I wish I could hear him screaming my name one more time. I hate knowing I'll never get to see him or feel safe with him again. I'll never get to feel his skin against my own or taste his lips upon mine. His kisses were the best thing in the world and the only kind I've ever known. At least I got to tell him I loved him before my life fell apart.

I can see his mouth moving in my mind. The words never come out, but it's just my mind replaying the last moment I got to see him. He's probably still screaming my name, struggling against Carter's grip to come after me. I'm so grateful for Carter holding him back like that. I really would have died if Ryder got hurt just to come after me. His image is starting to get fuzzy. I'm losing him and I can't fight through the pain long enough to get it back.

This is it.

This is my ending.

My thoughts are fading to the black death that is sure to consume me. My body is shaking even more now and my heart is going too fast for me to even determine if it's beating at all or if it's just one continuous pounding in my chest. There's blood in the palms of my hands from my fingernails digging into my skin. I keep my eyes shut tight as I take one last breath while everything else disappears.

* * *

"Bridget," a voice, barely a whisper, enters my ear, "Bridget, wake up."

Behind my eyes, the world is still black. No face, no image of the life I'll never have to take over the darkness. The pain has stopped and I don't feel like death anymore. I'm not shivering and the tears aren't rolling down my face. I actually feel fine.

"Bridget." I hear the whispering voice and I open my eyes.

I'm still in the bathroom, lying on the floor. The sun isn't shining through the glass window above me, but I can see everything as if it were. There's a set of muddy feet not far in front of me. No shoes I recognize although I'm sure I know this person. They know my name so I must.

"Get up, Bridget." The voice is louder this time, coming from a man.

I carefully set my palms of the floor, expecting pain to flood my body, and I push myself up. There's no pain as I get to my feet and brush the hair out of my eyes. I can see everything perfectly as though this room were lit by candles or the lights still worked. It's as though I have night vision or something.

The person sharing this room with me stands in doorway. His sweatshirt is torn by his neck and his hands and fingers are brown with mud. His black hair is a mess and there's a bite mark on his neck. I look into his familiar eyes and see sadness staring back at me.

"Charlie?" I ask, confusion filling my voice.

He nods, "Been a while, Bridget."

"You could say that." The lump is already forming in my throat as I stare at my brother's face.

It's been five years since I've seen him and it's felt like forever since I've heard his voice. Yet, here is his, standing a few short feet away from me, looking the exact same as the night we covered his body with dirt. He was eighteen when he died and still looks that way at this very moment. For the first time, I'm actually older than my brother.

I start moving my feet and it feels like I'm walking on air. I just want to touch him, to wrap my arms around him for the first time in years. I've missed him so much and seeing him now is more than I can bear. I need to cry on his shoulder. I need him to tell me things are going to be alright.

He raises a hand to stop me from getting to close to him, "Sorry, Bridget, you can't hug me."

I shake my head and stop moving, "Why?"

"I'm dead, remember?" he replies.

"Isn't that why you're here though? 'Cause I'm dead now too?" I ask.

"You're not dead, little sis." He states.

"What are you talking about? I was bitten, of course I'm dead." I retort.

He shakes his head from side to side and looks past me, "See for yourself."

Hesitantly, I glance over my shoulder and look down at the floor. A shivering, pain-filled Bridget is still there, convulsing from the pain she's in. Blood forms a small puddle by her mouth and it makes me sad. I can't stand the thought of seeing myself in so much pain like that. My body is dying and transforming into something I'll never understand. At least I had the common courtesy to kick myself out of my head while this is happening. I run my fingers through my hair and turn back to my brother.

"Sorry, sis." Charlie says.

"Nothing you could've done." I reply. "I couldn't even stop this from happening."

"Yeah, but you tried." He says.

"I failed, Charlie. I let all of you down."

He shakes his head again, "You didn't fail anyone. You made it farther than any of us could. You were able to save yourself *and* the lives of quite of few other people because you lack the ability to give up. You are not capable to let things go and you set out to make great things happen. Because of you, that boy you're so in love with is still alive."

"Ryder." My voice is hardly a whisper.

"Yeah, him." Charlie says.

I close my eyes and try to find his image in my thoughts again. The only thing I can see is the utter blackness in the void that has taken over my memory. I still remember his name and the times we shared together, but I cannot bring his image back. I could squeeze my eyes shut as tight as they'll go and I'll never bring his face back.

"Bridget," Charlie says and I open my eyes, "this isn't your fault."

"It *is* my fault." I say. "I didn't turn around fast enough. I didn't aim right or pull the trigger at the right moment. I know better than that. Dad *taught* me better than that. Why did this happen to me?"

He shrugs, "I've been asking myself that very same question for years now. All of us have been. Mom, Maggie, and, yes, even dad. We don't get why this had to happen and we're always stuck wondering why it did. It's like we're caught in limbo, but we've come to know that this isn't our fault. No matter what we could have done, we would still be in this position. I still would've gotten killed by that vamp, Maggie attacked by that zombie, and mom still would've killed herself because she couldn't handle the grief anymore."

"What about dad?" I ask. "Would he still be dead even if something had gone differently?"

Charlie nods, "Even him. He tried staying with you, sis, he really fought the effects from that vamp's bite for as long as he could. He stayed with you until he couldn't handle the pain anymore. But you made his final moments the best moments he could've wished for."

"How do you know this?" I ask.

He shrugs, "I was there. I've always been there, right by your side. All of us have. We were there when you buried dad in the rain. There when you couldn't sleep through the tears in your eyes and the sadness in your heart. When you fought those zombies and saved your boyfriend's life. My favorite part was watching you stand up to that town and save those people. Watching you fight the vamps for something you believe in, was the proudest I've ever been of you."

A small smile forms across my lips. Knowing all of them were there watching over me when I needed them the most, made doing those things worth it a little more. It makes this life a lot more bearable just to know they have been by my side since things went south.

"Where's everyone now?" I ask.

"They didn't want to see this one."

"Then why are you here?"

"Because I knew you didn't want to be here either. Someone needed to help you get out of your head while the madness takes over your body. I'm the escape you needed for this moment." He replies.

"You've always been good at being an escape for me." I say.

"That's what older brothers are here for. Well, in my case not here, but..." he smiles and looks up at the ceiling.

I take this second to look over my shoulder again. The real me is still on the floor. The shivering and shaking is slowing and the blood isn't dripping from her lips anymore. Her eyes are squeezed shut so tight, I can tell she's still in pain.

"See," Charlie draws my attention back to him, "I'm

already taking your mind off the pain you're in."

"What's going to happen to me now? What am I going to turn into?" I ask.

He shrugs yet again, "Honestly, I have no idea. No human has ever been infected by both creatures before."

"Will I still be myself?"

"With you, anything's possible. You got zombies to fight a battle with the vamps and kill themselves in the process. Whatever you'll be when you wake up, you'll be something this world has never seen. Something this world will never forget."

"You think I'll wake up from this? You think I'm not gonna die completely?" I ask.

He nods his head, "You're a strong, young woman, Bridget. You've overcome challenges no person should have to be faced with. I *know* you'll wake up."

"Well, that's good, I guess. If I run into someone out there, I probably won't last very long, but at least I'll wake up." I reply.

He smiles and shakes his head, "Leave it to you to let your sarcasm take a turn for the dark side."

He looks up at the ceiling again, then turns away from me. I let him get through the doorway before taking a step and stopping him.

"Wait. Where are you going?" I ask.

He turns slightly and says, "It's time for me to go back, sis. I knew this visit was going to be a short one and I have to go."

"I don't want you to go. I need you here with me." I beg.

This is the first time I've seen my brother or heard his voice in a long time. How can I just let him walk away from me? How can I let this moment be over before it really begins? I don't want to see him go again. A part of me died with him that night in the woods and a bigger part of me feels like its dying all over again just knowing he's leaving. This was probably the only time I'll ever see him and I don't want it to end.

Sadness fills his eyes and he says, "I wish I could. I wish I could *really* be by your side when you wake up. I know you'll need someone to help you through whatever happens next, but I'll still be watching over you with mom and dad and Maggie. We'll all be here to keep an eye on you, no matter what you are when you open your eyes."

"But I don't want you go." I feel my eyes tearing up and the lump expanding in my throat again.

"I know you don't and neither do I, but it's time. We all have to move on at some point and I can't be here forever. Just remember one thing, Bridget," he turns away from me and starts walking, "everything is going to be alright, because..."

"I love you, sweet dreams, and goodnight." We finish the lullaby together and he disappears from my life one more time.

It's like the first, worst day of my life is repeating itself. I close my eyes and let the darkness of my mind consume me once again.

Part Two

I have no idea how long I've been out. The sun was shining when I got here and, as I look through the skylight above me, it's dark outside now. I can see the stars shining in the sky and they look miraculous. They seem brighter, more amazing than the last time I saw them. I don't know if the reason for that is from my being infected by both beasts. It might have something to do with me still being a bit delirious from the whole ordeal. I mean, I *did* just have a conversation with my brother who has been dead for five years now.

Something else seems off as well. The floor isn't cold anymore. I'm either used to it or I can't feel it. The pain has faded entirely, but my body feels stiff. I've been lying in the fetal position for who knows how long and I'm afraid if I move again, the pain will come screaming back. I got lucky when I passed out earlier. Everything was so intense, which was probably the reason I kicked myself out of my mind and hallucinated about Charlie. It was the only thing to keep my mind off whatever was happening to me.

Speaking of that, I just now realized, I still feel like myself in my head. I know my name is Bridget, I know my family and I can even picture their faces when I close my eyes. My dad with his grey hair and smirk on his face. My mom with the sad eyes and hair just as brown as mine. Maggie and Charlie staring at me with goofy smiles just like they had when we were still a family.

I can even picture Ryder, which is just the best.

I can see him struggling against Carter's grip, trying to get to me. If I try harder, I can see him smiling. I can hear his laughter and his voice as he tells me how much he cares about me. I still remember his face and that's all I really care about.

I open my eyes and stare at the room around me. Even though it's dark in here, I can see everything perfectly as though the lights were on. The grimy tiles on the wall across from me. The wooden door is still wide open and I can even see the mirror I smashed when I saw my eyes change. That mirror makes me want to see them again. I have to know for sure what I am.

I put my palm on the floor, feeling the cracks in the linoleum, and slowly push myself up to my knees. Every muscle stretches and pulls against me like my body is telling me not to get up. My knees and elbows pop when I finally get to my feet. It doesn't bring a new pain, it just feels like I ran a marathon without training for it. I'm sore, but I feel fine on the inside.

I look around the room before turning around to the mirror. The trash can is still in its place and there's a small puddle of blood where my head was just on the floor. The redness glimmers in the starlight. It's amazing how I can see this well in the dark. It's like I have cat eyes now or permanent night vision.

I'm not going to lie, this is kind of cool.

My feet spin around and I stare into the mirror. I've changed since earlier. My hair doesn't look dull, it looks shiny and healthy as it hangs delicately on my shoulders. There's no bump from where my hair tie was and it looks better than any hairstyle I could ever attempt to do. My skin is slightly paler than before, but it isn't all veiny or death ridden. I take a step forward, feeling my weight shift to my left foot. It's awkward to walk being so stiff and my legs feel wobbly. I grab hold of the sink and lean closer to the mirror.

There is a trail of dried blood on the corner of my mouth and I wipe it away with the back of my hand. My skin feels so soft and I drag my fingers across my face just to feel the smoothness again. Ryder would love how satiny this feels. He'd probably never stop touching or kissing me again.

There's a small amount of blood on my shirt and I can see it dried on the collar of my hoodie. Not much I can do about that. Blood typically stains clothes. I ignore it and lean closer to the mirror and take a good look at my eyes.

Part of me was hoping I had imagined my eyes changing colors. Not part of me, but *all* of me was hoping for that. I never wanted to see what I'm currently staring at. They aren't the deep black of the zombies' nor are they the hazy grey of the vamps'. They're more like a metallic silvery color and they're kind of beautiful. My brown eyes were pretty boring and hundreds of living humans on the planet have that color of eyes. This silver that has overtaken them, is almost mesmerizing. I could get lost in my own eyes.

I step back and examine the rest of me. I brush my hair away from my neck where the vamp had clamped its teeth against me. *Odd.* The marks are gone. Not even a scar remains. I look down to my right arm and push the sleeve up to my elbow. I wipe the dry blood away and see the same result. The holes are still in my hoodie, but no evidence remains that I was ever bitten.

This is something different. Every zombie and every vamp I've seen or killed, has shown some scar from where they were originally bitten. That bite in the neck or the claw mark across the chest, there's *always* a mark. I don't have anything. I guess this is a good thing. I'd be able to blend in a little with humans and not have to hide anything, other than my eyes.

I raise an eyebrow and run my fingers through my

amazingly soft hair. The shampoo in the city would never make my hair this soft or this wild looking without me doing something else to it. It's so wavy. *I love it!*

I really can't lie about this at all. I love how wonderful I feel. Despite the stiffness in my bones and muscles, I feel like I was never in that much pain and it was a *severe* amount of pain. I keep my eyes on my reflection and a smile forms across my lips. A small amount of white from my teeth shines through and I'm even more relieved by that. They aren't disgusting like a good majority of the undead have.

"Amazing." I whisper, surprising myself again.

There was no hesitation, no stuttering to get that simple little word out. I just said it, plain as day. Another indicator that I'm not like what bit me. As Charlie stated in my dream, I'm something different. I don't know what that is yet, but I'm *almost* hoping to find out.

I pull myself away from the mirror and walk out of the bathroom. With every step, my body loosens and I feel even better. I feel stronger, like I could take on the world. I can see everything in this store as though the lights are on. Darkness doesn't seem to have an effect on me. I don't know what that will mean in the morning when the sun is out, but for now, it's a good thing.

There's a stack of clay pots right next to me. It's stacked about as high as my head with the bottom facing up. I place a hand on the pots and feel every rough spot in the clay. I can feel where the tiny bumps where the material didn't hold as well, something I don't think I would have noticed before. I take my hand away and stare at the very top of the stack.

"Vamps can jump even higher and not get hurt. Wonder if I can." I say to myself, elated that I can make complete sentences.

I step back and face the stack of pots. It doesn't seem *so* high. I think I can do it. I bend my knees a little, keeping my eyes at the top of the stack. As if I have done this a million times, I jump the five and a half foot high stack and land perfectly on the top. It wobbles a bit, making me feel off balance. That makes the stack start to tilt and I can feel it falling out from under me. I look around. There's an aisle nearby with a perfect top shelf for me to land on. Just as the pots tip over for good, I leap through the air and land with both feet on the shelf.

The crash from the pots echoes through the store and fills my ears with so much sound it's almost unbearable. Everything is louder than before and I have to plug my ears to drown it out. The pots stop breaking and the echoes stop bouncing from wall to wall. I uncover my ears and listen for something to come next. I don't think anything else is here with me, but there's always a chance. It is nighttime and vamps could be lurking in the shadows here.

I listen to the silent air for a few minutes and nothing happens. No groaning from zombies and no vampires rushing to get me. I'm completely alone and this is just like a big playground for a person who wants to figure out what all they're capable of doing.

There's a metal pipe above me with water spigots spread out to spray the plants. It's just a couple feet above my head. I don't think a normal human being could jump and catch it, but I have a feeling I can do that very thing.

I bend my knees again and leap into the air. I reach my hands out and grab onto the pipe and pull myself up, setting my feet on it to kneel. The pipe sways back and forth, but I feel stable. I feel in control of everything I'm doing and slowly begin to stand. There's nothing for me to hold onto once I let go of the pipe at my feet, but it stays steady. I'm not losing my balance and I don't feel like I'm going to topple over and crash to the shelves below me.

I take a few baby steps, just to get in the rhythm. The pipe moves slightly with each step. I put one foot in front of the other until it seems easy as pie, then I pick up the pace. The thing might be swaying under my feet, but I feel on top of the world right now. My feet move faster until I'm running across the pipe. I don't look down, I just keep my eyes ahead of me with a smile on my face.

The end of the pipe is coming up fast. There's a tall, metal gazebo not far from the end. I run a little faster and push myself off the pipe. It feels like I'm flying through the air as I reach out for the top of the gazebo. I grab one of the posts and flip myself around it, let go and land on the floor. I brush the hair from my face and look around for the building's exit.

The world outside should be even more incredible, more vivid with this new life of mine. I can't wait to experience it all. The door is just past a few dead plants on the ground, right behind the registers. *I wonder how fast I can run now.* Those vamps can run pretty fast and you can miss them if you're not too careful. I move away from the gazebo, making sure I have a straight shot to the door. There's a pallet with bags of dirt I'll have to leap over, but that's a piece of cake.

My hands clench into fists and I make a mad dash to the door. I can barely feel my legs moving as the rest of the store blurs past my eyes. The pallet of dirt came and went, not getting in my way at all when I leapt over it. I push through the door, letting the glass shatter as it hits the wall and I rush outside.

I stop running a few feet outside the store and look around. These new eyes of mine are amazing. Everything is so clear and magnificent. The colors are more alive. I've never experienced just how true every color I've come across really is until this very moment. The green of the grass, the grey rocks under my feet, even with the sun below the horizon, it's all so fantastic. The stars are like tiny candles sparkling against the dark canvas above me. There's millions of them, more than I've ever been able to notice before.

I breathe in through my nose, taking in every wonderful scent. Everything I smell is even better than before. The grass, the trees, even the air smells amazing. I can practically taste the things I'm smelling and I can't wait to come across other aromas.

I feel like I've been missing out on these senses my whole life and it's a great feeling to have them now. Knowing I can do things I was never capable of doing, or seeing things I could never imagine seeing before. For lack of a better word, it's so wonderfully amazing.

I look back to the world in front of me when something no so great passes through my mind. I just ran like a bat out of hell in that store. I'm not winded, I'm not tired, and I don't feel like my heart is going to beat out of my chest. In fact, I don't feel it beating at all. That's the least amazing thing I could feel right about now. It pretty much ruins everything I just thought was great.

Quickly, I lift my hand and place it on my neck, checking for a pulse. I don't get one. I press two fingers to my wrist. Still no pulse. Finally, I place my hands on my chest, right over my heart and focus on feeling the one thing I *need* to feel right now. It feels like years have gone by with me standing like an idiot with both my hands on my chest, not feeling the most important thing a human needs to feel.

I let my hands fall to my side and every feeling of glee and happiness escapes me. I died back there in that bathroom. My heart no longer beats. Of all the things that had to happen, this is the worst. This is the one thing that makes me practically identical to those monsters who did this to me.

Without a heart, how can I feel anything for anyone I come across? How could I face a human and be able to hide the fact that I am now a member of the undead? How could I ever face Ryder again if I were given the chance? Would he hate me or would he fear me?

I really hate when my mind thinks of all these annoying questions. My life is already hard to deal with. I don't need those to make things worse.

I turn around and sulk back inside the store. I still don't know what time of night it is and I'd rather not take the risk of getting caught outside when the sun comes up. There's no saying if I'll be like the vampires in that situation or not. Obviously, I'm hoping I'm not like them, but you never know. I am the newest being to walk the face of the earth and there's really no telling what I can do.

* * *

I found a nice spot under the cashier's desk inside the store after my unfortunate discovery about my new form. This spot is not the most comfortable spot in the world to hide. My knees are bent and my head is about an inch from hitting the underside of the desk. But, I figured when the sun comes up, I'll be safe. I don't want to risk being more like a vamp than I already feel. I've seen how so many of them die and it's not pretty. It actually seems very painful and I'm not much into that. After feeling my body go through the worst change on the planet, roasting in the sun is far from what I would like to do. Thinking about it kind of makes me feel sorry for the few I've destroyed that way.

I'm still trying to find a pulse somewhere on my body. I check every spot I know of and always come up disappointed. At one point, I even squeezed one of my fingers so hard, trying to cut off the blood circulation in hopes of feeling a pulse, and still there was nothing. My finger didn't even turn purple like it would normally do if there was blood flow in my body. It's a weird thought knowing I'm alive yet I don't have a pulse anymore.

Sleep is another thing I couldn't find overnight. I never

felt tired the few hours that were left of the night and my eyes never got heavy. I closed them, hoping I'd fall asleep just so time would pass by faster. Dreamland never came and I stared at the wall for a good majority of the night. One thing that helped time pass a little more swiftly, was thinking of Ryder.

I can still picture his face and see his perfect smile. His voice echoes in my ear and I thank my lucky stars that I didn't forget him. That would have destroyed me. I wish I knew what he'd think of me right now. I'm not really human anymore and I'm not exactly one of the other two things either. I'm my own being and it makes me wonder if he'd be afraid of me. He could take one look at me and see that I'm different then shoot me in the head to end it all. Or he could look past what I've become and still be in love with me. The worst part is not knowing how he'd react. I'll never see him again, so I'll never know.

Wow. That thought just about kills me all over again. Never seeing Ryder again is worse than anything else in the world. I'm sure they went back to the city and gave up searching for the village. No matter how hard Ryder probably fought to chase after me, they would have made him go back to the city with one less person in the group. He's safer behind those walls and he knows it. He doesn't need to risk his life to come after me. I could be an even bigger threat to the human race and I'd rather die than let that happen.

It's better this way. It's better that I never get to see him again.

So, here I am, still crouched under the cashier's desk with a stiff body. The sun came out a little while ago and I'm afraid to come out of hiding. With the skylights above me and the sun shining all over the place, there's not much room for me to hide in case the sun decides to boil my skin.

There's still some shade over this part of the store. The skylights are mainly over the mid-section to provide light for the plants that used to be here. I have *some* room to play with before worrying about the sunlight. I move my stiff body and crawl out of hiding. I feel every muscle stretch and pull against me as I get to my feet. I raise my arms over my head and stretch as much as I can to loosen up. A sharp cracking sound comes from my neck as I pop it. It sounds like it would have hurt, but I didn't feel much of anything.

I glance around the store. My eyes are having a hard time adjusting to the morning light. It kind of hurts looking around the place, not a bad pain, just an annoying one. I squint and move away from the register. My feet take me to the glass door at the front of the store and I keep my distance. The sun is shining even brighter right here making it much harder for me to see. I'm thinking it has something to do with the change in my eyes. I might have to do something about that.

I stop moving at the edge of the light coming through the doorway. I'll have to go outside eventually. I can't really stay in an old greenhouse for the rest of eternity. Not a lot of excitement to be had in a place with dead plants. At least we will have something in common, we're both dead.

Slowly, I lift my hand and ease it toward the light. This way, if the sun burns me, I'll only be hurting my hand and not the rest of me. I think I can manage life without a hand. It would suck, but I'd get over it. The light is getting closer and I slow down even more. The tip of my middle finger hits the light first and I brace myself for the pain that apparently isn't going to come. I move the rest of my hand into the sunlight and it's completely fine. No smoke rising from my skin and no blisters bursting with puss. I barely feel the warmth of the sun at all.

I smile and take the next couple steps to put the rest of me in the direct sunlight. My head is the only thing left as I take that final step outside. The second the rays hit my eyes I'm blinded with the brightest light I've even seen. Pain fills my head and my eyes feel like they're on fire. I close them quickly, still feeling the burn. I fall to my knees, then cover my face with my hands.

Fallback number two of this new creature I've become.

I don't have a heartbeat anymore and now I can't see during the daytime without catching my eyes on fire. What a *wonderful* life this will be.

I spin around and crawl back inside the store, keeping my eyes closed until I'm safe in the shadows again. It's still hard to see and they burn quite a bit, but I can make out the objects around me. I'll at least be able to see my way around the store without bumping against too many things.

If only I had something to cover my eyes so I can walk around outside. There's got to be something I could use to shield them from the sun. I'm *positive* there's something manmade that will work perfect for me.

Oh wait! There *is* something I can use. These fantastic things called sunglasses. They would work perfectly for what I need. I just have to find a pair.

It is still very bright, but my eyes don't hurt anymore as I stand. There could be a chance I'd find a pair of sunglasses in this place. The people who worked here did things outside and I'm sure they liked to have something to keep the sun out of their eyes. I have no idea where I'd find them, but I have to start looking or I never will.

I go back to the register and look around the computer. There's some old paperwork and a few pennies stashed in a pile. The drawer under the cash drawer is filled with yellowing receipts and trash. I move to the second register and find the same things, even a wad of cash lying next to the machine. It serves no purpose to me to have it, so I'll let it sit.

No such luck at the registers so I turn around. I squint a little and find a set of stairs leading to a small office with windows looking out over the store. I rush to the stairs, faster than I probably needed to and run up the short flight. The door to the office is locked, but the window on the door looks easy to shatter. With my elbow, I slam my arm against the glass, letting it crash to the floor in pieces. I reach inside and unlock the door to open it.

A pungent stench greets me and I almost don't want to go inside. Something has been in here, rotting for quite a while. I can smell everything about it. The dried blood, the decaying flesh, I can even smell the person's hair which is something I've never experienced before. I step into the office and take a left to go in further. The smell gets stronger and I see what's causing it.

He doesn't look that old, maybe sixteen or seventeen. His body lies on the floor with blood stains in the carpet by both of his arms. The knife is still in his grip from when he cut himself. The smell made it seem like he's been here awhile, but this looks a little fresh. His skin is still peach colored and the blood hasn't faded to that nasty purple color it likes to change to. I guess this kid couldn't take the world any longer and found a way out. Not like this is the first time I've seen a suicidal human before. That family in the rest area was the worst, so seeing this kid is nothing.

I can't believe how strong the scent of his blood and flesh are to me. I never would have noticed these smells before I got infected and I hate to say this, like *really* hate to say this, but it smells enticing. I can feel my mouth watering as that horrid scent drifts further up my nose. I move closer to him, staring at his lifeless form at my feet. There's a strange feeling going through my body. Something I think I'll have to learn how to control if I'm ever in the vicinity of a *living* human. I can feel myself wanting to taste the flesh that I smell, take a sip of the blood that has poured from his wrists.

It's intoxicating.

I bite my lower lip as my eyes devour the dead body. It's disgusting that my mind is even considering taking a bit out of him. Every other thought has left my mind and all I can think about is eating this corpse. I don't know what would happen to me if I did and I'd rather not find out. It's just really hard to keep my mind from thinking about what he'd taste like. It feels like there's something rising inside of me that wants to gain control over my body and do whatever the hell it wants.

What if I'm by a human and I get this urge to try a bite? Will I be able to control it or will this new form of mine take over and turn me into a monster I'll hate?

I'm wasting too much time trying to figure out what I'm going to be. Eating this dead man's flesh and tasting the blood that's still in him isn't an option. I absolutely refuse to be like the things who turned me into this. I can't afford to be something else the planet is forced to fear.

I turn my eyes away from him and take control over my mind and body. The manager's desk is pressed against the wall right under a window looking out to the store. A coat is draped over the back of the chair and, with any luck, I'll find what I need and get out of this place. I step over the corpse and walk quickly to the desk. I push the papers aside and sift through the drawers only to come up empty handed. It's in the pocket of the coat where I finally find what I'm looking for.

The dark pair of shades is just the thing I need. They aren't too big, so they won't cover my entire face, and they aren't too small to let sunlight shine through. They are just the right size and I slide them on my face. Instantly, my eyes can see without the tiny hint of fire burning through them. The light isn't bothering me and I don't have to squint in order to see anymore. I admire myself in the reflection on the window and smile a bit.

"I look pretty damn good in these things." I say to myself.

The things that make me happy from now on are definitely going to be different.

* * *

The sunglasses were a great find. It is intensely bright outside, even with the shades covering my eyes, but they aren't on fire and that's a plus in my book.

I'm following a gravel road away from the greenhouse. I believe it's the driveway that would take me to some main road I'm sure. I figured I'd follow this for a little while, then turn into the woods. I've always been one to stray away from the trees when vamps are known to hide there, but I think I'll be safe now that I'm not exactly *human* anymore.

Out here in the open, it's like a whole new world. I can see much farther than I ever could before. All I have to do is focus on a bird flying in the sky and it looks to be right in front of my face. I can hear things that aren't even close to me. If I focus hard enough, I can concentrate on just one thing and not let everything take over. I can smell things I've never smelt before. Flowers, leaves in the trees above my head, the flesh of an animal running through the woods. That scent is what's overpowering the most.

There is a stream up ahead that flows under the gravel road. This section of the path was made into a bridge with wooden beams for railings on either side of it to prevent people from falling over the edge. The railings aren't real tall, so I doubt they did a decent job. I move closer to them and stop for a moment. There's a message spray painted in white colored graffiti on one of the wooden barricades. Someone decided to let the world know where they thought heaven and hell were. There are arrows next to both words, pointing up to the sky. I guess this person thought that no matter where they go, it'll be hell for them. It's a sad world when people are forced to think that way.

Good to know, I still don't believe in a man in the sky

watching over us.

I walk across the bridge and figure it's time to venture into the woods. I'd hate to run into a human trying to find safety out here. Being hidden by the trees is the best place for me to be. I'll blend right in with the vamps out here.

I see a deer cross into my path. It's not really in front of me by any means. It's more like a hundred yards away and I can see it perfectly. I can smell the flesh on its body, the blood coursing through its veins. It is so mouth-watering that I can't stand it. The hunger is growing inside of me and I wish there was something I could do to get rid of it. I know what I'm craving the most, but I don't want to be this *thing* who eats living creatures while they are still moving. I'm not against eating meat, but when its heart is still beating while you take your first bite, that's going a little too far.

Every animal I come across has that same effect on me. I have to pause, take a deep breath, and try focusing on something else. The smell of them only makes the hunger grow and it becomes harder to focus on anything else. No matter how wonderful the idea sounds, it's equally disgusting and I hope I can control it.

That sounds easier than it actually is.

I jump over a fallen tree without any effort at all. There's evidence of a campsite on the other side of the trunk. It's old, no one has been here for a long time, possibly years. I can see the pile of sticks they put together to make a fire and a small log they set up for a place to sit. Reminds me of the first night with Ryder. Sitting under the stars and talking about random things in our lives. I didn't know I'd fall in love with him at that moment. We were just two complete strangers who didn't want to travel alone.

I wish I wasn't alone right now. Having no one to talk to is boring and lonely. It makes the day go so much slower and it feels like I'm never going to make it anywhere. I mean, have nowhere to go, but I don't want the rest of my life to inch its way by either. I could always befriend a fellow member of the undead, but they wouldn't make for good company.

I move away from the old campsite and pass a few more trees. The smell of the bark creeps up my nose. I've never been able to smell a tree like this before. Smelling the wood and the sticky sap running down the bark. It's so different now and it'll probably take a while to get used to all these new changes.

I hear movement to my left and I stop walking. It didn't sound big, like a person. It was small and I turn my head toward the sound and sniff the air. The smell of flesh fills my nose and my stomach is begging me to put something in it. It aches and growls and I know I won't make it too far without eating something. I take a few steps toward the rustling sound and wait. The bush right ahead of me is moving and the branches creak as they sway.

I tilt my head to the side and watch a small, brown rabbit hop out of the bush. It pays no attention to me as it sniffs the ground searching for something to eat. My hands are shaking as I stare at this wonderful creature. It would make a nice meal. I know I could catch it. After running that fast in the store last night, it would be easy. And all it would really take is one bite to kill the little guy. I could make it instant so he won't feel a thing, then I'll be able to fulfill my stomach's needs.

I shake my head back and forth. That sounds horrible. The thought of eating that tiny little animal. It probably has a family of even smaller bunnies waiting for him. How could I take him away from that? I can't kill this poor, innocent creature who has done nothing wrong to me. I can't rip the flesh from its bones and let the taste of its blood flow down my throat. I can't give in to the monster growing inside of me and let it have what it so desires.

What am I thinking? *Of course I can.* I'm hungry and there is a perfect meal sitting on the ground a few feet away from me.

I take a step, as quietly as I possibly can, closing the distance between me and my dinner. My mouth waters as I get closer and closer to it. I can't control myself any longer. The hunger for this thing is too strong and I *need* it. I need to let the monster out for a moment and get what it wants so I can keep moving. I need to let the taste of that thing fill my urges and take the hunger pain away.

I get a little closer and it notices me. Its ears perk up as it stares my way. The chase is about to begin and there is no delaying it. I take that last step and the rabbit takes off like a bat out of hell. A smile forms across my lips as I dart after it. I leap over small bushes and plants while the rabbit is able to run underneath them. I'm sure its little heart is pounding faster and faster as it tries to get away from me. I think it's having a bit of an issue seeing as how I'm closing in on it pretty fast. Just a few more feet to go and it's all mine.

The rabbit jumps over a tree root sticking out of the ground and trips over its big feet. That gives me the advantage and I throw myself on top of it. I have no control over myself right now as I clench onto the furry body of this animal. It wriggles and squirms in my grip as I sit up on the ground. I can feel its heart beating faster than mine ever has. My eyes widen as I stare at the succulent flesh. The smell is even more fantastic and I don't waste any time sinking my teeth into its tiny body.

I rip a chunk of flesh and fur from the rabbit's body, letting the blood slide down my chin as I chew my meal. The rabbit's life ends in a matter of seconds and I take another bite, ripping more flesh and muscles from its bones. I close my eyes, eating the only thing able to meet my demands. Everything in my mind rushes by in a flash. Vivid colors and textures I've never seen before. I take another bite and another rush flows through me. The monster is finally getting what it wants and I know I've made it happy.

It takes a few, short minutes to finish eating and I toss what's left to the ground a couple feet away. I look down at my hands and see the blood seeping between my fingers. I wipe my mouth with the back of my right hand and see even more of the rabbit's blood. For some reason, I don't want this to go to waste. I lick my lips, letting the blood flow down my throat before I slurp up what's on my hands. The small amount that's left, I wipe on a few dead leaves on the ground. I get as much of the blood from my face before I finally take a breath.

During this moment of relief, control finally comes back to me. My mind and body are mine once more and I realize what I've done to that poor little creature. It didn't deserve to die like that, having some undead thing eat it raw while its heart was still beating. If I can't control this craving around an animal, who's to say I can control it around a human. I feel horrible right now knowing I'll never be my full self again. I'll be this demon who needs some sort of fresh meat in order to stay alive. I've only been like this a short while and already it's hard to stop myself from getting the flesh and blood that I want.

Not to mention, it's absolutely disgusting what I've just done. I ate a rabbit. It was still alive and struggling in my grip when I took that first bite. I wish I could force myself to throw up but that would only drive me to want more of something else. I just hope an animal is that something else and not a human.

There's movement coming from behind me, bringing me back to reality. Heavy footsteps and I know they're coming from a human. They don't smell dead or rotting. They smell fresh and alive. The smell of their salty skin climbs up my nose and a frenzy erupts in my stomach all over again. The rabbit wasn't enough and I find myself wanting this new smell. My mouth waters as it gets stronger and the footsteps get closer. I wipe my mouth with the back of my hand again, getting the last trace of blood from my lips.

I stand slowly and turn around to face whatever's there. I expected to see a person or an animal or even a zombie. I'm prepared for all that. Only there's nothing other than thin air and trees for me to be prepared for. I can hear the footsteps like they are right next to me. Crunching over leaves and twigs as they walk. It's clearly a human of some kind. I spin around, searching every direction for whoever is out here with me. I see a bunch of trees, some bushes, a few leaves floating to the ground. Just no sight of a person walking near me.

This hearing of mine is very deceiving, not to mention confusing. I'm obviously not alone in the woods right now and I would love it if I could pinpoint exactly where these footsteps are coming from. Right now, being so new at trying to focus on one thing at a time, I can't tell at all. Every direction I look, it seems like they're coming from that way.

I take a deep breath, inhaling through my nose, and close my eyes. The smell isn't confusing. Their flesh is alive and burning through my nostrils. The blood in their veins tells me which way I'd have to go to find them. It's easier to concentrate on the smell other than sight or sound. I guess being a blood or flesh hungry monster will allow you to do that.

With my nose in the air, I move around until the odor is at its strongest point. My body wants the person walking through the woods. It wants me to run after them and devour their heart and soul without thinking twice about it. My mind, being the logical part of me, tells me otherwise. It wants me to run away and put as much distance between this human and myself as possible. Whatever's inside me might be very strong, but I know I can force the human part of me to be stronger and try not to give in when a human is around.

I open my eyes and stare in front of me. The footsteps are getting louder. At least I'm not nervous or terrified right now. Fear was the one thing that used to hold me back in certain situations. It was fear that made me hesitate whenever I was face to face with a vamp.

I hated that feeling and I'm glad it's gone.

It isn't here to tell me to be afraid of running into a

human out here in the woods. It's not here to tell me to run away and never have contact with anyone ever again. Courage and the insatiable desire to meet this stranger is keeping me in place. I stand still, letting the footsteps grow louder with every passing second. I can actually hear them breathing now. I can hear their hearts beating in their chest.

This is so strange.

Finally, I see the person coming into view. It's a man and he isn't too far from me. He's not paying attention, his eyes are focused on the ground. Not the wisest thing to do in the woods, but to each his own. He's carrying a backpack on his shoulders and a gun holstered to the belt around his waist. He steps over a small branch and I notice a smaller human right behind him. She's younger than me, maybe fifteen or so, and the man she's with has to be a few years older. She has jet, black hair that's pulled back into a tight bun and a serene face. Her clothes are dark, matching the shade of her eyes.

The girl is the first to notice me.

Our eyes meet and she freezes in her tracks. She grabs the man's wrist and he stops walking. Both of them are staring at me and I feel like a deer caught in headlights. The man's hand quickly goes for the gun at his waist and he aims it at me in a flash. I'm sure if he saw my eyes under these sunglasses I'd be dead in a second. Seeing those metallic orbs is a surefire giveaway that I'm not human. Luckily, he can't see them and I'm not about to take these shades off just to show him.

"What are you?" he shouts and moves a little closer to me, "Are you human?"

How should I answer this one? I've never had to think about this before. Never thought I'd have to. Lying is the obvious choice, even though it doesn't feel like a lie. I've been a human my whole life, so forgive me for thinking it's weird to say I'm not one all of a sudden.

"Answer me before I shoot." He demands.

I shrug, "Do I look like anything that's not human to

you?"

He stops moving and takes a moment to go over my answer. It's not necessarily a lie. I just went around the answer to let *them* decide what I am. Everything about my appearance is human, other than my eyes and the blood on my clothes. I'm not pale and veiny like a vamp and I'd be frying right now if I were. I'm standing in a direct ray of sunshine. My skin isn't rotten or decaying like some of the zombies and I can speak in perfect sentences. To the untrained eye, I am still a human.

Good thing this man can see all the human things about me. He lowers the gun and stands up straight, putting the gun back in the holster. The girl has her hand tight on his wrist as they slowly make their way toward me. Their aroma gets stronger and I start thinking that it might've been a good idea to run away. I still don't know how well I can control this new desire of mine.

* * *

The smell of their flesh drifts up my nose and that horrifying hunger pain is starting to take over my stomach again. I keep my eyes on the man and focus on only his scent. The salt of his skin, the sweat on his brow, the smell of his blood coursing through his veins is much stronger than before. My mouth starts to water as I stare into his eyes. I know in my mind I could catch him much easier than that rabbit. It would lead to a pretty good fight, but I'd win in the end. I have a feeling the monster inside me is much stronger than this strange man and the girl he's with. Both of them would be so filling and so rewarding with all I've been through since I woke up.

The man is well built, slightly bigger than Ryder, with shaggy blonde hair and deep blue eyes. His tan skin and those tight muscles under his shirt look delicious, I can practically taste him already. The girl is a tad on the scrawny side with long, black hair. Her dark eyes stare right through me, questioning why I'm staring so much. Her flesh and blood would be pretty tasty as well.

Hold on a second. I'm not seriously considering eating these people, am I? That goes against *everything* I believe in.

What the *hell* is wrong with me?

I *can't* eat them. They are two, simply travelers, most likely out here in search of food or shelter. I can't be the one bad thing that stands in their way of that. I *have* to control whatever the hell is going on inside me. I don't want to add to the pandemic that has already destroyed the planet.

"You alright?" the man asks, as he stops moving and stands right in front of me.

I shake the demonic thoughts about eating him out of my head and run my fingers through my hair. I nod and keep my mouth shut. That gun is still holstered to the belt around his waist. If I show any signs of not being human, a bullet could go straight into my brain. I have no idea if I'm quick enough to evade the deathly outcome that would bring me and I'm not ready to find out.

He squints his eyes as he stares at me, "You know you have blood on your chin? And on the collar of you hoody and even some on your shirt? You mind telling me what that's all about?"

I shake my head and quickly wipe the rest of the rabbit's blood from my face, embarrassed about it being there. I have to force myself to keep the urge of wanting to lick it off my hand. It was so good the first time, I know it would taste the same now.

"I cut myself a little bit ago," I reply, "that's all it is."

He raises an eyebrow and says, "Sure," he doesn't believe me one bit, "What are you doing out here in the middle of nowhere then?"

I shrug and say, "Nothing. Just out for a hike."

He smiles a pretty gorgeous smile and I can see him relaxing as he says, "A smart ass, I like it."

"A girl has to be when she's faced with a world full of monsters." I reply. "What are the two of you doing out in the woods?"

He shakes his head, "We're headed back to our village. We went looking for supplies," he notions to his backpack, "and it's about another day's walk before we get home."

"I see." I reply.

The girl steps around him and asks, "Aren't you afraid of getting eaten?" her voice is soft and sweet sounding.

"Not anymore. I have no reason to be." I reply, keeping the truth all for myself.

"Why?" she asks.

I shrug, "There's no point in spending your life afraid of them."

"Where's your weapon?" the man chimed in.

"Ran out of bullets so I ditched it. Don't need it anyway." I say, thinking about the gun my father gave to me.

At least that wasn't a total lie. I'm pretty sure I was out of ammo when the gun fell out of my fingers at the overpass. It serves me no purpose anymore. I think I could handle my own if I'm face to face with a vamp or a zombie. There's nothing either of those things could do to me that would further ruin my life anyway.

"You're a weird girl," he says, stating the obvious, "Name's George and this is my little sister, Kelly." He sticks out his hand to shake mine.

I stare at his outstretched hand while he waits for a response from me. I'm a little afraid to touch his skin.

Controlling myself, I am learning, is going to be a hard task and touching the flesh of a human, something I'm craving at the moment, might drive me over the edge. However, in order to keep passing as a human, I'll have to force myself to take chances like this one.

"I'm Bridget." I say, taking a firm, yet shaky, grasp on his hand.

The second our skin touches, the frenzy in my mind begins again. I can feel the blood flowing in his hand. His rough skin wouldn't be so hard to get through and it would only take a few seconds and his agony would be over. My lips are quivering at the thought of devouring another living creature. This would be more fulfilling than the measly little rabbit lying dead a few feet from where we're standing.

I can't do it. I can't go against the things I stand for. The human race still needs to go on and still needs to win the war against the vamps and zombies. I'm not going to allow myself to stoop to the levels of the creatures destroying mankind.

It pains me to do this, but I peel my hand away from his and force a smile to my face. George smiles in return and raises an eyebrow at my lack of commitment with my own. It's hard to fake a smile when my body wants something I refuse to give it.

"What's with the shades? It isn't that bright out here with the trees to block out the sun." He asks.

I shrug, "The sun hurts my eyes. What's with the million questions to a complete stranger?"

"It's rare to come across another human in the woods. Normally people stick to the highway since vamps roam this part of the world. Our village isn't really near a highway so the woods are the easiest way to get there." He replies.

"Then I should let you get back to your village. I'd hate for you to keep your family waiting." I say, then step aside.

"Where are you headed? To the city?"

The city. I hated that place at first, wanting to feel like I mattered in a place filled with hundreds who could care less about me. But I made something for myself there. I made sure I still mattered and was still able to contribute to the survival of mankind. I made a home in Des Moines with close friends that were more like family and Ryder being the number one best thing about that place. He's all I really miss about it right now and a lump forms in my throat just thinking about him.

"I can't go back there." I say, quietly.

"Why?" Kelly asks.

I shake my head, hoping to drop the subject, "I just can't."

"Okay. Keep your secrets," George states, "You can come with us if you want. We don't have a lot, but you could stay for a day or two until you figure something out."

That could be the worst decision I'd ever make. Being in a place with other humans might be bad. I'm new at this and it'll take a while to get used to things and how to control myself. If something goes wrong, that village could witness the beginning of a horrible monster unleashed to the world.

On the other hand, I hate being alone. I hate thinking that this is how it's going to be from now on. It would be nice for some company and the last time I traveled with a stranger, it wound up being something spectacular. There's a good chance that won't happen with George and Kelly, but I could at least entertain the idea of traveling with them. This will just have to be another learning experience on how to control myself.

"Sure." I say, hoping this doesn't come back to bite me in the ass.

He smiles, "Okay. I just have one more question before we get moving."

"Go for it."

"You have no idea who we are or if we're even telling the truth, how are you so trusting?" he asks.

I raise an eyebrow and tilt my head to the side, "Well, for starters, you're not nervous enough to be lying to me. You

seem confident, like you care to get back to your village without bringing harm to an innocent young woman. Secondly,
you wouldn't be walking around the woods with your little
sister knowing full well there could be vamps all over the
place, just to find someone to hurt or kill. A normal person
would be scared shitless to do such a thing."

He smirks and nods, "I guess you're right. Let's get
going."

* * *

George really doesn't like to travel in silence. He's basically
told me his entire life story in the short couple of hours since
we met. I got to learn that he came from a very wealthy
family of doctors and lawyers. He was on the path to be-
coming one himself when the cure was developed. His
mother was one of the doctors who injected quite a few
people with the cure and had a hard time living with herself
after that. She wound up injecting herself and sat out in the
sun to seal her fate.

His father is still alive and helps run the little village.
George told me it's just what's left of a very small town.
Most of it has been destroyed and only a few houses remain.
The humans trying to survive haven't been there for long and
only plan on staying until the vamps or zombies get wind of
them. This would also be the very same village that small
family told me about. The very reason all of us left the safety
of the city walls. At least I can find comfort in knowing it still

exists and isn't full of bad guys like Dwayne thought.

George's sister, Kelly, hasn't said much since I joined them. She keeps quiet and only speaks up when she has something to add to a story George is telling. He whispered to me how she's still upset about their mother dying. She never really got over it and has been quiet ever since. I can't blame her on that one. I know what it's like to lose a mother who chose to kill herself. I just refuse to stay quiet most of the time.

"Tell me about you, Bridget. What's your life like?" George asks.

"Not much to tell. I was a traveler, then went to Des Moines and lived there for the last year and now I'm back out here. Pretty boring." I'd rather not tell them too much about my life.

"Okay, you obviously don't want to talk about life in the city. Tell me about your family, then. What are they like?" he asks.

"Dead." I say, simply.

"Oh," he says, "Sorry to hear that."

"Don't be. I was able to take a lot of anger out on the creatures who did it and that helped quite a bit. The zombies tend to be my area of expertise when it comes to killing them." I say.

He smiles, "Yeah, they are the easiest. Have you run into any of the ones who sort of hesitate when they see a human?"

I nod, "Yeah, still haven't figured out why they do that."

"No one has, but it's got all of us confused and some are afraid that they're about to change into something worse."

I raise an eyebrow, "I highly doubt that. An entire group of them committed suicide to save me and a bunch of other humans from being a midnight snack for the vamps. I don't think they're going to change into anything different at all."

He snaps his head in my direction and seems taken aback, "What? What are you talking about?"

"Oh, before I came to the Des Moines, a friend and I

found this small city down south, Hatfeld. They were trading human travelers to the vamps for safety in their city. They took my friend and I did what any girl would do to get him back. I went after the bad guys and kicked some ass." I told him the rest of the story and he seems completely mesmerized by my every word.

"I don't get it. Why would they attack the vamps like that if they knew they would die in the end?" George says, surprise to his voice.

"I don't know. My assumption is that they still had a bit of human left in them and didn't want to live life as a zombie anymore. Or they didn't want to see innocent humans being killed at the hands of the vamps." I reply.

"Strange. I can't wait for my village to hear your story." He says.

We walk in silence for a little while. I can feel his eyes staring at me from time to time. He doesn't seem too concerned with me so far. It's his little sister that worries me. I can feel her eyes glued to me the entire time. It's as though she can tell I'm hiding something and she is waiting for me to spill the beans. I hate to break it to her, but the only way I'll ever admit to not being human is if something accidental happens on this journey. I'll take this secret to my grave.

That thought brings a smile to my face.

We cross a small stream, it's about five feet across to the other side and the water is only a foot deep. He walks through it, getting his boots and the bottom of his black jeans soaking wet. I don't think as I hop over it before he makes it to the other side. I didn't need a running start or even need to push off of anything to make the jump. It was just so easy to me. George seems surprised by it, but Kelly insists on giving me a suspicious stare.

"That's a pretty wide stream you just leapt across." He says.

I shrug and tilt my head to the side, "Didn't want to get my boots wet."

That's a logical excuse for a girl. We never want to ruin our shoes by getting them wet and we will do amazing things to keep them in perfect condition. Granted, that was not the real reason I jumped over the stream. It's just fun being able to do things without having a running start at it.

"Okay," he says, then takes his backpack off when he makes it to this side of the stream, "I'm gonna refill my water bottle while we're here."

He takes an old, plastic bottle out of his bag and kneels down to the water to fill it. I stand a few feet away from the stream and let him do as he pleases. Kelly stands behind him, her eyes are constantly questioning everything I do or say. I don't know if she has the random ability to read minds or if she can just tell when a person is lying. All I know, is that she's really starting to creep me out with all the staring.

George stands up and faces me again. He takes a drink of water, then offers the bottle to me. I haven't tasted water since I've been bitten. I don't know how it would taste or how I'd even react to it. As far as I know, I could die from eating or drinking human food. I'd rather not risk it nor would I want to risk drinking from the same container as George. I could infect him and things could get really bad, really fast.

"No thanks." I say.

"C'mon, we've been walking for a couple hours and I haven't seen you take a drink of anything. You've got to be thirsty." He says.

Oh, I'm thirsty alright, just not for water, "Trust me, I'm good. I've gone further without drinking water before, I'll be fine."

He hands the water to his sister and she takes a big swig of the clear liquid, "Okay, just let me know if you get thirsty. I'll consider sharing it with you." He says.

He smiles and walks past me leaving me to get yet another awkward glance from his sister. She slowly puts the lid back on the water bottle and shoves it inside her brother's pack. I wait for her to say something, to ask me a question about why I'm so different than a normal human being. I might not have the greatest answers for anything they have to throw at me, but I'll be damned if I don't keep trying to pretend to be human. I'll never be ready to give that up.

* * *

George found a small clearing to make camp when the sun went down. He built a fire and made himself comfortable on the grass across from me. Kelly sat with her legs pulled up to her chest right next to him. When she wasn't staring at the open flames, her eyes were burning a hole in my head. It's like she's this obsessed teenager and I am the object of her desire.

George spent a few minutes trying to talk me into eating some of the beans he cooked over the flames and I had a hard time refusing his offer. He handed a bowl to me and I stared at the meal in disgust. The food didn't even sound good. I had a feeling that the second that first bite hit my tongue, I'd regret it and want to throw it back up. But, in order to keep this human persona under wraps, I forced it down my throat and pushed through the pain in my stomach after eating it. The taste only got worse with each bite I took and my stomach did not approve of this meal.

I wish I knew why food doesn't taste the same anymore. When I was traveling with dad, it was the most wonderful thing to come across a can of beans or a can of *anything* edible. It was a delicacy to me back then and now it's repulsive. The smell of it makes the pain in my gut expand and it took a lot to shove the few bites down. I had to use the excuse of not being very hungry in order to get out of eating anymore of it.

That little dinner was about an hour ago. The stars are out and I can't get enough of looking at them. Even with the shades still on my face, I can see them just as bright as if they were off. They glimmer and sparkle against the black canvas they're painted upon. All the millions of lights shining above us provides enough light so we can see. The full moon adds even more light to the woods and it's absolutely beautiful.

"Why won't you take those sunglasses off? It's dark outside, I highly doubt the sun will hurt your eyes now." George says and I turn my attention to him.

I shake my head, "The flames are just as bright. I can't stand bright lights for some reason. It really hurts my eyes." I'm getting good at not using complete lies.

He rolls his eyes and smiles, "You are confusing, you know that. You won't tell me much about yourself and I'm probably the first company you've seen in days. I know you are to us."

"Trust me, you don't want to know my life story. It's sad and doesn't end well." I reply.

"Does this have something to do with why you can't go back to Des Moines?"

I nod, "Somewhat. There are other reasons, but I'm not going to tell you."

"Won't you miss it? Don't you want to try going back there?" George asks, poking a stick at the fire. "Surely you have friends who live there."

I close my eyes, letting the montage of the people I love flash through my head. Sherry and her new family with Seth. They'll live a long, happy life together with her father and Dillon to watch out for them. Carter, the guy who's sole purpose in life is to make sure his best friend's girlfriend doesn't get herself killed. I hate to think this, but he sort of failed on that part. There's also Dwayne, who might be a little on the crazy side for believing this world will ever see peace again.

Then there's Ryder.

As much as I love seeing his face flash through my mind, I hate seeing it just the same. I hate seeing the reminders of what I'll never have again. Those memories that should have been lost right along with my beating heart. It's a tough battle to love and hate something at the same time. Especially when it involves the one person I never want to live without.

"You have a guy back in Des Moines, don't you?" George asks, after my long moment of silence.

I open my eyes and nod my head, "I do."

"Why isn't he out here with you?"

"It's complicated."

He smiles, "Every girl's excuse for being in a bad relationship. It's not complicated to see that he doesn't deserve you."

"You have no idea what the hell you're talking about." I feel the anger rising through me. "It's not Ryder's fault why I'm stuck out here. It's mine. I made a stupid mistake, one that I'm forced to live with for the remainder of my life, and it's my fault that I'll never get to see him again. This isn't a matter of who deserves who. We both deserve each other and I screwed that up when I stepped foot outside that gate. You'll never understand what I'm going through right now."

He raises his arms in defense and says, "I'm sorry, I don't understand. I'm just so used to meeting girls who say one thing but mean something completely different. I really didn't mean to upset you."

I take a moment to calm down. It's hard to do when someone says the wrong thing about the man I'm in love with. I'm sure if Ryder was given the choice, he'd have come with me. If Carter wasn't there to hold him back, he would have followed me and stayed right by my side throughout my night of pain and dying. I'm glad he wasn't given a choice.

He didn't need to see me like that.

"You alright? Are we good?" George says.

I stare at him, the shadows of the flames dance across his face, "For now. You just need to know not to say anything bad about Ryder. You know nothing about him or me and you never will."

"I understand." He replies. "You must really be in love with that guy to get *that* pissed off about it."

I nod, "You have no idea."

"I might. I used to be in love with a girl, not too long ago. She was supposed to be with me forever, but got scared and went with a group to the city to be safe. Only they didn't make it and we found their corpses a few days later." He states, "I should've went with her, but she told me to stay. The city life wasn't a life I wanted and I'd be unhappy if I went. It's true, I'd hate it there, but I still should have went with her."

"Sorry you had to go through that." I say.

"What about you? How do you know that Ryder is your one and only?" he asks.

"I met him on the road and we spent a few nights alone together. I knew after our first kiss, I only wanted to be by his side. He's the reason I went to Des Moines in the first place and he's the reason I wanted to stay there." I reply.

"But you're out here now. I just wish you would tell me so I can finally get some clearance on your whole story. This secret can't possibly be that bad." He says.

If he only knew.

Before I'm given the chance to answer, a sound catches my ears. I can't tell exactly where it is or how far away. My eyes grow wide and I stare at the woods behind George. Another stick breaks and echoes through my mind. He isn't reacting, meaning it's still too far for him to hear it. His sister, on the other hand, still has her eyes on me. She can tell just by the look on my face, that I know something neither of them don't.

"I think I know your secret." Kelly asks, her first words since we got to the clearing.

I raise an eyebrow, "Oh yeah?"

"What do you think it is?" George asks.

She clutches her hands around her knees and says, "I don't think you're a human like you told us."

George lets out a loud laugh that seems to echo in the trees around us, "That's a good one, sis."

"Yeah," I say, without a smile at all, "good one."

I hear another sound, more like a footstep and I stand, ignoring Kelly's statement. I take a look around, scanning the trees for movement of any kind. I expect a vamp to jump out from the darkness. Those creatures love this time of night and love preying on unexpecting victims like these humans sitting around the fire. I close my eyes and try focusing on the sound. It's definitely footsteps, labored and stumbling quickly through the leaves. Doesn't sound like a human or an animal. I inhale through my nose, hoping to catch a hint of the creature. I get something, the smell of death and I open my eyes again.

"Bridget, what's wrong?" George asks, getting to his feet and looking around for himself.

"We're not alone." I say, simply.

* * *

Things always have the tendency of happening as though they are on cue after I say something. Take right now for instance.

The second those words came out of my mouth, I hear the groaning coming from behind me and see a horrible look of terror all across George's face. He looks like he's never seen something horrible like this before. I've been in his shoes and used to get so scared I just wanted to run and hide. Those days are long gone.

He turns to his sister and she stands up to be with him. They cower together, without thinking to get the gun from the holster on his belt. That would have always been my first go-to thing the second a zombie came within firing distance. I guess George isn't as confident as he likes to claim he is.

I turn around to see the zombie lumbering toward us. Her red hair blends in with the blood stains on her white sweater and blue jeans. She doesn't look as gross as some of the others I've come across. Her eyes are still black, but she's not all rotten or starting to decompose.

She must be new at this.

She's obviously not the type to want to hesitate either. She's hungry and I can see it in her eyes. It's the same hunger I felt burning inside me all day. She lets out her annoying and deathly growl as she runs through this clearing to get to us. If I had a gun, she'd be dead by now. That seems a little too easy now that I have some cool, new abilities of my own. Killing her with my bare hands should be just as rewarding and maybe even a little fun.

I step away from the fire, moving closer to the stumbling zombie. I probably look like a complete idiot approaching something as deadly as this. Good thing it doesn't matter anymore.

"Bridget, what the hell are you doing?" I hear George's question, but I'm too focused to care what he's saying.

My mind is solely set on destroying this zombie. She marks one of the reasons why I am the way that I am right now. Her kind ruined my life and I'm about to ruin hers. I pick up the pace, closing the short distance between us, and tackle the thing to the ground. She lets out a shriek when her body hits the grass. I position myself on top of her and grab a handful of her hair. The ground is soft so this could take a while. I slam her head against the ground as hard as I can. Nothing cracks or breaks in her skull and it only seemed to piss her off even more.

She reaches both hands up and claws at my face and neck. I lean back far enough so she can't get me, but she's pretty strong. She swats at my face, catching a finger on my sunglasses. She pulls her hand away to swing at me again and the shades go flying. I'm a bit preoccupied at the moment to watch where they land, but I hear them crash somewhere close by.

I feel her nails scratching the skin of my right cheek. There's a small amount of pain coming from the scratch, nothing I can't handle but enough for me to notice. It's just like a paper cut. Annoying for about two seconds, then fades away. I take her hair and slam her head against the soft grass one more time. Still, nothing breaks and she only gets stronger underneath me.

A loud wail comes pouring out of her mouth and she lunges up from the ground, tackling me this time. She digs her fingers into my shoulders and pins me on the ground. My back hits the grass with a thud and the weight of her body has me stuck in place. Her eyes might be hungry and I'm waiting for her to dig those yellow teeth into my flesh. I'm anticipating it actually. Instead, she simply kicks me away from her and gets to her feet. I'm not on her menu tonight and she lumbers toward the meal she truly desires. I roll to my stomach and stare at George. Kelly is hiding behind him and he still hasn't gotten the gun out.

I jump to my feet and quickly chase after the zombie. She's close to the humans and the fire isn't enough to stop her. She steps around it, her feet kicking a piece of the wood out of place and the fire goes dim for moment. I can see perfectly in this darkness. The one thing I'm really enjoying about this new life of mine.

She's too close to George and Kelly for comfort. She has them backed against a tree and they are too afraid to run away. I pick up the pace and sprint toward the zombie. The air rushes past me, whistling in my ears as I run. The world flashes by and in an instant, I'm leaping into the air coming down on the back of the zombie. She falls to the ground one more time and starts clawing to get away from me. Her fingers are digging lines in the grass and dirt.

"Not this time, bitch." I say, feeling very tough at the moment.

I know slamming this thing's head against the soft grass isn't going to do anything. I don't have time to steal the gun away from George and I'm having enough fun as it is. As I pin her to the ground, the wind soars through the air around us. I catch a scent, something I'd rather not want to enjoy. I can smell whatever blood is flowing through her body. It might be dead blood, but it's still intoxicating. It's hard for me to not want to try some. It's hard for me to stop myself from wanting a taste and bringing an end to my hunger.

I hate myself for the thought that's going through my mind. It's disgusting and dangerous, but it might be the only way to put an end to her miserable life without the use of a gun. If I'm lucky, it won't put an end to mine as well. With my mind screaming at me not to go forward with what my body is forcing me to do, I grab this zombie's arm and clamp my jaw down, hard on her wrist. I feel the skin breaking under my teeth and the flow of her black blood oozes between them as my monster finally get what it wants. She screams loud, blocking out whatever George is yelling. The blood flowing through my teeth is different than the rabbit's. It tastes old and even a little dirty, but it's calming my aching stomach.

My mind races as I suck a little more of her blood into my mouth. I even taste some flesh and let a little slide down my throat. I don't feel myself getting weak or feel like I'm going to *actually* die. I feel stronger now that my stomach is finally getting what it wants. My mind has even shut up and isn't yelling at me for doing this. If this is what I have to do to stay alive, then I'll just have to get to use to it.

The shouting coming from the zombie is fading, as is her struggle against my grip. She stops clawing at the ground to get away from me and soon stops moving altogether. That's my cue to let go of her arm and throw it on the ground with the rest of her. I lick my lips and wipe her blood from my mouth.

God I'm disgusting. I can't help it anymore though. This is all I have to keep myself from eating a human and I'm going to do it. I don't really want to, my mind hates me right now for doing it, but it solved the problem. I killed the zombie. George and Kelly are still alive and they can thank me for this later.

Speaking of those two, I snap back to reality and turn my attention to them. I quickly get to my feet and wipe the remainder of the zombie's blood from my face. George is stunned and shocked as he stares at my eyes. Without the shades on, there's nothing to block what they look like. Not that it matters anymore now. I can't pretend I'm human after sucking the blood from a dead woman's wrist. That sounds weird just thinking about it.

I take a step toward them and *I'm* the one who gets the reaction the zombie should have gotten. He quickly pulls the gun from the holster and aims it at me. I stop moving, staring down the barrel of his small pistol. If he shoots me in the head, I'm sure to be a goner. There's got to be something to keep him from doing that.

"George," I say, hoping against hope that he doesn't shoot me for speaking.

He opens his mouth and shaky words come out, "What the hell are you?"

"I was hoping I never had to tell anyone my secret."

He raises the gun and shouts, "Just tell me what you are. You're not human and you're not a vampire or a zombie.

Please, just tell me what the hell you are."

I nod and here goes nothing, "You're right, I'm not human anymore and as much as I wish I could make things go back to normal, I can't. I was bit by a vampire first, then backed up into a zombie and it got me as well. I don't know what I am and I don't know of any other way to explain this to you. This is the reason I can't go back to the city and why I shouldn't have gone with you in the first place."

The gun is shaking in his grip and he says, "I don't know if I'm supposed to be afraid of you or not. I mean, you just saved our lives, but you're not human. Do you even have a heartbeat?"

I shake my head.

"How long have you been like this?"

I shrug, "I don't know, not long. I was with a group when this happened, but I ran away from them to keep them safe. I blacked out in some greenhouse and woke up like this."

"So, what's with the sunglasses?" he asks.

I shrug, "The sun burns the hell out of my eyes if I don't have them on. I found that out the hard way. I'm not like *them* though." I point to the zombie on the ground, "I'm not going to bite you or your sister. I just want to be as normal as possible. That's why I didn't tell you anything."

"That zombie kinda ruined your plan on keeping things a secret. Why did you do go after it like that? Why didn't you just take the gun and shoot it?" he asks, lowering the gun to his side.

"I don't know. This thing that's inside of me, has a hard time not being in control when I'm hungry. And I have a difficult time controlling it as well. This morning, right before you found me, I was eating a rabbit and I couldn't stop myself. I couldn't keep myself from killing it and it wasn't enough to ease the hunger burning inside me, but I was able to control it around you." I reply.

"How do I know you're not going to kill us?"

"Because I were going to, you'd be dead by now."

He stares at me for a second. I can see the judgment in his eyes. I wouldn't blame him for killing me right now. I'm a little surprised he hasn't yet. I am a monster after all.

George takes a breath, then lowers the gun to his side completely and must know I'm telling the truth. I have no intention of hurting him or any other human on the planet. I didn't even plan on killing the zombie the way I did, but it had to be done. Glad I'm not dead by drinking her blood, that's for sure. The vamps died pretty quickly after the dead blood hit their lips and I'm still standing. I must be something so different, who knows if I'll ever fully understand it.

"I guess you're right, we would be dead by now if you were lying." He lets out a sigh.

I nod, "Killing a human is something I never plan on doing."

"You better keep that promise." He orders.

"If I don't, you have my permission to kill me." I reply.

I wait for him to holster the gun, before walking away from him. I need to find those sunglasses in order to make it through the morning without plucking my eyes from my skull. I walk back to the place where I tackled the zombie and search the ground for the shades. There's a small trace of blood, from one of us and I remember the scratch she gave me on my cheek. I wipe where she scratched me, but don't feel a mark. On my fingers, I see the blood from the wound, yet there's no wound for the blood to come from anymore. Quick healing must be another new power of mine. One that will come in handy someday, I'm sure.

I spot the sunglasses a few feet from where I'm standing and walk to them. The stars reflect off the lenses and I pick them up from the grass. Luckily, they aren't broken or scratched. There's no saying when I'd find another pair good enough to shield my eyes from the sun. I hang them on the collar of my shirt and head back to the campsite. I can see even better at night without them.

George is busy getting his gear back together when I

make it to the fire. He shoves all of his cooking utensils in one compartment along with his bottle of water.

"I knew I was right." Kelly says as I approach them. "I knew you weren't a human right off the bat."

She seems pretty smug with herself. I would be too if I were so right about something.

"I take it this was why you didn't want to eat or drink anything I had to offer?" George questions.

"You would be correct." I reply.

He smiles, "Yet, you seemed to enjoy the blood coming out of that zombie. That's pretty gross if you ask me."

"Yeah, things are confusing right now."

"Not gonna argue with you on that one. I don't think we should stay in this area any longer. Who knows if any other zombies are around." George says once he has his bag packed up.

"You probably don't want me to come with you anymore. Could prove to be a bad thing if I go to your village." I state.

He shrugs and gives me a questionable glance, "I don't know. I believe that you don't want to harm a human, but if someone else gets wind of this, who knows if they'll feel the same. They probably won't be as nice as I am and they could pull the trigger. It might be best if you..."

Before he can finish speaking, a loud gasp fills the air and both of our eyes dart to the only thing around to cause it.

* * *

She gasps and coughs, trying desperately to catch her breath. George has his hand hovering over the gun at his side while I slowly make my way to the zombie. She was dead a few minutes ago. I felt her die and her body went limp in my hands. Yet, here she is, rolling onto her side, still attempting to take a calm breath. I'm not sure what's happening to her. She grabs a handful of grass as a pain-filled look crosses her face. She turns to us and opens her eyes just enough for me to get a look at them.

Something's not right.

They aren't the same shade of black they were when I tackled her to the ground. They aren't black at all. She opens them again, this time all the way, and I can see the white surrounding the hazel colored iris of her eyes. My jaw drops and I honestly have no idea what I'm supposed to think right now. She *was* a zombie. She shouldn't be staring at me with eyes filled with life. The color shouldn't be coming back to her face and the veins shouldn't be fading from sight.

But, that's what is happening.

George steps to my side, obviously noticing the same thing. He kneels to the ground next to her and she looks at his face. Kelly stays by the fire with her eyes glued to the girl. The woman on the ground darts her gaze to each one of us and looks terrified.

"Where am I? Who are you?" she asks, frantically.

Something else that shouldn't be happening to this girl. Zombies don't talk. The only sound they make is the annoying groaning coming from their dead throats. She's defying all laws of what I know to be true about the creature.

She quickly sits up and brushes the hair out of her eyes. George turns his head and looks to me with wonder written all over his face. I have nothing to do other than shrug in response. *Hell*, I'm not even sure what to think right now. I watch as the girl looks at her hands and the blood stains on the sleeves of her sweater. Her hands shake and she breathes heavy.

"Why is there so much blood on me?" she asks.

"You don't know what just happened?" George asks, trying to sound as calm as he can.

She shakes her head, "The last thing I remember, I was standing outside of a house with someone," she seems confused, then shakes her head again, "No, that's not right. I was somewhere else, alone maybe? Something came out and attacked me, I think."

"What's your name?" Kelly asks, stepping closer to us.

The woman on the ground looks around. She opens her mouth, like she's going to say something. Aggravation fills her eyes and she quickly shakes her head one more time.

"I don't know." She says, sadness in her voice. "Does this mean I'm dead?"

George slowly lifts his hand and places two fingers on her neck. She doesn't protest or try eating his arm as he touches her skin. We patiently wait for the verdict as George takes his time feeling for a pulse.

After a moment, he turns his head toward me and smiles. I guess he's expecting me to smile back, but I don't know what to do. How is this possible? There has never been any talk of a zombie coming *back* to life. Then again, there's never been talk of a zombie being bit by something that's never been created before. In other words, me.

George turns back to the girl and says, "You're alive. I don't mean to scare you, but you were just a zombie a few minutes ago."

"I was?" she questions.

He nods, "Yeah, but you're alive now."

I can see a faint smile across her thin lips, then she asks, "Who are all of you?"

"I'm George, that's my younger sister, Kelly," he points to her standing beside me. "And this is Bridget."

"Are all of you alive?"

George nods, "My sister and I are. Bridget, well, we

don't know exactly what she is. She's the one who brought you back to life."

Her eyes dart to me and I can see the tears building inside them. Tears of happiness I bet. I guess I should be a little happy that something is able to bring these things back from the dead. A little weirded out that that something happens to be me. Not really sure what I'm supposed to do with this new power of mine or how I'm even supposed to react. I guess shocked and confused will work for now.

"Is that true? she asks, her eyes pleading for an answer.

I nod my head.

"How?"

"I bit you, you died, and now you're back." That's putting it short, sweet, and to the point.

She takes a deep breath and smiles. Her teeth aren't black or blood soaked anymore. They are white, just like a human. Her skin doesn't show any signs of being dead either. She's still a bit pale, but healthy looking. The only part about her that's off in anyway, is the blood on her hands, face, and clothes. She just needs to get cleaned up and a new outfit, then she'll look as good as new.

"Let me get you some water or something. You must be thirsty." George offers, reaching for his backpack.

"I am, thank you." She says, her voice is quiet and polite.

He takes out the bottle of water and hands it to her. As clumsy as her human hands are, she drops the bottle and some of the water spills out. George smiles and helps her lift it and even helps her take a drink. He's such a nice guy, but I really wish I was sharing this moment with Ryder. He's the only one who would help me understand what I need to do. What I'm supposed to be doing right now. I'm just so confused.

Kelly stays quiet, her eyes now focused on the life I just gave back to the strange woman on the ground. It's a good thing she's not giving me the look of death anymore. She got the answer I'm sure she was looking for and knows the truth about me.

I glance back to the girl. This is a miracle to be witnessing the rebirth of a human after being a zombie for who knows how long. I'm the miracle to give that human life back to her. That's a lot to take in on top of trying to get used to my new form and trying to control my hunger for disgusting things.

"Where are we?" the girl asks, interrupting my thoughts.

"In the middle of the woods. We're headed to my village and you can come with us. We'll get you cleaned up and spread the word about this to everyone." George replies.

"Us?" I ask.

Kelly's the one who answers me, "Yeah, you *have* to come with us now. You can cure the zombies." She sounds really excited about this.

I, on the other hand, can see this thing going badly, "How exactly do you plan to explain this to everyone?"

"Exactly how it happened." George states.

I run my fingers through my hair. It's still just as soft as it was when I opened my eyes last night. Telling people exactly what happened in order for this girl to miraculously get her life back, seems quite difficult to me. There are certain details to the story that might get peoples' attention in the wrong way. For instance, once they learn about what happened to me in order for this miracle to work, they might not like it. Some could even go as far as wanting me dead instead of trusting our word that whatever's flowing through my veins is the cure for the zombies. That could prove to be unbelievable to some of those on the receiving end our story.

"Bridget," George says, "I know you're thinking the obvious right now. *A lot* of people won't believe this. They'll probably try to kill you as soon as those words come out. Even if they don't believe us..."

"They still need to know." I say, quietly.

He nods, "Yeah, regardless what happens. You owe it to the rest of the world to share this new cure with them. People deserve the right to believe they can have their loved ones back. They deserve the right to believe the world has a chance."

"It would be selfish if you kept this from everybody." Kelly says, sounding a bit demanding. "You have to tell everyone, even if they want you dead."

I liked her better when she was quietly staring at me. She actually seems like she wants to make me go with them, like I have no other choice.

"Bridget," George says, a little nicer than his sister, "I'm not going to make you come with us. I'm just saying it would be a good thing if you did. The world would thank you for it."

I know I have to go with them. I'll probably die after his village hears about this, but I hope it will be worth it. The world should know about the cure for the zombies, even though it's absolutely disgusting how it was discovered.

"I'll go." I say. "We should camp here for the night so she can eat something and you guys can get some sleep."

"Good idea." George states. "If we leave after the sun is up, we should get to our village around noon or a little after."

"Can't wait." I say, a hint of sarcasm to my voice.

I turn away from them and stare into the emptiness behind me. I hear Kelly's footsteps as she approaches her brother and helps the woman get her bearings. Being able to cure the zombies will be a good thing. The world will be a much better place with one less demon here to destroy it. If only I could feel excited about spreading the news to everyone.

I guess I'm too paranoid about having a bullet enter my brain to entertain the idea of saving the world.

* * *

I stand alone in the clearing, staring into the vast emptiness that is the night. I was voted to keep watch since I apparently don't want to sleep anymore. It also doesn't hurt that I'm quite stronger than the others in case something else decides to show up.

It's well past midnight now. The red head fell asleep first, then George couldn't keep his eyes open, and Kelly was the last one to drift off. I don't even feel tired at all. Maybe that's what this is going to be like from now on. I can't eat regular food and I can't sleep like I used to. I can't touch the flesh of another living being without hunger burning in my stomach.

I truly hate how messed up I am now.

I look up at the stars, eyeing the constellations and think of Ryder. I can't get him out of my head. Never getting to see him again is the worst part of everything. I need him to be with me, to be by my side on nights like this one. When I need someone most of all, he's the only one I want. He took the pain away when I lost my dad and he kept that pain far from my heart after that. I know that once we get to the village, it'll be really hard to control the hunger that courses through my veins. I feel that if Ryder were here with me, he could help me control everything. He could hold my hand when I need him to and tell me things are going to be alright.

I close my eyes and I can see him again. The same scene playing over in my mind. I hate seeing the look on his face when he realizes both of our worlds have been shattered by two simple bites on my skin. The pain on his face seems much worse than what I felt that day.

"You know, if you keep thinking about it, you'll never be able to move on with your life."

I recognize that voice. It's been a while since I've heard

it, but I could never forget what she sounds like. I slowly open my eyes and see her standing a few feet in front of me. Her dark blonde hair is a mess and her clothes are dirty. This is just like when I saw Charlie. I needed an escape from my head when he came along. I wonder if Maggie is here to do the same thing.

"You're not dying this time, Bridget." She says with a smile.

I look to the ground just to be certain I'm not going to see myself writhing on the grass in pain. I did bite a zombie a few hours ago and there is always a chance for something else to happen to me. Thankfully, there is no other me lying on the grass. I'm still standing with no clue as to why my mind is coming up with my older sister right now. I'm not going to complain about it though.

"It's nice to see you, Maggie." I say, quietly.

"Same here, Bridget. I've missed you." She says.

I nod, "I missed you too. A lot. There were a million times when I needed you and you weren't there."

"I know, but I'm here for you right now." She says.

I let out a sigh, "Not really."

She smiles, "You're mind wants someone else to be here with you other than those other people over there. Some part of you wants to see me, so here I am."

"Just for a few minutes though. Then you're going to leave me like Charlie did." I say.

"We don't want to leave you, sis, but you know we can't stay forever. But, a part of us is always with you, every day of the week." Maggie takes a small step closer to me.

"You better be." I say. "Tell me something, why does my mind want to see you right now?"

She takes another step, then says, "You know, when I left college to come home, when all the madness started, I was leaving someone I fell head over heels in love with behind. I thought it was the worst thing in the world, but we both knew we wanted to be with our families. It was the right thing to do."

"Are you trying to tell me to get over Ryder and save the world?" I ask.

She shakes her head, "That's not what I'm saying at all. The love story you share with Ryder is the most beautiful thing I've seen. It's my favorite part about watching you. You love him so much that you've risked your life on numerous occasions only to make sure that love never dies. Just like you did when you were bitten. You left him, even though it was the hardest thing to do, but it was the *right* thing to do. You now have the chance to make the world a better place, to save as many people as you can and still be in love with the man of your dreams."

"How can I do that when I'll never be able to see him again?"

"Maybe you shouldn't think like that. You thought you would never see Charlie or me again and yet here we are. I might just be something your mind wants to see in order to help you through this, but I'm just as real as you want me to be." She replies. "If you keep telling yourself that you'll never see him again, then you never will. If you think you still have a chance at catching even the slightest glimpse of him, you might get just that."

I raise an eyebrow, "Never thought of it like that."

"That was always your problem, little sis, you don't think like me." She says.

"Even for a figment of my imagination, you still prove to be a little better than me." I say.

Maggie shrugs, "That's my job as being your older sister."

I hear a shuffling sound coming from behind me. Foot-steps, quiet ones, and I spin around to see who's causing them. It isn't George, he's still fast asleep next to the fire with his sister lying by his side. It's the red head. Her legs are a little wobbly from being a zombie for so long and I can tell she's nervous. Still, she approaches me, biting her lip along the way.

"I heard you talking and I came over to check on you." She says, quietly. "Are you alright?"

I glance over my shoulder. Maggie's already gone and the area is clear. It was a much shorter visit than I had with my brother and it's just as painful to know she's not there anymore. My mind might have been the thing that brought her here, but it's also the thing that wants more time with her. I haven't seen her in years and a few, short minutes isn't enough time.

"Bridget?" the red head gets my attention again and I face her.

"I'm fine." I say with a small smile. "Are you?"

She nods, "I think so. I'm actually glad I get to talk to you."

"Why?"

"So I can thank you." She smiles a little wider, "You brought me back from something so evil and I can try to be myself again."

"Are you starting to remember things?"

She shrugs, "While I was sleeping, I got short visions of things. I was in all of them and I think they might be memories. They seem so familiar and wonderful. I was happy as a human and I want to be happy again. I want to see more of what my life was and I want to remember. I just don't know how."

"I wish I could help you, but I don't know how to bring your memory back either. I didn't even know I could cure anything with how I am." I say.

"It's a miracle that you can. People will love this and be grateful for the gift you give to the world." She says.

"I hope you're right." I say.

"I have faith that I am."

"You believe in God?" I ask.

She nods, "For some reason, I know that I do. I feel that faith was one of the strongest parts of my previous life that I can remember and God seems to play a big part of it. Do you believe?"

Not sure how I should answer this. The last time I told someone I didn't believe in God, she kind of yelled at me. I know this girl doesn't really remember too much about her life, but she believes God is a big part of it. Who am I to make her see otherwise.

"Not really, no." that's how you answer that question.

She looks puzzled now, "Why?"

"Well, if there were a god out there, why would he put me through so much pain? Why would he take away everyone I love and leave me standing here as something I don't want to be? Why would he let *my* life go to hell?" I say, not really meaning to get a little testy about it.

She opens her mouth to speak and I can see her lips quivering, apparently I said too much of the wrong thing, "You're here for a reason, Bridget. You might think it's something horrible, but it's something great."

Not another word is spoken and she doesn't give me the chance to respond. She spins around and walks back to the campfire. *Way to go, Bridget.* You managed to make the human you saved hate you. I can only hope she sticks around to be the proof we need in order for George's plan to work. It'll still be hard to get people to believe us even with this girl, but she might be able to convince them. As long as she stops hating me long enough to do so.

* * *

Morning's here. Midmorning actually. We've been walking for a while and we're very close to George's village. We found a beaten path that he says will take us right to it. The woods are starting to grow thin. The girl, who George decided to call Rose because of the color of her hair, hasn't said much. The few words she did say, were strictly to George or Kelly and she hasn't so much as glanced my way. I even tried to apologize and she simply smiled and kept moving. Maybe that's her way of accepting it, I don't know. If this new life gave me the ability to read minds, I might have an answer.

George leads us out of the woods and the beaten path takes us to a broken street. Cracks and potholes have taken over the concrete giving way to small trees and grass to grow through. I catch the scent of life not far away. A lot of life actually and my mouth begins to water. The hunger is starting to boil in my stomach and it knows there's fresh meat and blood up ahead. I hope it also knows that I'm not giving into it. I'll starve before I let that happen.

Other than the scent, I can hear the human life. People talking and a few kids are laughing. It's faint and I can't quite make out what's being said, but I can hear it if I focus. Those people are happy, I can tell by how they talk about life and hunting and friendship. The closer we get to them, the louder the voices and the happiness seem to get, and the more my nervous hands begin to shake.

Old houses come into view on either side of the road. Some are in shambles and one is completely burnt to the ground. There's an ashy square of where it used to be along with a few burnt support beams sticking out of the ground. Most of the houses are boarded up and locked down completely. Until we get to the end of the road, a cul-de-sac, and these houses are all in decent shape. Boards cover the windows with enough of a slit in the wood for people to see through in case of danger. Dusty cars are parked in some of the driveways and even a few on the street. This place is nothing other than an old neighborhood on the outskirts of a rundown city. Not a city like Des Moines. This is a smaller one that failed.

We walk to the middle of the cul-de-sac and a few men with guns look our way. Their weapons have my mind wondering about which one will notice I'm not human first and pull the trigger. George nudges my shoulder and passes me a reassuring look when he notices how tense I am.

"The one with the hat is my father. He's reasonable and he's the one we want to talk to first." The man he's talking about is tall with a brown hat on his head. "The one with the black jacket sort of runs this place, Adam. He's not as reasonable and doesn't really like visitors."

"That's comforting." I say.

"Don't worry." George states. "My dad will help us get them to understand."

Kelly darts past us and runs straight for her father. I watch as she instantly wraps her arms around him and squeezes him in a tight embrace.

"I'm sure he can, but we have to get him to believe us first." I say to George.

"Just have some faith, Bridget." Rose states.

The man in the black coat approaches us. The rifle propped against his shoulder looks intimidating. Definitely something that could kill me in an instant. He's taller than George and his grey beard tells me he's older, like my father's age. His eyes pass over the three of us, ogling Rose, who didn't get very clean in the small pond we found. He skips over George and his eyes stop at me. Rose might have blood on her sweater, but I'm the one who doesn't look human anymore. My hoody is torn at the sleeve and there's blood stains on it as well as my jeans. The shades covering my eyes don't help me much. They kind of make it look like I'm *trying* to hide something.

"Who are your friends, George?" Adam's deep voice is

intimidating. "You know we don't like visitors. Explain."

George motions to the two of us girls and says, " This is Rose and Bridget, I met them yesterday. Bridget saved me from a zombie, so I figured I'd let them come with me after that."

"How? I don't see a gun." Adam asks, his eyes glaring at me.

By now, many other people in the village have swarmed around us. Men, women, a few teens and children, all circle around. A few watch from the lawns in front of the houses and I can feel myself fighting the urge to end the pain in my stomach. Their skin looks appetizing, I can practically taste it already. I can smell the blood flowing through their veins and I only need one of them to satisfy my needs. One measly human will do, but I know I can't do that. I need to ignore those thoughts and focus.

"I'm just that awesome." I say, feeling smug and forcing down my hungry thoughts.

He steps closer to me and tries peering through the sunglasses to see my eyes. Good thing they're pretty dark. I'd hate for him to see the metallic silver of my eyes right now. The way this guy looks at me and with how many guns I see in the hands of the inhabitants of this village, I wouldn't last very long if the news about my *non-humanness* came out.

"Bridget, huh?" he questions.

I nod, "That's right."

"What's with the sunglasses? Not a lot of people wear them anymore." He says, still trying to see my eyes.

I shrug, "Sun hurts my eyes and I like to make a fashion statement."

This Adam fellow, moves his eyes over the rest of my body. Probably noticing the blood on my clothes. He takes a glance at Rose and sees the same thing.

"Is there a reason for all the blood?" he asks.

"Tough life on the road." I reply.

He nods, "That it is. How long are the two of you planning on staying?"

Jeez, this guy must really enjoy playing twenty questions or something. He won't leave me alone with all of this nonsense. Why can't the people here be like everywhere else and let us get on our way without going through an interrogation?

George steps toward me and says, "They're just here for a few days. Rest up and get some supplies for the road. Then they'll be on their way."

"Supplies? You two have nothing to trade for anything we have here. What makes you think we'd give anything up for you?" Adam asks, glaring at me.

I could tell him I have the greatest gift the world could ever ask for in order to shut him up. I think that should grant me all the gold in the world. I just don't see that working right now and it could get me killed faster.

I look him in the eye and say, "Figured we'd just wing it and hope for the best."

Adam takes a step back from me and smiles, "I like you. You're a smart ass, something this world doesn't have enough of anymore. Stay for a few days and we'll take care of ya. George can show you around."

"Thank you." Rose says, with a cute smile.

The village goes back to their business, some are still passing us awkward stares. Adam walks away and joins his bud-dies in whatever they have going on. I take a moment to look around the rest of the place. There are only houses and a few sheds in the backyards of some, no businesses or shops. Gardens have been planted outside the houses. The corn has all been harvested as well as the other fruits and vegetables. There's a large chain-link fence surrounding a grassy lot. A few cows and five horses reside there with plenty of hay to eat and water to drink. This place seems like a nice, homey place to live.

All of the houses are boarded up and the people here have taken the necessary precautions in case vamps or zombies show up. Most of them have weapons and some have even booby trapped the lawn in front of the houses with metal stakes sticking out of the ground. Zombies are pretty dumb and would run right into those things without taking a second glance. I even spot a few, metal bear traps barely showing in the grass of one house. That would catch a vampire if it weren't paying attention.

I turn back to George. He's staring at the only man left in our immediate vicinity. His father. They look almost exactly alike. Same blue eyes, same pointed nose, his dad is just a hair taller than he is, but definitely a spot on match. Kelly must take after her mother. Right now she's busy talking with the other girls around her age, ignoring the rest of us.

"You and your sister leave for three weeks and make me think you're dead." His father says, anger to his tone.

"I'm sorry, there was something I needed to do." George replies.

"I hope it was worth it."

George nods and says, "Can we talk somewhere in private? I have something really important to tell you."

His father sighs, "Yeah, we'll go to the house. After you tell me who these two girls are and why they're both covered in blood."

George shakes his head, "That's kinda why we need the privacy, dad."

His father raises an eyebrow and glances to both me and Rose. I can't tell what he's thinking as his eyes pass me over, but he doesn't appear to be a bad guy. Maybe he'll be another person in this town I can trust.

"Fine, follow me." He says, then turns around and leads the way.

The wind blows through the air, sending all sorts of smells up my nose. Most of them are human and the blood flowing through their veins. It is tempting and I could use another meal, but they're humans and I am vowing never to eat or drink a single one of them.

There is another scent that gets my attention. Something

familiar, something I haven't had the privilege of smelling for what seems like ages. It's not a dead smell or another rabbit or animal. This aroma is much better. It might be faint, but it's enough to get me to stop following the others.

I sniff the air again, only to make sure my mind isn't playing another trick on me. The scent is gone this time and I find myself losing hope in everything all over again. Just thinking there was a chance he'd be here, looking for me, that made things worth so much more. But, I got my hopes up. My nose got my hopes up. I'll never see Ryder again and sooner or later. I'll have to accept that.

"Bridget, you coming?" George calls to me and my feet start moving again.

* * *

"I don't understand." George's father stares at the three of us with a look of extreme confusion on his face.

We spent the last couple of hours trying to get him to comprehend the situation we're all in right now. It took a while to tell my side of the story and that seemed to put him on edge. The gun hasn't left his hand since I told him I was bitten. Made him even more nervous once we were able to prove that Rose used to be a zombie and I *magically* brought her back to life with just one bite. So far, he hasn't killed either of us, but there's still plenty of time for that to happen.

Right now, he's sitting on the other side of an old dining room table with George sitting next to him. Rose sits in a chair across from him while I stand and lean against the faded white wall in the dining room. There are a couple of lit candles on the table, enough for us to see since the windows are completely boarded up. Not that I need any help with seeing in the darkness. Already proved to myself that I'm great in that department.

"What don't you get? We told you everything." George states.

"I don't know. I just don't get how any of this could be true." His father replies. "This girl, *both* of these girls look human, I don't get how you expect me to believe something without any proof."

"We have proof, the blood on Rose's sweatshirt and the bite marks on her wrist. She's healing like a human would heal. Isn't that enough?" George retorts.

His father shakes his head, "I'm sorry, but a little bit of blood and a few marks doesn't tell me that she used to be a zombie. It makes me nervous as hell with these strange stories and I don't feel comfortable with them around. But, if you think you can get the rest of the world to believe you have the cure for one of the problems in the world, you'll need something else. Something no one has ever seen before. Just stating that you have a young woman who claims to be the cure for this, isn't enough. You can't even get me to believe what you're saying."

George lets out a sigh of despair and stares at his hands on the table. I had a feeling it would take a lot to get someone to believe us. This does seem pretty farfetched and will have the tendency to not be taken seriously. But, his father is right. The world will need strong evidence in order to even give me the chance to show them that I cured a zombie. Other than biting another beast of the undead, which isn't exactly a smart thing to do right now, there is one thing I can do to show him I'm not human anymore.

I pull the chair out next to Rose and sit down. His father looks at me and tries to give me a sympathetic smile. He clearly wants to hear nothing more unless it's something that shows him we aren't lying. I lift my hands and grab the sunglasses from my face. Slowly, I take them off and set them on the table. My eyes are the proof he might be searching for and I'm thinking I probably should have done this in the first place.

"Holy hell." He whispers as he stares at me.

I can see perfectly in this darkness and the look on his face is priceless. His mouth is agape and his eyes are wide open in shock. He's never seen eyes like mine before and he might never see something like them again.

"Is this proof enough?" I ask.

He takes a deep breath and says, "They're amazing and beautiful. This is why you wear the sunglasses? To hide your eyes from the world?"

I nod in agreement, "Not just to hide them. The sun burns the hell out of them during the day, I have no choice but to wear them."

"Wow," he says, "So, you really aren't a human anymore?"

I shake my head, "I guess not."

He runs a hand through his hair and leans closer, still staring at my eyes, "If you're not human, do you have a heartbeat?"

Again, I shake my head, "You can check if you want." I offer him my wrist to feel for a pulse.

He sets the gun on the table and hesitantly presses two fingers to my wrist. With all that's left of my heart, I wish a beat would be found right now. The look on his face tells me he didn't find one either. He takes his hand away, quickly, and gives me another confusing look.

"You were bit by a vampire *and* a zombie." He says in disbelief, "What the hell are you?"

I shrug, "I haven't figured that out yet."

"She's something wonderful." Rose chimes in, "She saved my life and I wish I could prove more to you that she really did. She's the thing that can save the rest of the world."

George's father turns his gaze to Rose and smiles, "If she really brought you back, why don't you remember anything? Why can't you remember your name?"

Rose shrugs, "I don't know. I keep getting more and more images flashing through my mind, giving me some things that I feel really happened. I see an older woman. She has red hair just like mine and I think she's my mother, but I don't know for sure. There's nothing more to tell me who she is and why I keep thinking of her. I wish there was something to tell me what my visions mean and give me some direction of who I used to be. I only know who I am right now and I know it's only been a day, but I know I'm human again. I can live the life I was meant to have. The life God gave me."

There she goes with that religious talk again.

"Dad, you have to believe us. I wouldn't be begging you this much if I hadn't seen it with my own eyes. I swear to you, Bridget holds the cure for the zombies." George says in his most pleading sounding voice he has.

His father passes his eyes between the three of us, landing on me. I can tell his trying to believe us, trying to put the pieces of our messed up little puzzle together. He knows I'm not human any longer and that's a big piece that fits in with this. Again, this would be so much easier to prove if I had another zombie around to give this man a live-action view of how it works. That isn't something I'd really look forward to, no matter how hungry I am right now. However, once you get past the rotting flesh smell and the fact that you're eating an undead creature, it's not half bad.

"What about the vampires?" George's father asks.

"What about them?" I ask.

"Can you cure them too?"

I shrug, "I don't know. Haven't had the *privilege* of running into one since this happened to me. But, I did cure a zombie somehow, I'm sure anything is possible."

He takes a deep breath and says, "Okay, let's say I believe you. Let's say you aren't just another monster trying to hide out in a village filled with humans waiting for the perfect time to attack," his eyes are deadlocked with mine, "How do you suggest we get the rest of the people here, or the world, to believe that you are some sort of cure for the zombies? You can't expect something like this to go over very well at all."

"Well, if it goes bad, at least I'm already dead. What more could they do?" I reply.

The old man smiles and says, "Okay then. It might take some convincing, but at the bonfire tonight I'll pull Adam aside and see what he thinks. It's best to keep this secret small at first. He'll know what to do from then on and he'll figure out if he wants to believe your story. I mean, you got the eyes and the lack of a heartbeat, girl, but a cure for the zombies, that's far from believable without seeing it actually happen."

"I agree." I say.

We might have one person on our side. It's still questionable, but I don't think he's going to kill me. Not right now anyway. I think I can trust him enough to attempt to spread the word about this cure through the village. That actually seems like a pretty tall order to fill and I can only hope, with every fiber of my being, this man will do what he says he's going to do and get another person to believe this. Otherwise, I can kiss this weird new life of mine good-bye.

* * *

I hid inside the house for most of the afternoon. The smells coming from outside were too much for me to handle. Human blood is mouth-watering and just being in this house with three others, is enough to get that familiar frenzy boiling in my gut. I can't risk that frenzy turning into something I can't control.

I'm still so new at this.

One day isn't long enough to learn everything about being part of the undead. I'm a *new* kind of undead. A kind that can control their hunger much better than the vamps and zombies. Still, I can't take that risk and I absolutely won't let myself kill human.

The bonfire started a few minutes ago. The sun is starting its descent and the sky is slowly growing dark. The people in this small community have armed themselves with guns in case something chooses to go bump in the night. George tells me that once that happens, the group packs up and finds someplace new. A place to start over until the next horde destroys it.

I've never met people who live like this. It doesn't seem like a very fun way to live. Once you get used to something and really like it there, something bad happens and you have to get used to something else. Makes me glad my dad and I never stayed in a place long enough to get used to it. *Hell*, I've lived in Des Moines for a year and I'm still not used to it. There are just certain things in life we have to force ourselves through in order to survive. I'm sure this isn't the life these people had planned out.

I'm a prime example of that one.

I didn't plan on losing my family or going from place to place hoping to be safe for a day or two. I never thought I'd have to live as someone who may or may not hold the key to human's survival. Then again, I never wanted to live a boring, sit behind a desk, pushing paperwork day in and day out kind of life either. I wanted to live in the moment. Be the one who tells the stories of all the amazing things that happened all over the world. Instead, I *became* one of those stories the world will share till the end of time. Not quite sure how I feel about that just yet. Give it some time and it might sink in.

I finally found the right moment to go outside and join the rest of this civilization. The smoke from the fire drifts up my nose as I hop down the two steps to the dirt on the sidewalk. George and Rose are waiting for me by the bonfire and I can see them sitting on an old wooden bench waving for me to join them. His father gave Rose some clean water and soap, along with new clothes so she could freshen up. She no longer looks like something the zombies discarded. She looks human. I was offered the same, but refused. I don't feel dirty or gross. My clothes might beg to differ, but the rest of me feels clean and amazing. My hair is still so soft and tangle free, never how it used to be. That, and there's no sense in wasting something good on someone that's not exactly human when it should go to the living.

I walk to the bench and force a smile when Rose and George notice me. Both of them have a piece of chicken to munch on. Everyone surrounding the fire has either chicken or beef to eat as their dinner. I'm sure it tastes amazing, but I'd rather have something a little more rare.

The eyes of the crowd are glued to me as I sit down. They're still getting used to seeing two newcomers in their community. I'm sure it has *nothing* to do with the fact that I'm a strange girl wearing sunglasses when the sun isn't shining or that there's blood stains on my jeans. No, it must be that we're new here. That's all it is.

"Hungry?" Rose asks as I sit beside her.

I raise an eyebrow and pass her a smirk, "Believe me, what I'm hungry for would be frowned upon here."

"I'm glad you have a sense of humor about your situation. George's father is already trying to convince that Adam fellow about you." She retorts.

I shrug, "My sense of humor is the last thing to die on

me. Besides, I'll need it when I'm held at gunpoint for being a monster amongst a clan of humans. Might make my last few moments of breathing tolerable."

"Bridget, you can be so cryptic when you want to be. Is this how you were before you were bitten? When you lived in the city?" George asks.

"Quite a bit." I say with a smile.

"You would think being undead would change all that." He says, taking a bite of his meal.

"You would think that, but you'd be wrong." I reply.

"It doesn't look like your father is having much luck over there, George." Rose says, staring across the street.

His father is talking to that guy, Adam, by an old light post. I can tell he's having issues trying to get Adam to understand everything. By the way that man is glaring at me, I'm sure it won't be long before the guns in this place change their aim to me.

"He has to believe us." Rose says, quietly.

"Oh well, just finish eating and we'll head over there." George goes back to his small meal and Rose takes a sip of water.

I keep my eyes on Adam. His arms are folded across his chest and I can see his lips moving. They're too far for a human to hear what's being said. I guess it's a good thing I'm not one of those anymore. I stare at them, focusing only on what they are saying and drowning out the others around me.

"I can't believe you let your son bring one of those undead creatures to my community. You're going to get us all killed, Greg." Adam argues.

Finally, I got to learn George's father's name. Through this entire day, he never once thought to mention it.

Greg frantically shakes his head back and forth, "I don't think she's going to kill anyone here. I sat down with them and not once did she give me any sign of hurting me, my son or that other girl. It might seem hard to believe, but I think they're telling the truth. I think she might actually be a cure."

"I don't care what you think. If that thing doesn't have a heartbeat, it doesn't deserve to live anymore." Adam says.

That hurts a little. Never been called an "it" or a "thing" before.

"Please, Adam, you and I have been friends for years. Right after this thing really went out of control." Greg sounds like he's begging, "I'm asking you to just give me a chance. Just hear them out and if you don't like what they have to say, I'll give you my own gun to kill that girl."

I can see the look of frustration on Adam's face as he contemplates what his friend is trying to tell him. He doesn't seem at all convinced by any of this and I wouldn't blame him for pulling that gun out of the holster on his belt and shooting me in the head. I'd probably consider doing the same thing.

"I'm sorry, Greg," Adam states, "maybe if there was more evidence and not just that red head's word about the other one being a cure. Maybe then I could believe it. I just can't and I have more important things to do right now. That thing is your responsibility and I'm going against my better judgment by not killing it right now. Whatever happens with it around, is on your head. I'll let you make the call on letting it live or not." He walks away from his friend and heads for one of the houses.

Greg solemnly looks down at his feet, ashamed at himself for not getting Adam to believe him. Good thing we didn't tell the whole world right away. It's hard enough trying to convince one person to convince someone else about this thing. It might be best if I left before these people get too suspicious of me.

"Your dad couldn't get him to believe us." I say, turning back to stare at the fire.

George passes me a confused look and says, "How do you know that?"

"I could hear them." I reply. "I think I'm just gonna go before they kill me."

"What? You can't go." Rose protests.

I stand from the bench and say, "It's for the best. You're human now, so you can live the life you want and be happy. I don't have that privilege anymore."

I don't get more than one step away from the bench before the breeze comes swooping in. An array of wonderful scents fill my nose. The humans, their blood, the salt of their skin. I want it so bad, leaving would definitely be the best choice for me to make right now. All of this temptation isn't good for someone like me. I just want to make this last little aroma stay with me for a while.

I let another whiff of their scent fill me up and I close my eyes so I can feel what they would taste like. I imagine it's the best, sweetest taste in the world. Better than any rabbit or zombie on the planet. Probably more filling as well. This would be so much easier to leave if my stomach wasn't trying to keep me in place. I take another sniff of the air and my eyes open again.

There's something familiar looming on the air. The same thing I noticed earlier when I thought my mind was playing around with me. It's stronger this time and I know it has to be real. I know he's got to be here somewhere. I'd never forget his smell, not in a million years. I move further away from the bench and the fire, scanning the area for a sign that might point to him. Something to tell me he's close by and I'm not going crazy with my imagination.

There's a hint of fear mixed in with his aroma, only making me nervous about what he's going through. I take a few more steps down the middle of the street, sniffing the air as I walk. I'm getting strange looks from a couple kids passing me by, but it's easy to shrug them off when I'm so focused on finding the source of this scent. The further I get away from the fire, toward the way out of this place, the stronger the smell gets.

Something catches my ear and I stop dead in my tracks. A voice. One I'd never forget. He's yelling for help and I know he's got to be close. Maybe he's running from something. A zombie or a vamp most likely, but maybe he's running here. I could save him. I could stop whatever is chasing him.

"Help!" his voice is definitely louder this time and I'm not the only one who can hear it.

The talking behind me steadily grows quiet. There's a few hushed whispers from people trying to figure out who is calling for help. I can feel all of their eyes staring the same way I am. The sun is practically gone now and the whole place is dark. Too dark to see with these damn shades on anymore and I take them off, hanging them over the collar of my shirt.

"Someone help us!" I hear him calling again and I can now make out the sounds of his footsteps.

He's not alone.

* * *

He's definitely not alone, like I said a moment ago. I sniff the air and can tell he's with a friend, another human. There's also something dead running right behind them. The closer they get to this village, the louder their groaning gets. Zombies, but I can't tell how many. I guess it could be worse. I expected vampires to rip into this village considering as how everyone's out right now. It's a good thing zombies are chasing them instead of the vamps. I'm pretty sure I can handle this.

I take a step forward, hearing the mechanical sounds of guns being cocked and ready to go. If only they knew what I am capable of doing, they wouldn't need the guns. I just need time that I don't have to get to the undead before these people start shooting at what could be alive in a few minutes. With me and this cure in the picture, I can't just sit around and let these humans destroy a chance at getting the world back on track. I might be a little dead myself, but I still want the human race to survive.

They are coming into view. The humans around the fire gasp and a few run for the houses to gain safety. There are three zombies, two male and one female. They don't appear to be too badly decomposed. My cure will hopefully work on them, if I'm given the chance. The two people they're chasing, two people I thought I'd never see again, are running at top speed trying to get away. These zombies are slightly faster than most and are catching up rather quickly.

They get closer and a few men come around me. Their guns are aimed and ready to go once the zombies get close enough. I turn my head from side to side, frantically looking at the eager faces ready to kill something that doesn't need to be killed. *Man*, listen to me showing compassion for a zombie. Those things have ruined my life more than once and here I am caring about them all because I hold a cure for their illness.

"Don't shoot them." I say, getting a few awkward sneers thrown at me, "I got this."

I highly doubt they'll listen to my words, probably even shoot me in the process of trying to take out the zombies. Still, I have to do this. I have to do what it takes to bring back three people who hopefully remember none of their horrible lives as a zombie. If they're anything like Rose, they won't.

"What the hell are you doing?" I hear a male voice calling from behind me as I walk.

It's easy to shrug them off as I walk swiftly down the street, keeping my eyes on the one person I'm really doing this for. He needs my help once again and dammit I'm going to give it to him. I can see Carter pumping his arms and legs, trying to outrun the zombies behind him. He's ahead of Ryder, but keeps glancing behind him to make sure his friend is still there.

Ryder, to think I'd never get to see him again and here he is, running toward me. He might not know it's me just yet, but he will. I watch him move his legs faster, looking over his shoulder to see the zombies coming up on his tail. His eyes don't see the pothole he's headed for and there's no way for me to stop him from twisting his ankle and falling to the ground.

Of course, that's exactly what happens. Life can never be easy when you want it to be and I have to pick up the pace.

Carter doesn't notice that Ryder has fallen behind. He doesn't even see me when I rush right by him. My legs are moving so fast, I can't tell if I'm really moving them or if the world is spinning faster so I can get there. The zombies are closing in on their prey. He's trying to pull himself up, crawling away from them. All of the creatures stop running and know they have what they want without even trying. Their growling gets louder and Ryder rolls onto his back, staring up at the things about to devour him. I can smell his fear more than anything else and it has the monster raging deep in my gut. It's even more pissed off than when I won't feed it.

One of the male zombies closes the gap between him and Ryder. I can smell the death protruding from his skin. That rotten scent drifts up my nose only driving me into an even deeper frenzy. It must know that nothing is allowed to put its gnarly hands on the man I'm in love with. I'm the only undead thing allowed to touch him.

I'm still a few yards away when I leap through the air and dive into the male zombie standing over Ryder. I tackle him to the ground, toppling over him, and landing on my stomach a few feet away. The zombie doesn't pass me a second glance as he pulls himself back together and goes for Ryder once more. I'm beginning to notice that these things have no desire for my flesh whatsoever. The other two going after Ryder are paying no attention to me at all. This might be a good thing. I don't have to worry about zombies or vampires trying to eat me anymore.

I jump to my feet, thrusting myself through the air and bringing the zombie down again. I hear a crunch when his shoulder hits the concrete, but that can be fixed once he's human. I pin him to the ground, feeling his claw-like finger-nails digging into my boots, not strong enough to break through the leather. He growls at me, trying with all his might to push me off of him. This thing might be strong, but I'm even stronger. I grab a handful of the stringy hair on his head, forcing him to sit up and look at me. The black eyes stare back and he spits his nasty saliva on my face.

"That's not very nice." I say, then take a breath and bring my mouth to his neck, sinking my teeth deep into his skin.

I can't believe how hungry I've gotten since last night. I break the skin on his neck easily, letting that dead blood pour down my throat. It's so amazing, so disgusting, yet all so filling at the same time. His groans are drown out by the frenzy taking over my mind and destroying every ounce of me that's human. All I want is more of this. More of this nasty new thing called a meal. It's refreshing and the only thing to calm myself.

As soon as his screaming fades and he is lifeless in my grip, I let him fall to the ground and turn to the other two. Ryder is currently holding off the female zombie. Her hands are clutching the collar of his hoodie while his arms block her from biting into him. I wipe the blood from my mouth and get to my feet. I stomp angrily across the concrete and reach out for the zombie. I take a handful of her nasty, brown hair and yank her away from Ryder. She growls at me, her arms still reaching out for her meal as I fling her to the ground.

"Bridget?" I hear a shocked Ryder say from behind me.

The zombie quickly gets to her feet and glares at me.

Hatred burns in her black eyes and she lunges at me. She digs her nails into my back and I can feel them breaking the skin. It doesn't hurt, just like when Rose scratched my face last night. Nothing but an annoyance and I can deal with that. This one tries throwing me to the ground. She's able to grab my hoody and swing me away from her a bit. I stumble, but never do I fall. Her hungry eyes focus again on Ryder. I'm sure she's peeling him apart right now with those black orbs. She takes a heavy step toward him, falling almost on top of him. I'm right there to catch her and drag her away.

A loud scream escapes her throat, filling my ears as I stand in her way. If there was a way for me to tell her that I'm about to make this all better, I'd be doing that right now. I could speak to her, she'd never understand the words coming out of my mouth, but I could try. That sounds foolish and it's easier to jump the gun and go for what I want. I let her rush me again, coming within inches of taking me down. With a swift move, I lift my leg and kick her in the stomach, causing her to double over.

That raspy breathing, the sound that has haunted my dreams for so long, is about to be ended in this woman. I kneel down beside her and she quickly starts clawing at me again, trying to push me away from her. She swings her arms at me and I grab one of them and bite down hard. Her blood fills my mouth, dripping down my chin, staining my shirt and hoodie even more. She claws at my grip on her arm, unable to make a sound after the kick she took to the gut. I can see her in the corner of my eye as I take the dead life away from her. Slowly, very slowly, I can see it fading from her eyes and she falls face first to the ground. I let go of her arm and wipe the blood from my chin.

Another one down, but my monster still remains.

I pull myself to my feet and turn around. There's one last zombie standing over Ryder. There's something familiar about this one. I've seen him before, back at the wall. This is the hesitant zombie that chose to walk away instead of eating us. I let him live and this is the thanks I get. I glare into those black, lifeless eyes that aren't paying any attention to the fresh meat on the ground. Instead, all of his attention is on me. This one isn't like the other two.

He's hesitating.

Maybe he can understand me. Maybe the hesitant ones are different. I move toward him, stepping between the zombie and Ryder. I can feel a small part of the human me returning to my brain so I can gain some sort of control over my body. The zombie doesn't move or try to attack. He just stands there and I'm about to do something crazy. It might not be as crazy as biting a zombie to gain sustenance, but still crazy in my opinion.

"I can fix you." I say to him. "I can make you human again."

I see his black eyes dart to the woman lying on the ground. Any moment now and we should hear two gasps for air. They'll be human and by the look on his face, I think he knows.

"Let me cure you." I say.

He lumbers up to me, closing the space between us. I'm not sure what this thing is doing to be honest. He's not really giving me a sign or coming out and telling me. He stands within an inch from my face and cocks his head to the side. I start to wonder if he remembers me from back at the wall. If he does, he might be slightly grateful I spared him. Then, he looks down at my arm and I feel a tight grip on my wrist. I feel his fingers tightly wrap themselves around me and lift my arm to his mouth.

This time, I do feel the pain as he chomps his teeth down against my hand. The skin breaks instantly and I even feel the veins bursting and blood flowing out. I tighten my eyes and clench my teeth. The pain is searing and I don't understand why. I've gotten scratched by these things and felt nothing, but this bite is the one thing to bring me pain. Maybe it has something to with the zombie taking my blood for once and not the opposite.

I don't like it.

A few seconds pass and the tightness and pain in my hand eases as the zombie releases his jaw and falls. I take a breath and open my eyes to check out my hand. There's a jagged cut on it with red blood oozing out. I wipe some of it away and can see the wound healing itself already.

"Bridget." I hear a whispered voice from behind me.

My head snaps back to reality and my mind belongs to me again. I'm no longer trying to control my hunger for the flesh and blood of a zombie. I turn around and look to the ground where Ryder is still sitting. His eyes are open wide. I guess he's not used to seeing a dead girl like me.

Past him, I see the shadows of people moving in toward us. Their guns are raised and pointed at me. This would be the perfect time to run, but I can't. My feet won't let me move and I know I need to stay. Not just for the fact that Ryder is lying at my feet, but I need to be here to prove to the people that I am the cure this planet has been looking for.

"What the hell is going on out here?" I recognize Adam's voice and see him running out of the house he disappeared inside a few minutes ago.

He runs to the street and heads my way. His eyes widen as he sees the three zombies unmoving on the ground. A few others are gathering to get a look at the mess I've created. Carter is amongst them and he pushes his way through in order to get to Ryder.

"Bridget? That was you?" he sounds surprised.

I shrug, "Yeah, it was me."

"What the hell?" he says.

A loud gasp escapes the throat of the first man I took down. Everyone's eyes dart in his direction and so do mine. I see him coughing, gathering whatever air his lungs will allow him. George runs to the scene and quickly gets to the man's side, helping him sit up so he can breathe easier. I see his eyes flutter open and I smile when the brown hue comes to view.

"What the hell is going on?" Adam asks.

I turn to him and say, "I cured him. I don't know how and I definitely don't know why, but I cured them all."

The woman's gasp comes next and Rose rushes to her side, "They're changing back to human." She says as she kneels beside the woman. "The same thing happened to me when Bridget bit me last night."

The few people in the crowd are astonished as they stare at the people on the ground. Both of them are opening their eyes and seeing the world as a human again. The guns slowly lower and I think they realize I'm not a threat to them.

"Where am I?" the man asks as he looks around.

A few more people move closer, answering whatever questions he may have. Others join Rose in assisting with the woman and Greg, George's father, goes to the third one's side and waits for the gasp that comes from his throat the second Greg's knees hit the ground.

I stare at each one of them. The human color back in their eyes and faces all because of me. I'm just as amazed as when Rose first opened her eyes. It doesn't feel like I did anything at all, but I brought them back. I am the miracle Rose keeps insisting I am.

"Bridge?" Ryder's voice catches me and I turn to face him.

Carter helps him to his feet and the two of them stand together, staring at me, "Hi." I say.

Ryder smiles and I can see tears building in his eyes, "I thought I'd never see you again."

I nod, "Same here. I guess I have a lot of explaining to do."

"Damn right you do. What are you?" he asks.

I shrug, "No clue."

"Your eyes are different now. They're beautiful."

I smile, "Just one of the perks of this."

"Glad to see you're still yourself, Bridget. You might

have blood dripping from your face, but it's good to see you." Carter chimes in.

Embarrassed, I quickly wipe the rest of the blood from my chin on the sleeve of my hoodie and pass Ryder a smile. He can't stay away from me forever and he limps the few, short steps to throw his arms around me. I can't protest being this close to him, no matter how wonderful his flesh might smell. The monster in my stomach has gone away and is allowing me to wrap my arms around the man I love.

I hold onto him, gripping the back of his shirt with a clenched fist. The warmth of his body is the only place I truly feel safe. Even now, after changing into whatever I am, in his arms is the only place I want to be. The world cannot hurt me in the small bubble he forms around the two of us.

He pulls himself away from me and I know exactly what he wants to do now. He closes his eyes and moves in for the kiss. I don't know what would happen to him if he got the taste of whatever is on my lips. Not only the zombie blood that's most likely left behind, but the poison in my own blood. I can't let the same thing that changed me, turn him into something of the same caliber. I can't let him go through that pain.

It kills me to do this, but I put my hand on his chest and stop him from coming closer. I feel his heart beating in his chest and it needs to stay that way.

"You can't kiss me." I say, quietly.

"Why?" he argues.

"I can't destroy your life." I reply. "I don't want you to feel the pain I felt when I changed into this."

He sighs and nods his head in understanding, "This is going to suck."

"I know, but I can't hurt you." I say.

"I understand." Ryder says, quietly.

"Bridget?" Adam interrupts our little reunion and the two of us turn to face him. "You really cured them?"

I nod, "I did."

He raises his eyebrows and nods his head, "You need to come with me."

* * *

Adam took me to the same house I saw him walking out of right after he missed my little battle with the zombies. Ryder and Carter came with us as well. I wouldn't have gone with the man if they weren't by my side. In this world, you can never be too safe, even when you're something like me. We left George and Rose in the street with the newly cured humans and disappeared with Adam into the small, white house.

The front door creaks open and the place smells dusty. There's a fire going in the fireplace on the far wall of the living room. It's not the first thing I notice when I enter the house. That happens to be the boxes of ammo and the many weapons being cleaned and loaded by a few people who apparently didn't want to attend the party outside. All of their eyes turn toward us when we walk into the room. A dark skinned woman with short black hair, goes on full alert the second our eyes meet. She pulls a gun out and aims at me.

"I saw what this one did outside. Why would you bring her here." She asks.

"She's not a threat to us, guys. She might be the most valuable asset to this planet." Adam states and leads us further into the house.

The woman reluctantly lowers her gun and steps aside.

This allows us to enter the kitchen. A dinghy, white room with dust layered on everything. There are still dirty dishes in the sink and the smell of mold consumes the place. We move to a wooden door, which Adam unlocks and pulls open. It leads to the basement and he descends down the stairs. Carter follows first, then me, and Ryder comes down last.

It's darker down here than in the rest of the house. The small windows at the top of the walls are boarded up, hiding any trace of sunlight that could possibly come into this room. A few lamps are spread about the place to give off enough light for the others to see. There are two men down here. A tall, skinny man who looks like he hasn't eaten anything in weeks and a shorter man with a long beard and dark hair. He's sitting on an old bar stool in front of a long black sheet. This is where we come to our stop.

I stare ahead of me with awe written all over my face. I've seen curtains like this before. They're meant to hide something and the last time I encountered one of these, the result from removing the curtain ruined my life. I sniff the air, trying not to focus on the humans I'm trapped down here with. I can't let myself drool over them. Outside of their scent, I catch a hint of something that doesn't belong. Something that isn't alive anymore, yet doesn't smell dead enough to be a zombie.

I *really* don't like this.

"What's going on, Adam? You've never brought others down here." The bearded man says. "Especially ones with eyes like hers."

Adam steps in front of me to block any sort of attack this man might want to throw at me and replies, "She's here to help us, Michael. Now grab that end and let's get this sheet down."

This man, Michael, stares at me for what seems like the longest minute ever. His eyes are telling me something, telling me not to trust him. He doesn't appear to be someone who would associate himself with the likes of a person like me. I hope I'm wrong and my intuition is fooling me right now, but I think I'll keep an eye on him until I figure him out for sure.

He nods and gets off the stool. Both he and Adam grab ends of the black sheet and yank it down from the nails holding it to the ceiling. They toss the sheet to the side and quickly step away from what's in this corner of the room.

Just as I figured, a vamp in a cage.

This cage is better welded in the corners and the door looks more secure than the last time I saw something like this. There's a small cot in there with the vamp, not like she needs it. She's standing inches from the bars, staring out at all of us. She's young, maybe fifteen or sixteen and she's shorter than me. Her hair is long, blonde, and faded matching the haze covering her eyes. Her clothes aren't torn or bloody like some of the others I've seen. She actually looks human, despite the paleness of her skin.

"This is my daughter, Katie." Adam's voice sounds hoarse and sad. "She was bit about six months ago and I couldn't bring myself to kill her. I took her just before she changed and locked her in this cage."

I step forward, keeping my eyes on the vamp, "How do you feed her?"

Adam lifts a sleeve of his jacket, revealing a few scars on his forearm, "I'm not a horrible person. I rely only on myself to keep her alive instead of giving her other means."

"Does she know who you are?" Carter asks from behind us.

Adam shakes his head, "I don't think she does. I've told her time and time again that I'm her father and she uses that to taunt me. She gets me to think that she's not a vampire anymore and I want to let her out. That's why Michael is down here, to make sure I never do that."

This would be the hardest thing a father could ever do. Watch his daughter live as a vampire, bleeding himself so she could stay alive. My father would never do such a thing. He wouldn't allow us to suffer. If he were here today and saw me get bit by both of those things, he would've ended things before I had the chance to run away. It actually might be a good thing he's not here right now. The world wouldn't have its cure for the zombies.

Adam turns to me, his eyes are sad and full of tears, "Bridget, I wasn't lying when I met you this morning. I like you and even more now that I saw what you did out there. You brought those people back to life. You made their hearts beat again."

"You still wanted to kill me though." I reply.

"Yes, this is true but," he takes a deep breath, "after witnessing a miracle, killing you is the last thing I'd ever dream of. You are a new hope for the humans."

I shrug, "Not the first time I've heard this today."

"That's why I'm asking you to cure my daughter."

He didn't need to ask for me to know what he brought me down here for. He saw how those people came back after I bit them, it's only natural for him to assume I can cure a vamp just the same. There's just one problem with his assumption.

"I don't know if I can." I reply.

"You have to." Adam pleads.

"Look, I honestly didn't even know I could cure those zombies. When I attacked Rose last night, it wasn't because I knew I could change her back, it was because I was hungry. Killing George or his sister wasn't an option and the zombie was the next thing around with the right ingredients to calm my stomach. Seeing her wake up as a human was just a perk of the game." I say, "I don't think I can risk the same thing with your daughter not knowing what will happen. I don't know if she'll wake up a human or if we'll both die."

He nods, "I get that you don't want to risk it, we can cut your arm and let her drink your blood for herself. These vamps don't turn down blood."

I run my fingers through my hair and say, "The zombies

don't detect me as being alive. They don't want anything to do with me. I *highly* doubt a vamp will be any different."

He turns his watery eyes to his daughter, letting a few tears drift to his cheeks. I know how I said my father would've killed me if he saw me change into something like this. I also know, if there was the possibility of a cure staring him right in the face, he'd do what it takes to make me human again. Even if that meant risking my life and losing me anyway. If my mother were here, she'd want me to do this. Helping people was one of her things and she hated seeing someone sad.

"I'm not promising I'll bring her back. I'm not even going to promise she'll be alive after she gets a dose of whatever is in my blood. But I'll do it." I say, "I'll try to make her human again."

Adam smiles and turns to me, "Thank you so much for this. I'll get a knife and we'll try getting her to drink your blood first."

I shake my head, "That will take too long and I know she won't go for it. I'll actually prove that to you right now."

I walk away from them, approaching the bars of the cage. The vamp on the other side stays put and glares at me. Both of us sniff the air when I'm close enough to her. She smells different than the zombies. The salt on her skin smells sweeter as well as the blood underneath. My body can't tell the difference and wants to try a taste regardless of what happens to either of us.

The vamp looks me up and down before taking a step back. Just as I figured, she wants nothing to do with me and can most likely detect I'm not human. That's one of the few problems with this cure of mine. I'll have to do a lot of work in order to get close to anything without having a human nearby to trick them.

"I...don't want...you." she says, her voice raspy just like any other vamp.

"I...don't...care." I say, mocking her.

"Not...alive." she says and backs further away from the bars, out of my reach.

This is going to be difficult. I look around the bars, searching for the handle to get inside. There's no handle, just a metal chain wrapped around two of the bars with a padlock to keep it closed.

I turn to Adam and say, "Do you have a key?"

Michael's the one who reaches into his pocket and fishes for the key. He tosses it to me and I quickly go to work on unlocking the padlock. The vampire, Katie, moves even further away from me until she's pinned herself against the opposite wall.

"Bridget." Ryder calls when I let the chain and lock fall to the floor.

I look over my shoulder, seeing the concern on his face, and say, "It's okay."

I pull the metal door open and step inside the cage, letting the door close a little. The vamp glares at me and moves into the corner. If this cure ever goes global, these people are really going to have to put it some kind of dart gun or something. I can't put myself into situations like this anymore, hoping things will turn out okay. A dart gun would be much faster *and* safer for me. If this works today, I'll be sure to suggest it.

I move toward Katie, making sure I block her from getting to the door. If she gets out, she'll be shot and I can't be responsible for that. Adam would kill me just for letting it happen. She has nowhere to go in here. If she tries to lunge at me, I can take her down. I'm not sure how strong I am against a vamp so this will be a learning experience.

"I...don't want." She seethes as I stand less than a foot from her.

"I might be able to cure you. Why wouldn't you want that?" I ask.

Her response to my question burns a little bit. She raised her hand so quick, I didn't see it coming. Her fingers scratched my face and I can feel a slight burning sensation in each cut. I stumble away from her and hold my face for a second. I don't really like how this is going so far. I wipe the blood from my face and glare at her. The burning in my cheek isn't enough to keep the anger from sending a frenzy of hunger through my body. Anger seems to make it worse and I tend to get stronger right along with it.

Katie tries clawing at me again, but this time I'm prepared for it. I reach up before her nails can connect with my skin and grab her arm. She screams and I pull her closer. With her free hand, she digs her nails into my shoulder. More burning pain soars through my body and I let out a grunt. I grab her hair and slam her against the wall. Another wail comes out of her mouth and she digs her nails deeper into my skin. I quickly tilt her head to the side until her bare neck comes to view and I lean in for the bite.

She's a lot stronger than I thought she would be. She lifts her leg and jabs it into my stomach, sending me across the cage until I meet with the bars. I catch myself before I fall to the floor and stare at her. She hops onto the bed and is making her way to the door. I hear the metal of the guns behind me getting ready to take aim and it's now or never for me to make this happen.

I push through the pain in my shoulder and lunge at her before she's able to get the door open. I slam her against the wall and don't give her the chance to push me away this time. With a mouthful of her blonde hair, I clamp my teeth against her neck, right above her shoulder. I pin her against the wall with one hand keeping her head in place and another holding back an arm. She's too busy screaming and shouting and banging her fist against the wall to fight back anyway.

Her blood tastes different than the zombies. Bad different. It's like when you drink cough syrup that's way past the expiration date. Cough syrup is disgusting on its own, but expired, it's much worse. Her blood burns my tongue and the back of my throat and I can feel a dizziness taking over. My head is spinning and begging me to stop, trying to get me to let go. I can't, not until she stops moving and the screaming grows quiet. Only then will I know the vamp inside her has died and there might be a chance for her human form to come back.

Although, it seems to be taking too long for her to stop moving. Her body isn't going limp and it doesn't appear like she's going to fall from my grasp. The painful shouting still fills the air. It sounds different, but it's not going away. I try holding on a bit longer, letting this poison fill my throat. I just can't take it anymore and I'm forced to let go. The taste is too much for me.

I pull myself away from her and spit out what's left of the blood in my mouth. The burning only seems to get worse and the room is spinning violently. I grab onto the bars closest to me to keep myself from falling over, but fail when I realize I've grabbed the door of the cage. It swings open and I fall backwards to the floor outside. Katie is still pinned against the wall, her head shaking back and forth, screams escaping her throat. We're both having a bad reaction to this.

"Bridge!" Ryder's voice sounds distorted and his face is spinning as he kneels beside me.

I feel his hand on the back of my head and he cradles me in his arms. I can't keep the pain from coursing through my veins and squeeze my fists so tight I can feel my nails cutting into the palms of my hands. I grab Ryder's hoodie and hold on tight while the pain takes over and the world spins. He lifts me off the ground a little and I can see Katie slowly sliding to the floor as well. Her screaming has ceased and her eyes are closed.

Another shot of pain flows through me and I can feel it in my gut, like someone stabbed me with dry ice. The spinning world is growing faint with every passing second or minute or hour. I can't tell how fast time is moving. My mind is shutting down. I can feel it. The pain is too much for me to tolerate, even the muscles in my hands start to relax.

"No, Bridge, you have to stay with me. Keep your eyes open." Ryder's voice doesn't even seem real.

I can't tell if it's real or if it's just a tape recording playing over and over in my head. His face is distorted and I can't really see him all that well. The spinning is too much and my head is pounding from the pain. If I close my eyes, it will stop. It's the only thing to ease the pain enough for my mind to take me elsewhere.

I let them fall shut and the blackness of my mind consumes me.

* * *

I don't recognize anything when I finally open my eyes again. There are flowers all around me in fields as far as I can see. The sun is shining in a bright blue sky over my head and it's not burning the hell out of my eyes. I don't even have the sunglasses on and I'm fine. I guess I must really be dead this time. You know, the kind of dead that *doesn't* come back to haunt the world.

I can't believe I failed so soon after something amazing happened. The world was given another chance of keeping the human race alive and, because I chose to risk it all by saving one young vampire, more humans will die. I might be in an extremely beautiful place right now, this has to be heaven, but I feel like I'm in hell for failing the world. It was my responsibility to keep the cure safe and it's dead right along with me.

"You're not dead, Bridget." I hear a woman's voice coming from behind me.

I don't want to turn around though. I know that voice and it kind of scares me to face her. I'm afraid to see the look on her face after she witnessed me turning into something she would be afraid of. She took herself away from my world so she wouldn't have to face the monsters anymore.

"I'm not upset with you, sweetie." Her voice is heartbreaking just to hear it, "You can turn around and look at your mother."

I bite my bottom lip and hold my breath as I allow my feet to spin around in the grass. The last time I saw this woman was a lifetime ago. She was unhappy and depressed over losing Maggie. We all were, but she took it harder than dad and I. She couldn't eat or drink anything and she looked like she had aged ten years in just one night. But here she stands, a few feet in front of me, looking as beautiful as ever. Her hair is perfectly curled, just like mine, and she's even wearing a bright pink sundress that matches her fluffy personality.

"Mom?" I whisper.

She nods, "It's me. I'm here for you."

"Where am I?" I ask.

She smiles, "Someplace your mind wants you to be right now. A safe place with someone who cares about you."

"That's a good place to be." I reply, my eyes are starting to water.

She moves closer, floating on the air under her feet. Everything about her is exactly what she would want. This flower-filled place in the middle of nowhere, the bright sun in the sky, she loves this sort of thing. Her dress is clean and even brighter in the sunlight. The exact opposite of me. My clothes are holey and stained and I'm sure I'm a little ripe by now. Being dead probably isn't the best smell in the world.

"My little Bridget, you are so grown up." She says.

"This life was sort of thrown at me, so I had to grow up."

I reply.

"It's okay if that happens once in a while. It's how we know we're doing the right thing." mom states, "and you, my little Bridge, are doing the best thing."

I shake my head, "It doesn't seem like it. Not after changing into whatever this is that I am now."

"You are." She reassures me, "You always have done the right thing. Whether that was ignoring your chores or helping your father fight off the monsters out there. You have never done anything to make me see you as a bad person."

"So you're proud of me?" I ask, feeling the sudden longing to know the answer.

"I've always been proud of you. Why would you ever ask such a thing?"

I shrug, "It just never seemed like you noticed me as much as you noticed Maggie. You always loved what she wanted to do with her life and didn't seem like I could ever measure up. I know I'm a tomboy at times and can be a smart ass all the time, but I never thought you were ever proud of anything I've done. Maggie always seemed like your favorite."

A tear falls from her eyes and she says, "No, all of you kids are my favorite. I love each and every little thing about all of you. Your perks, your faults, all of your abilities. I don't have a favorite, Bridget."

"Then why did you kill yourself? Why would you leave us like that?" I can feel the lump forming in my throat and the tears in my eyes.

"I had to. It was best for you and your father. Leaving you was the hardest thing I could have ever done, but I would've slowed you down." She says.

I shake my head, "We would have waited for you. You didn't need to go. I didn't want you to go."

Her eyes are bloodshot as more tears fall from them, "You might not understand things now, but you have to know I did what I knew was right. I miss you more than anything else in the world, but I'm able to see you in a way I've never been able to before. After watching you all this time, I was finally able to prove myself right."

I raise an eyebrow, "What do you mean?"

She smiles, "The day you were born, you were unlike any other baby in the nursery. You refused to cry, even when the doctor gave you a little tap. You sniffled and whined, but never cried. When I held you in my arms, you smiled at me and I knew you were going to be something great. Something that would make you the best person you could ever be."

"You never told me that before."

"I never thought I'd have to." She replies, "Bridget, from the moment you knew what you wanted to do with your life, you have always been the best. I'm not talking about when you were in school and wanted to travel the world collecting stories. I'm talking about from the moment you killed your first zombie with dad and I saw something change inside of you. Something that told me you were going to do something good for this world. It's what you were destined for."

I take a deep breath, letting the smell of flowers fill my nose. The lump is still sitting in my throat as I stare at my mother. She's never once told me how she thought I was destined for anything other than being another part of society. She would tell me how I could do whatever I wanted, but never be the one thing that would change the world.

"Bridget, you need to know that what you're giving to the world is the best thing it could ever receive. The fighting chance it didn't know it could ever have. I'm glad I get to watch you through all of this and see how well you'll do with the gift you've been given." She says.

I wipe the tears from under my eyes and say, "I'm really glad to hear you say that."

She smiles, "I know, sweetie."

Her feet slowly move away from me and I know it's her time to leave. I hate seeing her go, but my mind has reached a point of serenity to allow it. Just seeing her and knowing she cares about me and what I can do for the world, is all I need to keep going. To push through whatever hardships I know I'll come across. I know I'll be the best damn fighting chance the world has ever seen. I'm going to do whatever it takes to make sure she's always going to be proud of me.

Curing a lot of people seems like a great start.

* * *

I open my eyes to stare at a white ceiling above my head. The fan is covered in dust and there are chips in the paint around it. My body is stiff, once again. Not as bad as the first time, but my bones crack the same when I move my arms and bend my knees. I'm lying on a couch in some old living room. Good to know I'm not lying dead in that basement like I thought was going to happen.

I sit up on the couch and look around. The flat screen in front of me has a nice crack down the middle of it. There's a sliver of sunlight drifting in through one of the windows that wasn't boarded up properly. That tells me I've been unconscious for at least one night. I spot Ryder asleep on the love seat with a heavy blanket draped over him. He looks so peaceful. I wish I could cuddle with him. There's not much room for me and I really don't want to wake him since he looks so cute being asleep like that.

Above him, hanging on the wall, is an old photograph of the family who used to live here. There's the mom and dad, both wearing matching Christmas sweaters, three kids, two boys and a girl, each with identical, ugly sweaters. A Christmas tree is in the background of the photo with a bunch of presents underneath. All of them look so happy, regardless of how cheesy the picture looks. Seeing it makes me wish I had my photo album with me. I don't think I'd look at it right now, but it would bring comfort just knowing it was nearby.

I hear footsteps walking this way and I instantly get to my feet. Feels like some protective instinct is taking over because I thought Ryder and I were the only two people in the house. I turn my head toward the footsteps. There's a dark hallway leading to another part of the house. Carter stops walking and sees me staring at him. He's holding a small bottle of water and motions for me to follow him. I run my fingers through my hair, thankful there wasn't anything hiding in this house.

He leads me to the kitchen to a breakfast nook at the back of the house. These windows are boarded up as well with two peepholes carefully placed for someone to look out. They don't let enough light in to hurt my eyes since I don't have my sunglasses on. Not sure where those things are exactly. They were still hanging over the collar of my shirt the last time I saw them and they aren't there anymore. Hopefully, Ryder has them somewhere.

"Glad you're awake, Bridget." Carter says as we sit across from each other. "We weren't sure if you were alive or not."

"Yeah, hard to tell without a heartbeat." I reply.

He smiles, "You don't breathe very much either."

"All part of the package."

He takes a drink of the water and sets the bottle on the table. By the look on his face, I can tell he's distraught. I would be too if I just saw a good friend of mine tear into a few zombies and a vamp in one night. Probably freak me out for a few days.

"You probably want to know what happened last night." He suggests.

I nod, "A little bit, yeah."

"First you should know, that this last week has been hell for Ryder. Last night is the first time he's slept since you ran away from him at the overpass." Carter says.

"It's been a week since that happened?" no wonder I was so stiff when I woke up the other morning, I was lying dead for a few days.

He nods, "Yeah, a week."

"What happened?"

"Dwayne got nervous and didn't want to go any further. He was worried about what happened to you and didn't want to lose anyone else. So, we found a different way back to the city and called it a day. It took a lot, but I managed to get Ryder all the way to the gate." He says, then takes another sip of water, "Right after they scanned him, he took off running back the way we came. I had no choice but to follow him. He's one of the only good people I know in this world and I wasn't about to lose him because he couldn't accept what happened to you."

"He wanted to find me, didn't he?" I ask.

Carter nods, "Yeah, he told me he just needed to see what happened to you, to get some closure. Once he got that, he'd let me take him back to the city and he'd go on with his life. We searched for the last couple of days until we ran into those zombies last night. Ran out of ammo and had to run away. I spotted the smoke from the bonfire here and we ran like hell hoping someone would help us."

"Then I came along."

"Exactly." He says, "I didn't want to think it was you at first. It would've been horrible to see Ryder get killed at the hands of his girlfriend. Then I saw how you took out the zombies with no intention of going for any of the humans around. Made it even better when those three came back to life. You have no idea what that means for the world."

I shrug, thinking of the conversation I just had with my mother in my head, "I think I might."

"After what happened in the basement, we all thought you were dead. The vamp too. You stopped moving and we waited a good hour before anything happened. The girl, Katie, she opened her eyes and was herself again, not a vampire. She knew who she was and knew her father, she just can't remember anything after being bit."

"Probably a good thing." I say, not sure if I should be relieved by this news or not.

Curing a zombie seems so easy compared to what will happen if I go for a vamp. I can't pass out after I try to save them. Especially if there's more than one at my doorstep. A dart gun would be a definite need in this case.

"I hope you realize how valuable you've become." Carter says, keeping his eyes on the table.

I raise an eyebrow, "What do you mean?"

He takes a deep breath, "You're the cure for whatever all of this is. You can end all of the bad things happening to the humans on this planet. Once word gets out, and I'm sure it'll spread fast, people everywhere are going to want a piece of what flows in your veins. They can bring back those they care about and stop it from ever happening again. If you fall into the wrong hands, terrible things could happen to you and the world. Humans could start a war over you and we would have more than the zombies and vampires to worry about."

I guess I never really thought of things like that. Never thought of myself as being worth anything until finding out what I can do. I don't understand why someone would want to use my gift as anything other than a way to save this planet. As Rose always likes to say, I *am* a miracle, whether I want to see myself as that or not. There's no reason the whole world can't enjoy this cure of mine. I can't let someone take it away and use it for evil.

"Someone could take over the entire world with *you*, Bridget." Carter says, staring me in the eyes.

Well, *that's* certainly not a terrifying statement, "I understand and I'm not going to let myself fall into the wrong hands."

"Neither will any of us. Everyone here, those of us who saw what you did last night, are willing to do whatever it takes to make sure this new cure stays safe." He states.

"What exactly is the master plan on making sure that happens?" I ask.

"We're going to the city." Carter replies. "It's a three day hike from here back to Des Moines. They'd have the resources available to reproduce the cure in your blood in order to distribute it to every corner of the globe."

I nod, agreeing with his idea, "That's a good plan and all, but how do you expect me to get through the gate? They don't need to scan my eyes to know I'm not human anymore."

"We have proof." He replies. "You showed us what you're capable of doing last night. Seeing that would get anyone to believe anything that comes out of your mouth."

"That would work, but" I say, "I had to physically show everyone what I could do in order for you to believe it. It's disgusting and horrifying and I'd have to bring one of those things with me to show them that the cure is real. You, more than anyone else, knows that is a bad idea. They'd kill me and the zombie right on the spot."

He nods, "This is true. It would be really bad if they don't believe us or even want to try believing. There isn't a perfect way for this plan to work. We just have to try and pray to God one of them manages to see what you can do."

I nod in agreement. Other than roaming the countryside, bringing every zombie and vamp I run into back to life, there really isn't another option. I'd get pretty tired of biting all of those creatures and passing out after every vamp I touch. That and it's *really* gross regardless if my stomach finds relief in eating one of those things.

"When do we leave?" I ask.

"Soon," he says, "Adam is rallying the village and gathering supplies. The whole place is going, just like you and

Dwayne wanted. I know this is the place that family came from and I'm actually surprised we found it. At least we're saving all of these people and getting to do something even more amazing in the process."

"You got that right." I say, "There's something I want to tell you now."

He raises an eyebrow, "What's that?"

I run my fingers through my hair and think of Ryder, "Thank you for holding Ryder back after I was bitten. I'm glad he didn't have to see what I went through after that."

He gives me half a smile, "I'd do it again, but you shouldn't be thanking me for that."

"Oh yeah?"

"You should thank me for not shooting you in the head afterwards. I just couldn't go through the verbal torture Ryder would give me for that." He says.

"Well, thanks for that too, I guess."

He chuckles and takes the last sip of his water. Carter very well could have shot me dead while I was standing with them at the overpass. I guess that's why this world has irony. If I would have gotten killed back there, we never would have discovered the cure and this world still wouldn't have a future. Good thing Carter and the others didn't care about how much I'd suffer after being bit. I guess suffering is all part of the big picture.

* * *

Ryder is still sleeping and I plan on letting him stay that way for as long as he needs it, no matter how bad I want to crawl on that loveseat and cuddle with him. I can't help it, he just looks so darn cute and comfy right now. I guess this must be the part of my love story Maggie likes the most. The parts where I actually act like a girl and express that *lovey-dovey* side of me. Maybe she enjoys knowing her little sister has a girlie side and not just the side that likes shooting a gun or being a tomboy. It's just so weird to admit I *have* a girlie side. I can't let too many people know about this. They might think less of me.

I found my sunglasses sitting on one of the end tables next to the loveseat. Ryder must have kept those safe for me after I passed out. He's such a good guy to keep around. Always makes sure I have what I need even when he doesn't know why I need it. Carter found his way outside after our little conversation. He's going to talk to Adam and help all of them get ready for our journey.

My feet carry me through the short hallway in the house until I find the bathroom in a small room on the right. It's darker in here than anywhere else in the house because there's no window. Just the depressing, moldy shower and the yellow sink to match. I'm not sure where the toilet has run off to. There's a place for one and the pipe it's supposed to connect with, it's just not here anymore. I don't plan on asking what happened because, let's face it, that's a waste of time and the answer might be disturbing.

The mirror takes up half of the wall above the sink. An open medicine cabinet hangs next to it and all the shelves are empty. I ignore it and focus only on the girl staring back at me. A good part of me wishes I wouldn't be seeing those metallic eyes and the porcelain skin in the reflection. My hair that is still so messy and wild, yet softer to touch than it ever has been. Sure, I'd miss those few things, but I miss the girl who used to be looking back even more.

I miss the ugly brown eyes that proved me to be human.

The hair I hated wearing down because it *always* got in the way. I got so used to having a ponytail I thought that bump in my hair would be permanent. My skin wasn't so soft but there also wasn't dried blood all over my clothes and under my fingernails. It's only been a week, or two days depending on how we're counting, and I feel like I've been this way forever. Being human seems like a lifetime ago and it will take another lifetime to get used to admitting that I'm not anymore.

If only there was a way I could have gotten myself prepared for being this new thing roaming the earth. My dad never told me what to do in this situation and I wouldn't even know where to begin if he were here now. It's hard for me to think that he'd probably kill me if he saw what I've become. I don't think dad could look at me the same anymore. I'm not his little girl like I used to be.

I can't eat food or drink water or even be out in the sun anymore without it causing me some kind of pain. Forcing myself to do those things isn't possible no matter how much I wish it were.

I have to quit thinking of the things I'll never have again and go on with the present. I know my dad is gone and I've had a year to move on from that. It sucks day after day being the only person left in my family, but I *am* still here. I'm alive and able to survive with the added bonus of helping thousands of people in the process.

I take the sunglasses and slide them over my nose to cover my eyes. The metallic hue disappears and I actually look human again. Despite the fact that no one wears sunglasses anymore and I could be the only person on the planet who has a pair. At least I can roam this place looking stylish.

The house is quiet and Ryder is still snoozing on the couch. His breathing is all I hear as I make my way to the front door. He'll be alright by himself and I'll make sure I'm easy to find when he wakes up. I just want to take a few minutes to be alone in this place and see the people who live here and the people I saved last night. I grip the doorknob and twist it, pulling the door open. The sun is bright and it takes my eyes a quick moment to adjust, even with the shades on.

I close the door quietly then jump down from the porch. At the house across the street, an older couple is sitting on a porch swing, rocking back and forth. I see the grimace on the old man's face when he spots me while his wife smiles and waves. I nod to her and head for the middle of the street. A small group of women is in a vegetable garden harvesting whatever foods they can before it's too late. I can smell the sweat protruding from their pores and I force myself not to let the frenzy begin and walk on.

A few kids, teenagers and younger, are in one of the driveways playing basketball. The pole is rusty and the net is missing from around the hoop, but the kids are having a great time playing outside. There's even an audience, sitting on old lawn chairs, laughing and having a good time.

I stand at the end of the driveway and stare at them. There was a time when I would have had fun playing ball with my brother. We didn't have a basketball hoop, but we'd spend hours in the backyard playing catch and hitting a base-ball to each other. Those were good times.

One of the kids eyes me from her seat in the audience and shouts, "Hey look, it's that woman who brought those people back to life."

The ball stops dribbling and all of the kids turn their eyes to me. I feel out of place all of a sudden. Like I shouldn't be standing out here in the open watching these guys have fun with their game. I half expect them to shout at me to leave or start throwing things at me. I'm a freak to them, a monster to some, I'm sure. Instead, I'm greeted with smiles and talks of praise. They're happy, even though they're young and might not remember what the world was like before the original cure came along. They cheer for me, telling me how amazing it was that I saved a handful of people and gave them a life again.

It should be great to hear all of this coming from the kids. I should smile and thank them for being this happy. I guess I'm still a bit confused and have no clue what to do. There's really only one thing I'm glad about all this, none of them are afraid of me. That alone brings the forced smile to my face as I back away from them.

They go back to their game while I go back to walking down the middle of the street. Why can't I be happy about this like everyone else seems to be? Why is there something so wrong with my mind that it cannot comprehend the ability to grateful that a cure has finally been brought to the human race? Why is my life just one big unanswered question?

I walk to the spot where the bonfire was held last night. The picnic tables and a few scattered chairs are still setup and some are filled with people. A horse-drawn wagon is being filled with food and supplies and more ammo. Three men are busy loading it while some of the women are getting bags packed and food prepped for the trip. Of the few people sitting in the chairs, I spot four of the five I brought back to life. George and his father, Greg, and two other humans surround them, laughing and smiling. Talking about memories and what they've missed. The woman with brown hair, the zombie I brought back last night, sees me standing a few yards from them and she stands from her seat and walks up to me.

The others take notice of this and are quick to get to their feet with smiles on their faces as they head my way. This is the sort of thing that always makes me nervous. Meeting new people normally is, but I saved these people and I'm having issues about everything right now.

"You're Bridget." The brunette speaks with a smile, "I'm Annah. I've been waiting all morning to get to talk to you and I wanted to tell you how thankful I am for you. You saved my life."

"You remember your name?" I muster the courage to

ask.

She nods, "Yeah, we all do actually."

I glance to Rose and she shrugs, "I guess your cure works differently after the first person, but my memory is slowly coming back." She says.

The older man with grey hair, the zombie who tried attacking Ryder first, steps up and says, "Name's Hank and I just want to say that you are the best thing to happen to this world. People everywhere are going to be more than grateful when they hear the news of your cure. Thank you for giving me my life back."

Katie, Adam's daughter, rushes up to me and smiles. She's giddy and bubbly, reminding me of someone I've already met and really miss right now.

"I might not remember much from when I was a vampire, but I remember how you saved me last night. You were in my head for the shortest moment and I'll never forget it. You somehow ripped the vamp out of me and gave me back to my dad. You truly are a blessing in disguise and I hope you realize all the great things you're going to do from here on out." She says.

Yeah, she's exactly like Sherry, right down to the blonde hair. She talks fast and sounds happy all the time. I could use my best friend right about now. All of these great things being said to me are starting to be too much for me to take and Sherry is good to have around in situations like this. She could make me feel more comfortable around everyone.

I stare at each of their faces and my mind is starting to wander. I'm jealous of each and every one of them. They all have their human lives back. They can walk around without being second guessed about what they are.

What do I have? Night visions and a few new abilities that make me stronger and faster. Not to mention my disgusting new appetite.

Where's my cure?

Rose steps closer to me and raises an eyebrow, "Bridget,

are you okay?"

I guess there's a pained look on my face to match how I'm feeling inside. I don't want to be around these people anymore. I can't feel happy for them when all I want is to be one of them again. To be human.

My feet start moving backwards, inching myself away. The smiles on their faces begin to fade and I shake my head back and forth.

"I have to go." I say, quietly.

I spin around and walk faster to get away from them. The kids in the driveway start cheering for me again and I pick up the pace. I'm finding hard to handle the acceptance and praise coming from all these people. I can't take it anymore and I need to be alone. I need some time to think about where my life is headed if I'm the miracle the world has been waiting for.

There's got to be something wrong with me other than the obvious issues I'm having. If I can't accept their gratitude over what I've done for them, how will I be able to do the same for the entire world without feeling some sort of jealousy? When all of this is said and done and the cure has spread throughout the globe, I'll be the only thing left without a heartbeat.

How will I ever be able to live in this world if I might never have a cure?

* * *

I don't stray too far from the village. I figured too many people might get *really* upset if I took off and never came back. Ryder is among the top two of those people. I don't really want to leave him again anyway.

There's an old park not far from the houses, amid the rubble of what's left of this small city. There isn't much left to this place. The swings are broken off and the chains are rusty. The merry-go-round hasn't moved in so long the wind can't even move it anymore and there's a decent sized hole halfway down one of the curly slides. Also, there's a few junk cars parked around here. One is crashed into a tree and two more look like they were left in their spots in a hurry. Probably has something to do with the vampire and zombie apocalypse going on.

I stand in the middle of all this mess around me, the weeds and grass are tall enough to reach my knees. My mind is so befuddled. Being around those people isn't good for me right now. It's better to let them be happy without me being there to ruin everything.

Things seemed to make more sense before I was bitten. My mind wasn't all wrapped around not wanting to hurt another human being or trying to figure a way out of this mess. A way to get the world back on track. I became that way the day my life was taken from me and I can't find a way to be happy about it. I can't smile about bringing those few people back from the dead.

They're all giddy and full of life now and all I can think about is how lucky they are to be alive again. To be able to do *normal* things that *normal* humans can do. They can love each other and touch each other without getting the constant desire to taste their flesh and blood. I might be able to love someone as well, but it's not the same without that special feeling a kiss can give you. There's no saying what I'd do to Ryder if our lips met and I'm not willing to risk it just to find out.

A sigh escapes me as I lean against a car crashed into the

tree. I wish this new life of mine was easier to deal with. Being the cure for all things horrible is great and all, but no one told me how hard it would be to go through all this jealousy towards the ones I save. I wish my dad was here to help me through this. He'd tell me to buck up and be happy that I'm able to give the world what it needs.

The breeze feels nice against my skin and I close my eyes hoping my mind will clear itself. The blackness isn't enough to take the annoyance out of my brain and the smell of humans seems to make everything worse. That smell is really clear out here. I know nobody followed me and it doesn't smell like Ryder. I open my eyes and look around. The swings are empty. The few cars are clear. The bench sitting next to an old, nonworking fountain is the only thing harboring the cause of the scent.

His black hair blows in the wind and I ease myself away from the car I was leaning against. He's completely alone and doesn't bother turning to face me until he hears my footsteps approaching.

The hesitant zombie from last night. The one who chose to bite me instead of letting me do all the dirty work. He looks much better now that he's a human. I can actually see his face. He is a couple years older than me and his eyes are just as dark as his hair. His skin is pale, but darker than one of the undead. I know I have Ryder and all, but this guy looks pretty good.

"What are you doing out here?" I ask.

He shrugs, "Just want to be alone. Why aren't you back there celebrating with everyone else?"

I sit across from him on the concrete edge surrounding the old fountain, "Needed to get away. What's your name?"

"Jason," he states, "and you're Bridget, the girl with the cure."

"I guess." I say, "Aren't you going to tell me how I'm so wonderful and the best thing to happen to the world since sliced bread?"

He shakes his head, "I'm sure you've heard that all morning."

Good. He gets it.

Jason looks away from me, his eyes are sad and full of shame. His arms are folded across his chest and it looks like he doesn't even want to be here. There's something on his mind and I have a gut feeling it might have something to do with why he was a hesitating zombie. I've wanted to know for over a year why some of those things choose not to attack humans and just stand there like an idiot instead. If he knows the answer to that, it will get rid of one annoying question I have.

"Can I ask you something, Jason?" I say.

He sits forward on the bench and says, "You want to know why I bit you last night instead of going after your friend."

I nod, "Something like that. I take it you remember a lot from being dead."

He takes a deep breath and says, "I remember everything. Every disgusting detail and the people I killed over the last two years. I remember my life before I was turned into that zombie and I can tell you every horrible moment I went through changing into it."

I raise an eyebrow, "How do you remember all that and the others can't recall a thing?"

He shrugs, "I don't know exactly, but one day I was lumbering along as a zombie and I got a flash of my life. I had forgotten everything until that moment and it all came back. My parents, my sisters, my friends, the bastard who bit me and tore of a chunk from my leg. At first I thought I was changing back to human, that I was finally going to have my life back. I spent days waiting for my heart to start beating again and it never happened. Then I started to remember all the people I killed and changed while being a zombie and I hated it. "

"So what did you do?" I ask.

"Since I knew I was still a zombie, I stayed as far away from humans as possible. I didn't want to hurt them anymore and swore to never kill another one. I stayed by myself for a while until I met with a horde of zombies a few weeks ago and figured I'd hang out with them." He says.

"Great company." I say, sarcastically.

He smiles and goes on, "We chased some family through the woods not long ago and wound up at a huge wall. That's when I saw you."

"You remember me?" I ask.

He nods, "Yeah and I know you recognized me last night right before I bit you. I thought for sure you were going to kill me at the wall when I first saw you and I was hoping you would have. But, you let me go and I found my way to those other two zombies and came here."

"And that's when you chose to go after Ryder and Carter. I thought you gave up on humans. Why the sudden change?" I say.

"I got tired of waiting for my life to finally be over. I figured not eating anything would end it all and it didn't." he says, "I sought out the death I desired after you wouldn't give it to me. When I saw you again last night, I knew you weren't human anymore, but I also knew you weren't entirely dead either. Still, I didn't want to be a zombie anymore and I assumed biting you would get me shot or piss you off enough to take me out."

"I guess I ruined your little plan."

Jason shakes his head and says, "No, you changed it. The moment I tasted how different your flesh and blood was from other humans, I knew you were special. I could actually feel my body coming back to life and it was overwhelming so I passed out. When I woke up, I wasn't happy to be alive. I was just happy I wouldn't have to force myself to watch the world through undead eyes anymore."

I figured I'd be relieved finally getting to the bottom of the zombie hesitation. It's so much sadder than I expected it to be. Those things, as monstrous and disgusting as they might appear, have gained some part of their soul back and hate living with the memories. All they want is to be human again or die because they don't want to live like that anymore.

It makes me think of the few hesitant ones I killed the last time I was on the road. That woman when I was with dad, the old lady right before I met Ryder, each of them saw their life and couldn't ask for help to get it back. Dying was the next best thing. That little battle between the zombies and the vampires outside of Hatfeld makes much more sense now. They were trying to save us as well as end the suffering in their own minds.

"I told you my story," Jason says, interrupting my thoughts, "tell me yours. Why did you want to get away?"

I toss him half a smile and run my fingers through my hair, "Well, for starters, it gets very hard to control the hunger and thirst every time I smell a human. I can feel the frenzy burning inside when there's a lot of them around and I'm worried I'll lose it and attack someone. Secondly, I can't stand being around all of them when they are so happy and grateful and can't get enough of me. It's hard enough dealing with my newly found issues, adding jealousy to the mix doesn't sit right with me."

He raises an eyebrow and asks, "What could you possibly be jealous of us for?"

"You all have heartbeats. I don't have one anymore." I reply.

"Oh," Jason says, lowering his head, "didn't think of that."

"That's the worst thing about all of this. The world has something to end what shouldn't have started in the first place. There's just nothing to end what happened to me."

He doesn't say anything. He tries to smile, but I can tell a small part of him feels sorry for me. I don't need or want that sorrow. This is the life I was given and I'm going to live it no matter what it takes. Probably be hard every day of my new life, but I have no other choice.

"You know, you might think this is the worst thing to happen to you, but I'm positive it's not. This could be the best thing to ever happen to you and you just haven't realized it yet." Jason says, standing from the bench and joining me by the fountain.

"How is being a monster with a cure the best thing to happen to me?" I ask.

He shakes his head, "I don't know you very well, but I promise you're no monster."

That might be the nicest thing anyone has said to me today. Weird that it didn't come from Ryder. Normally he's the one who tells me nice things to make me feel better. I guess it's good to hear things like this coming from complete strangers. Having others think of me as something other than what I feel like, could prove to be beneficial.

I turn to Jason and brush the hair away from my face, "I think I'm gonna head back. I don't want them to think I ran off never to return."

He smiles and says, "Yeah, you do have something important to return to them. You don't want to worry them or your boyfriend."

"I'm not concerned about worrying anyone. I'm concerned about getting the word out there about the cure in my blood. It's important the world has it." I say, then stand from the concrete ledge.

He nods and stands up as well, "Maybe you should sound a bit happier when you say things like that. People will think you don't want the world to have this new cure."

I shrug, "Sometimes it's hard to be happy about something that will grant the world humanity without giving yourself the same pleasure."

My feet carry me away from him. I know he's a good person, he's just trying to make me see things the way the world is going to see it. My mind is so stuck on never having a cure for myself. I can't get it out of my head and nothing anyone will tell me could ever help.

At least he didn't bombard me with gratitude or thankfulness over saving his life. I'm sure to be greeted with that once I return to the village.

* * *

Ryder is waiting for me when I get back. He is sitting on the stoop of the house we slept in last night. No doubt he woke up and instantly got worried when he didn't see me lying on the couch. I'd be worried too if the roles were reversed.

He smiles and stands when he sees me approaching. Further down the street, the group of people are still getting things ready. Their cart is fully loaded with supplies and many of them are swinging backpacks over their shoulders and talking amongst themselves. If I were interested, I could focus enough to listen to every word they say. I'm just not too worried about what they have to say about me or this plan Adam and Carter came up with on getting to the city. As long as things go well, they'll make it there and will be able to start a new life. I, on the other hand, will be lucky if the city gives me a second glance. The shades are kind of a dead giveaway on a human trying to hide something about their appearance.

Jason followed me to the village. Neither of us said a word to each other and he is on his way to join the others in preparing for our little journey to Des Moines. Ryder must have seen him walking behind me. The smile fades from his face and a scowl crosses his lips.

"Do I need to be worried about anything?" he asks as I get closer to him.

I shake my head, "Absolutely not."

"Okay," he says, "Where did you go?"

"I needed to be alone for a minute so I could let all of this settle. I ran into him at this old park and we talked for a few minutes, then I decided to come find you." I reply, "I did find out something interesting about the zombies and why they hesitate."

Ryder's eyes light up in anticipation, "What's that?"

I take a couple minutes to explain what Jason told me. This information could be important to anyone who comes across a hesitant zombie. It's almost as important as spreading the word about my cure. People should know this. They'd be able to understand and maybe not pull the trigger when they're face to face with a zombie who just wants to be human again. Might sound a little crazy, but you get used to all the crazy nonsense in this world.

"Wow," he states, "what happened in Hatfeld makes more sense now."

I smile, "That's exactly what I thought, too."

"Have you talked to Carter already?"

I nod, "Yeah, he told me everyone wants to get me to the city in order to make the cure worldwide before the wrong people get wind of this. Apparently I'm valuable now."

"I guess," he says, then lets out a sigh, "I really missed you, Bridge."

I run my fingers through my hair and say, "I missed you too. It hurt a lot having to run away from you like that. I just couldn't take the risk of doing something to you."

"I know, I just wish I would have been able to follow you. I could've been there for you during whatever change you had to go through. I could've made it better. I hate knowing you were alone for all that." He says.

"I wasn't *exactly* alone. Someone was with me, sort of." I say, thinking of my conversation with Charlie.

He scrunches his face in confusion, "Who?"

"It's a little hard to explain. I was in a lot of pain and my mind sort of shut down for a bit and I saw my brother. He spoke to me and things got better." I say. "He told me all of them were watching over me and I guess it helped ease the pain."

I probably just sounded pretty crazy. Talking about how I saw my dead brother in my head while I was dying in the middle of nowhere. Not a lot of people say things like that and it takes someone as strange as me to be the first one.

Surprisingly, Ryder doesn't think I'm as crazy as I seem. He gives me a small smile and takes my hand. Instantly, I can feel the blood flowing through his veins and the tiny pulse beating in his fingertips. His warm grip on my hand makes me feel somewhat better about all of this. I don't feel as dead as I know I am. I wish I could kiss him right now. I wish I could taste his lips on my own and get that wonderful feeling of love going through my body again.

Wishes like that can't come true for me anymore.

"I want to kiss you, Bridge," he says, "I wish you would let me."

Great minds think alike I guess, "I'm sorry. I don't want you to go through what I did."

He nods in understanding. He shouldn't have to agree with me on this. We should be able to kiss whenever we want, to hold each other whenever we feel the need. I shouldn't have gotten bit by those *damn* beasts. I wouldn't be standing here worried about the possibility of the wrong people getting wind of the cure. There's a chance I'd be safe and sound behind the city walls right now.

"Bridget," Ryder says softly, "I have to ask, why do you wear those ridiculous sunglasses?"

I smile, clearing the bad thoughts from my mind, "The sun will light my eyes on fire if I don't. One great side effect to this otherwise *flawless* new form of mine. The shades aren't ridiculous though. I think I look good."

He chuckles and squeezes my hand tight. I'm glad he changed the subject so I could get away from painful memories of things I'll never experience again.

I hear a whistle coming from the group down the street. The two of us look that way and see everyone gearing up and on their feet. It must be time to start moving.

Ryder takes a deep breath and says, "I guess that means it's time to go."

I nod, "The sooner we get to the city, the sooner the world can get back to normal."

We step away from the house and head for the group. A gust of wind sweeps across the village and I'm caught with a smell that doesn't seem quite right. It's human. Their fresh blood flies through the wind to get to me. It seems like there's a lot of them and I know for sure it's not coming from anyone here.

I hear the sounds of heavy boots stomping on the concrete and grass. The sounds are coming from behind me, the only road that will lead us away from this place. These humans are headed right for us and I'm probably the only one who knows. I stop walking with Ryder and stand in the middle of the street.

"Something's not right." I say, quietly.

Ryder turns to look at me, "What are you talking about?"

I close my eyes and concentrate only on the sounds coming from behind us. The footsteps crunching over leaves and sticks, kicking rocks out of their way. Hushed voices of men and women talking about something, *someone* to be exact. The reason they're coming here. The only reason anyone would come to a place like this after something life changing has happened to the world.

"Someone's coming after me." I say quietly.

* * *

"Who the hell are those people?" I hear Adam's voice as he rushes to us.

I open my eyes and turn around to see what he and everyone else is seeing. A large cluster of men and women, more than what we have here, and they are headed right for us. Guns are in the hands of some and swords are in others. Ever since the apocalypse first took form, I have not once seen a human use a sword to fend off any creature. I guess these Midwestern people have a different way to kill them.

Carter and the others have joined us, guns ready in their grip. The rest of the people in the village are running indoors and locking themselves inside. I'm not the only one who knows something isn't right with this new group of people heading this way.

A tall, dark skinned man, riding a horse approaches. He looks military with his camo jeans and dark green t-shirt. The dog tags hanging around his neck are a dead giveaway on that assumption. He stares us down as the horse trots back and forth and his group stand tall behind him. He snarls at some of us as he scans our faces. Finally, he jumps down from the horse, bringing his rifle with him. He keeps the aim at the ground, but that doesn't stop any of my group to take their aim off him and his men.

Adam steps out in front of us and asks, "What do you want?"

The man smiles, his teeth are white and stick out against his dark skin, "Can't some people come here looking for friendship without getting guns aimed at us? We ain't gonna hurt you people."

Nobody lowers their weapon on our side. Carter moves up to stand with Ryder and I. He slips a handgun to Ryder who eagerly takes it. I, on the other hand, get nothing. I'm sure they think I can handle my own, which is *so* not a lie.

"What are you doing here?" Adam tries pressing for an answer.

The man smiles and asks, "Look, my name is Trevor. The guys behind me are good people, fighting for this world and trying to keep the few humans we find safe. I mean it when we don't want to hurt you."

"Sorry, but I'm having a hard time believing that when all of your men have weapons bigger than ours and don't look shy about using them." Adam retorts. "Just tell me what the hell you're doing here."

Trevor shrugs, "Fine," he says and the smile on his face fades, "We heard you found something that could change the fate of the human race. I heard it was something unbelievable and I want it." He talks with more assertiveness to his voice.

Adam shakes his head and replies, "I have no idea what you're talking about."

"I figured you would say that which is why I have someone with me who will prove the truth." Trevor states, "Come on out, Michael."

Adam lowers his gun as we watch Trevor's group of men and women move aside to allow the familiar bearded man walk through. He's carrying a gun just as large as the others and wearing a smile so sinister it makes me sick.

"Sorry, Adam, but these guys want the same thing I want." Michael says as he stands before us. "We all want a perfect world. One we can decide the fate of."

"And how to expect to get that?" Adam asks.

Michael scans our faces until his eyes meet mine and he smiles, "With her."

Trevor turns his dark eyes to mine and smiles alongside

his new friend. My hands are shaking as I stare at the assailants across from us. All of them are after me and I can tell they are willing to do whatever it takes to get me.

Ryder and Carter step out in front of me, guarding me from our enemies' prying eyes. I can't believe I'm thinking this, but it's a little strange having Ryder protecting me for once. Normally it's the other way around.

"You see," Trevor states as he paces in front of us, "I'm a man who loves power and being in charge. I'll do whatever it takes to get that. What that girl can do, will grant me the power to control everything and I'm going to have her."

Adam shakes his head, "I'm not going to let that happen. The world needs her more than you."

"Oh, I'll give her to the world, don't think I wouldn't do that," Trevor says, "It would be on my terms only. This world needs order. The new race of humans that girl can give us will need order. I'm the one who can control it and make sure people do what I say and we will have a more perfect planet. Which is why you are going to do what I say right now and tell your men to step aside and let me have what I came here for. Unless you want things to get messy."

Guns are raised by Trevor's men and all of them pointed our way. I can hear the hearts of those around me beating faster and their blood is flowing nervously through their veins. Their heavy breathing tells me that some of them are considering laying their guns down and going home.

This isn't what's supposed to happen.

If I'm such a *gift* to this world, those humans across from us should see me as that and lay their weapons down in order to help me get my gift to those who need it. This man, Trevor, isn't the type of man who deserves even an ounce of this cure to use to gain power over the human race.

"C'mon, pal," Trevor states, readying his own gun, "make your choice. You can save all your men and let me have what I want. Or I'll kill them all and take it anyway. It's up to you."

Adam doesn't say a word. The pistol is shaking in his grip, I can hear the metal rattling between his fingers. He doesn't want to lose any of these people he's tried so hard to keep safe. His daughter is amongst this group, standing behind everyone, and I know he would rather die than risk her life again.

He stares at the enemy and shakes his head, "I'm sorry, but you can't have what this world desperately needs."

"Wrong choice, pal." Trevor pulls out a small handgun from a hidden holster around his belt and aims it right at Adam's chest.

I stare at Trevor's beefy hand wrapped around the trigger of the gun. Everything seems to be happening in slow motion as I watch his finger tighten on the trigger. Adam is still a complete stranger to me but that doesn't mean I want to watch him die. I take a quick step backwards, away from Ryder and Carter, and leap through the air, landing on the concrete in front of them. I let the faces of everyone blur as I speed by them in order to get where I need to be. The trigger gets pulled and even the sound of the blast is faint as I run up to Adam. I knock him out of the way and he lands on the ground a few feet away from me.

Gasps fill the air and exclamations of wonder escape their throats. I feel a slight pinch in my left shoulder as I stand in front of Trevor and Michael. I turn my eyes to my arm, feeling a trace amount of blood trickle down. The bullet hit me instead of Adam and I honestly don't feel a thing. There's no pain or the need to scream out in bloody murder. I am quite angry that I have a bullet lodged in my shoulder and my favorite hoody is ruined beyond repair, but I'll heal and get over it.

"Well, holy shit." Trevor exclaims as he stares at me with his eyes wide open. "I didn't even see you coming."

I glare at him through the shades covering my eyes. It really wouldn't take much for me to destroy this man. The frenzy is already building in my gut and I would love nothing more than to rip open his flesh and enjoy the taste of human blood. The fear of what that taste will do to me is the only thing holding me back.

"You really aren't human anymore, are you?" he says, his eyes scoping me up and down.

I grit my teeth and say, "And you're really a pathetic asshole, aren't you?"

"I think we might have our hands full with this little girl, boys." Trevor shouts to his men standing behind him.

"You're damn right about that." I say.

I jump up and slam my foot into his chest, sending him flying through the air, landing on the street in front of his men. I can hear him gasping for air and he puts a hand to his chest. I have to admit, it felt pretty great taking some anger out on that guy. He definitely deserved it.

Trevor isn't exactly reacting the way I want him to. He's not bowing down in fear of me or what I could do to him. Instead, he's sitting up on the ground with a smile on his face.

"Let's see what else you can do." He says, attempting to catch his breath.

On that note, a woman charges me, a sword in her hand and a demonic look in her eyes. She's wearing an all leather outfit and part of her stomach is showing as she comes at me with her weapon raised above her head. This will be easy.

She slices the sword through the air, attempting to hit me, but I'm quick to swerve out of the way. A growl comes from her throat and she glares at me. I can't help but chuckle at this. She sounds like an angry cat with a hairball caught in her throat. She lunges at me and I leap off the ground and let her pass under me. When I land, I spin around and connect my fist with the back of her head. A slight gasp comes from her throat and she falls, face first, to the concrete at her feet.

Like I said, easy.

Trevor sends another one of his goons out. He's short and stout, with a black goatee. This one isn't coming for me and instead is heading for Adam with a gun aimed for his head. I take a quick step across the concrete and, just as the man pulls the trigger, I'm able to grab his wrist and bend it at an angle I never thought I could ever do. I hear the snap and feel the bone break against my skin. A shrill scream escapes him and the gun falls from his grip. I take his broken wrist and twist it behind his back. Then, I kick the back of one of knees until he's forced to kneel in front of me. I let go of his wrist, kick him in the back, and he falls to the ground knocked out completely.

"Thanks." Adam says, getting to his feet.

I shrug, "No problem."

I look to Trevor. He doesn't seem very impressed with the two people he sent after me. He seems rather upset that I was able to take them down without breaking a sweat. I watch him get to his feet and his eyes instantly glare at me. Michael stands next to him, looking impatient. He's itching for something, I can see his hands shaking at his sides.

"I'm tired of this." Michael seethes. "Let's get this over with."

The first gunshot breaks through the air as Michael quickly sends a bullet shooting to my group. What follows is chaos. Screaming comes from both parties as everyone breaks out into a small battle. People rush past me, anger in their eyes and their blood. I can't seem to move my feet. The sweet scent of blood fills the air and my mind. It's so close I can practically taste it. I *want* to taste it.

That magnificent odor makes my mouth water and the frenzy shifts from rage to hunger. It's enough to take my mind completely off of what's going on. The people around me change into something that isn't human anymore. They've shifted into something that's sending my urge to devour them through the roof. This is much different than the zombie or vampire blood. This smell, this new taste I'm can feel running down my throat, it's all that I want.

I bite my bottom lip and start searching for the source of the blood. I know it can't be too far away, it's so strong and wonderful. My feet spin me around and I push myself through the crowd of fighting humans. The smell gets stronger with each step I take. There might be more people getting hurt all around me, maybe even dying, but my mind is too focused on getting to the source of this amazing scent.

A young man steps in my way, a knife aimed out in front of him. I snarl at him as I rip the knife from his grip and let him stagger backwards. I grip onto the collar of his shirt and fling him to the ground with another man that has fallen victim to this meaningless battle.

"Carter," I hear Ryder's voice breaking through the shouting, "c'mon wake up."

I push someone else out of my way and reveal the source of the blood I've been smelling. I stare at him, lying on the ground with a puddle of his own blood surrounding his head. Ryder is kneeling at Carter's side, frantically trying to get him to wake up. Carter's eyes are closed and his chest isn't moving any longer.

He was a friend of mine. Someone who didn't deserve to die like this. Not at the hands of an enemy or the hands of anyone at all. He deserved to live a long, happy life in the world that I'm going to help survive. This never should have happened to him.

Ryder stares up at me, tears building in his eyes for the loss of a dear friend. I stand tall, my hands clench into fists.

"We warned you this would happen if you didn't co-operate." Michael's voice clouds my mind and I turn around to face him, "We will end all of this right now if you come with us."

I can't find my voice. Not that words are the best thing for me to use at this moment. Anger is burning through me and it feels like my whole body is on fire. The monster in my gut has been granted the ultimate permission to take over and destroy this man standing in front of me. I take a step forward and the fight around me seems to disappear. He's the only person my mind is letting me see right now.

Michael lifts his gun and aims for me, "Don't take another step or I'll shoot."

"Go ahead." I don't recognize my voice as I speak.

His hand is shaking furiously and his aim is staggering. He accidently pulls the trigger and I can feel a pinch in the upper part of my leg. I stop walking and look down to examine the wound. Like my shoulder, I don't feel a hint of pain, only the anger that comes from it. I lift my eyes to him once more and he lowers the gun.

I take all of my strength to push myself from the ground, leaping one more time through the air to come down on this man. I tackle him to the ground, the gun flies from his fingers, crashing to the concrete. He lets out a shout for help, but no one comes to his aide as I pin him down. He grabs my wrists, trying to push me off of him. His grip is tight, but nothing to stop me from twisting my hands around, digging my nails into his skin. He lets out a sharp squeal and lets go of my left wrist. I use my free hand to grab a handful of his hair and lift his head from the ground.

"This is for Carter and everyone else I care about." I seethe into his ear right before slamming his head against the concrete so hard that his skull splits and his eyes close for-ever.

I lift my head and the shouting around me starts up again. The fighting comes back to my view and I get to my feet. The monster is slowly making its way down to the pit in my stomach it calls a home and I turn around. Ryder is still knelt beside Carter, no one has bothered to go near him. I hear a blast coming from my right and I turn my attention to the sound. Adam stands with a gun aimed in front of him and he moves closer to me.

"Bridget, I think it's time for you to leave." Adam says, "I have the proof you need gathered behind the blue house back there," he nods to one of the houses at the end of the cul-de-sac. "Get them and yourself out of here. We'll fight them off while you get away."

"What about you?" I say.

Adam lets out a sigh and says, "Five miles from here, there's an old truck stop. We'll meet you there." He points toward an empty field behind the houses, then goes back to fighting.

I nod and force myself to walk away. As much as I hate to admit this, I'll be glad to get away from the fighting and the blood in this place. I make my way through the crowd and get to Ryder. I kneel down beside him and take his hand. He turns his red eyes to me and shakes his head.

"We have to leave." I say, quietly.

He nods, "I know."

He allows me to help him to his feet. He takes another, long look at Carter before turning away from him and running with me. Our goal now, is getting to the others and finding the truck stop Adam mentioned. As long as it's safe and we can hide there, I'm sure we'll be alright.

At least I hope we will be.

* * *

There are seven of us total and we're being followed. I can hear the footsteps running behind us and they're catching up quickly. Of course people would chase after us. This isn't a perfect world where we can just walk away risk free. But, to be honest, I'd rather have zombies chasing after us right now. I don't mind destroying them anymore. No matter how disgusting it is to think about.

I take a second to look over my shoulder. Three of them are sprinting toward us, one with a machete, one with a small pistol, and the other with just his bare hands. He's bigger than the scrawny young man running beside him and the brown haired beauty a few steps behind. She's the one with the machete and a horrible snarl on her face.

I look ahead, there's no hiding places for us. A cluster of trees and a small shed next to a burnt down barn. The woods would be ideal to hide in, but I know the humans with me would never go for it. Vamps are too tricky, even with me there to fight them. We'll never make it to our destination safely if we don't get these goons away from us. There's really only one option to get those three to stop chasing us.

My feet come to a complete stop and I let go of Ryder's hand. This next moment I would like to use to gather the strength I need to defend myself and the others against the three bad guys running toward us. I close my eyes and let the stench of their sweat and blood drift up my nose. It seems like the frenzy I allow to build in my gut from the smell of human blood is what makes me stronger. I can feel the hunger burning, feel the anger coursing through my body. All I want to do is rip these humans apart piece by piece. I want to release the monster inside me and let her do what she is meant to do.

"Bridget!" Ryder shouts and I can feel him standing a few feet away. "We need to keep moving."

Slowly, I open my eyes and look right through him. Hank is leading the three girls away from the madmen behind me. Jason and Ryder stay behind, smelling of concern and worry. That smell will help. It will aide in allowing my strength to grow to the right point so I can do what I need to do.

I turn around. The smaller man has stopped running, the pistol is shaking in his hands. The woman slows to a walk, readying her machete for use. The bigger man, stands behind them, arms folded across his chest and a sly smile on his face.

I pass him the same smile and take in a breath through my nose. The little one's fear is so intense I can practically taste him already.

The brunette storms across the weedy grass first with her machete pointed up to the sky. By the way she's moving, she has no idea what she's doing. I'm guess she is new at this whole thing and probably joined the gang because she was hungry and needed shelter. Fighting for her life right now is all she has. Unfortunately, she has to fight me.

This girl, dressed all in black clothes that are much too big for her, swings her weapon at my stomach and I leap into the air, avoiding any kind of scratch at all. I land on my feet, watching as she steadies herself for another swing. It comes right at my head and this time I reach out and grab the blade, feeling it slice into the palm of my left hand. A look of bewilderment crosses her face. Before she can pull the machete from my grip, I rip it out of hers and give her a swift kick to the stomach. The breath is forced out of her lungs as she flies a few feet backward, landing on the ground next to the bigger guy. He pays no attention to the unconscious woman at his feet.

I toss the machete to the ground and turn my attention to the young man. His hands are shaking as he moves the gun back and forth between Ryder and Jason. He doesn't appear to be the threatening type, not with how small he is and how young he appears to be. This kid is probably a teenager and was most likely threatened to do this. I don't really *want* to hurt him, but when it comes down to it, I'm going to do whatever I can. It's survival of the fittest right now and I'm pretty confident I'm at the top of the being fit list.

"If you don't come with us," his voice shakes as he speaks, "I'm going to put a bullet in both of them."

I raise an eyebrow and walk closer to him until I'm standing right in front of him. He stretches his arm out, the gun aimed at Ryder. He's not going to pull the trigger. His lips are quivering and his whole body shakes as he stares at me. If a bullet does come flying out, it will be completely accidental due to his shaking.

"I mean it, I'll kill them." He tries to threaten.

I shake my head and say, "No you won't."

He keeps his aim on Ryder, trying not to let what I said get to him. The fear is building in his eyes and I can smell it seeping through the pores on his body. I lift my hand and quickly grab the gun from his grip. With my other hand, I take his wrist and twist it around his back. He shouts and grunts from the pain. I can feel the bones popping the more I stretch his arm this way. He backs up into me and elbows me in my side. He jabs me hard enough to get me to let go of his arm. He spins around, rubbing his wrist and hand to ease the pain.

I guess this kid is stronger than he appears. It doesn't take him long to get over the pain in his arm and he's back in the game, charging toward me. I'm too late to react and he wraps his arms around my waist and tackles me to the ground. The gun flies out of my hand and lands somewhere in the grass. This kid tries staying on top of me. He grabs for one of my wrists to pin me to the ground. He gets my left one and goes for the right as I reach up and grab a chunk of his hair and pull as hard as I can until I hear a sharp ripping sound.

The scream coming from his throat is enough to scare the birds in the nearby trees. Their wings flap through the air as they fly away in terror. I didn't mean to rip his hair out or small bits of the flesh from his scalp. There's blood dripping from the roots of the hair in my hand and he topples to the ground next to me. His hands try covering the wound on his head, but it must hurt too much for him to touch it. My eyes stay glued to the hair and bits of skin in my grip. A few drops of blood run down my fingertips and I can feel the warmth from the thick liquid.

I sit up and let the hair fall to the ground. The human blood remains and I admire the beauty of the red stuff on my hand. This is the first time I've touched human blood since my change. This small amount is enough for me to want more. To taste it, to let it flow down my throat and cure the hunger in my stomach. To ease the longing pain I have for this strong desire. I bring my hand closer to my face and inhale through my nose. The sweet scent takes over me and everything disappears for a moment. My hands are shaking, I bite my bottom lip, forcing myself not to lick my hand clean of this blood. It's all I want and the smell is causing the frenzy to shift to something a bit more menacing.

The young human is squirming on the ground next to me. More blood drips from the wound on his head, wasting away on the grass he's lying on. How could I let it go to waste? I just need to bend down and take all that want and more. It would be so easy and I could end the suffering of this poor human. He's in pain and with my help, I could take it away.

I reach over, my hand hovering above the bloody mess on his head. He's still screaming and crying, the salty tears streaming down his face. He looks up at me with fear burning in his eyes. I could end his sadness and take him out of this hellish world. In the process I could end my own suffering. End my constant desire to feed on something I don't want to feed on.

Wait a minute.

I don't want to kill this human. I don't want to taste his blood just to get rid of the hunger burning through me. If I let even an ounce of that stuff touch my lips, I could completely turn into the monster I know is inside me. I could let her loose and this whole world could be at risk. That's not something I want to do in this lifetime or any other.

A loud gunshot filters through the air and I snap back to reality. Out of instinct, I jump to my feet and spin around, searching for the cause of the blast. Jason is standing a few feet away, the small pistol I took from the boy is in his hands. I follow his aim and spot the bigger man with his hands wrapped around Ryder's throat. There's a bullet wound in the man's back and blood is soaking through his shirt. His grip is still on Ryder's neck and I quickly move my feet to get to him.

Jason pulls the trigger again and the bullet shoots the man in his side of his stomach, just above his waist. I get closer. I see his grip loosening from Ryder's neck. The life is fading from the man's face as he struggles to stay on his feet. I grab his arm and yank him away from Ryder, then shove him to the ground to let him die. I smell his blood and it takes all I have to not let it get to me.

Ryder grabs my arm and my attention turns to him. He's coughing, trying to catch his breath after having it taken away from him for a brief moment. I can see a red mark around his throat and it's now when I realize just how much his life is in danger because of me. Because I'm in this mess and bad people are after me, he'll always be in danger. Trevor seems like the type of man who will use whatever he can in order to get what he wants. Ryder is a potential victim in that scenario and I'd much rather not see it play out where he is being used to get to me. I've had that happen once. It cannot happen again.

"We need to keep moving in case someone else catches up with us." Jason says, then starts jogging away.

Ryder takes another, deeper breath, then pulls me along with him as he runs. We still need to find the truck stop and find a way to get back to the city. I'm starting to think that won't be as easy as everyone had hoped.

* * *

The truck stop Adam mentioned sits on this lonely strip of highway. I can see the almost leveled town further down the road and it has that eerie vibe to it. It's looks like a place I'd rather not venture to, even in this undead form of mine. There are dry cornfields on both sides of the building separating it from the town. Two semi-trucks sit in the lot behind it and one of their trailers is overturned beside the gas pumps. A grey van is parked close to the building and, to my great surprise, the keys are still in the ignition. I highly doubt it starts, but it's rare to see a used vehicle on the road with keys still inside.

There are three different sections to the truck stop building. The first one is the main part, the convenience store and a place where truckers used to get their coffee. Next to that, a small deli where people could stop for a bite to eat. At the far end, is a car wash with one giant bay for the big rigs. The roof is caved in on that section so we won't be able to wash our vehicles on this little trip today. Good thing we walked here.

No one in this newly formed group of mine is brave enough to scope out the inner makings of the stop. Katie is busy drying her eyes with Rose and Annah. Hank stands close to them in case they need further comforting. They just got their lives back and they could've lost them so easily back there.

Jason, Ryder, and I approach the consoling new humans and stare at the building standing before us. The glass doors and all the windows are still intact. There is some graffiti in black spray paint all over the grey building and the trash cans are tipped on their sides. Through the windows, it looks dark and empty. There's a chance this place hasn't been visited for months. I remember the last gas station I ventured to that look abandoned much like this one. If I recall, a vamp was hiding in the shadows waiting for her next snack.

"We should go inside." I say.

The others snap their heads my way as if I just said the worst thing on the planet, "We can't go in there! What if there are zombies or vampires?" Annah exclaims.

"We can't risk going inside when there's only one gun to the seven of us." Jason adds, "That's not enough fire power in case we need it."

I roll my eyes and say, "Well, we can't really stay out here in case those assholes find us out in the open. It's better to keep hidden until the others join us, then we'll get on our way to the city." I start to walk away from them.

"Wait," Jason calls and I spin around, "You're not seriously going to risk your life just to find us all safety, are you?"

I shrug, but it's Ryder who answers as he walks with me, "You really don't know Bridge like I do. She's a bit crazy."

I smile and turn back to the building. Jason sounded like he was concerned for me. The look on his face before I turned around made that concrete. He has no reason to worry about me. I've got Ryder for that and he doesn't worry all that much. After saving him a few times, he really has no reason to doubt how amazing I can be in tight situations.

The handle on the glass door is caked with grime and dust. It looks like this door hasn't been used in a while. I try pulling on it and, of course, the damn thing is locked. Ryder pulls on the other door and gets the same result. Breaking the glass on the door is an option. It would be easy, but it would make a lot of noise which could draw in some unwanted guests. Silence is what we all need in order to stay hidden. I back away from the door and move my eyes up and down the length of the building. Like I mentioned, all the windows are still there. No holes or secret entrances pop into view, but there is another door down at the deli.

"Stay here." I say to Ryder and the others, "I'll find us a way in."

I let my feet do the work and carry me to the next door.

The air is quiet and I take a deep inhale through my nose. Other than the few humans behind me, there are no other smells. Nothing which causes me to go into another frenzy. I reach the door to the deli and grip the dusty handle. It's not as grimy as the last one and this door isn't locked. There's an obnoxious squeal when I pull it open and a very distinct odor fills my nose. Something I'm not sure I want to be smelling right now.

I keep moving, letting the damp air caress my skin as I walk inside. It's pretty dark in here. The small amount of light shining through the windows isn't enough to illuminate the inside of this place. The door slams shut and the sound echoes through the building. The odor is stronger now and I stay quiet by the door to listen for movement. If there were a human here with me, they'd stay silent for the fear of running into a zombie or vamp. They can be pretty smart about hiding from those monsters in order not to be eaten. I would have heard a zombie by now. They couldn't keep quiet if their undead life depended on it. The one thing I'm worried about, is the creature that has stealth written all over it. A blood thirsty vampire.

I know a vamp wouldn't care for me. Before I saved Katie, she wanted nothing to do with my blood. I guess I'm too dead for either of them to want to try a sample. There is just the matter of all those humans standing outside waiting for me to tell them that it's safe. If I take too long, someone could come in here and be a nice snack for a vamp.

I move further into the deli. Under the glass at the counter is completely bare of food and the cooler for drinks is empty as well. To my left, is a doorway leading to the con-venience store part of the truck stop. I take a deep breath, letting the aroma fill my nose. The smell seems to be stronger through the doorway. I let my feet carry me while I keep my eyes peeled for any other signs of life. This is the first time I actually don't mind if I run into a vamp. I have no reason to lure it out into the sunlight and biting it would be doing a good deed. I'd be unconscious for a few hours, which is the only downfall.

Many of the coolers in the station have been wiped clean, as well as the shelves that were once full of candy and chips. However, there are a few packages of food scattered about the place and even some bottles of water at the bottom of one of the coolers. It's almost like this stuff was left behind on purpose. I move onward, letting my dull reflection stare at me as I walk.

My clothes are looking a bit old these days. There's a hole in my jeans from where I was shot and another one on my shoulder. The wounds are gone, but the dried blood and hole in the fabric remain. By the look of me, one would think I've been out here for a year without bathing or changing my clothes. Hard to believe it's only been a few days.

I'll be passing for a zombie in no time.

I turn away from the coolers and walk by the cash register. The only thing on the floor behind this counter is a pile of cigarette boxes and some cans of chewing tobacco. I can't possibly be alone here. With the strong smell of death, I am certain there's something else here with me. I spin around, scanning the convenience store one last time. The aisles are clear and everyone is standing on the other side of the glass entryway. There's a rubber door half open in the wall next to the coolers. The "Employees Only" sign is crooked and the door is stained with blood. It looks fresh and I let my feet take me to it.

The smell is definitely getting stronger as I walk toward the door. I reach my hand out and touch the cold rubber and slide it open. It scrapes against the floor and gets caught on something before it can close after I enter the room. This room is where the employees would have gone to refill the pop and beer in the coolers. A few carts remain and empty soda cans are piled in the corner. I turn my head and spot the hunched over figure of a young boy pressed up against the wall. He's shivering and his face is covered with his hands.

His jeans are tattered and shredded by his bare feet. The shirt he's wearing is no longer white, but stained red with blood. I'm sure the mark on the back of his neck is to blame for that.

"Hello?" I call out to him as calmly as I can.

He jumps and raises his head. The paleness of his skin reveals that he is already changing. He's sweating like crazy, yet seems to be shivering at the same time. I recognize that look. It's the same thing my dad went through after he was bitten.

"You okay?" I ask.

He shakes his head and whimpers, "No."

"When did you get bit?" I ask.

He opens his mouth and forces the words to come out, "Yesterday...morning."

"You still remember it?"

He nods, "Why?"

"That means you're not quite a vampire." I say, taking a few steps closer to him, "I can help you."

He stands up a little and looks slightly relieved, "How?"

"I have a cure in my blood. Something that can change you back to normal." I reply.

"You do?" he says.

"Yeah," I say, taking another small step closer, "it might sound unbelievable, but I've already brought a few others back to life. One vamp and a few zombies. I can help you too, before you change completely."

He moves away from the wall and a smile forms on his purplish lips. I can't let him bite me and I can't bite him either. I'll pass out again and I can't risk not being awake right now. Something bad could come this way and I'd ending waking up in a bad place.

"How can you save me?" he asks in his tiny voice.

"Umm, I need to go get my friends. They're waiting right outside and you have to promise me something before I get them." I say.

"Okay."

"You have to keep yourself from wanting to bite them." I say.

He nods as he speaks, "I think I can...do that."

"Wait here, I'll be right back."

I quickly walk away from him and head for the glass door. Ryder and the others have crowded around it and are peering in through the dusty glass. They step back as I reach for the lock and push the door open. I stand in the way so they can't pile inside. It will be too much for the little boy in there and, if he's anything like me, he'll find the hunger frenzy hard to resist.

"We have a situation in here." I say.

The others look past me, scoping the place out and Ryder says, "What do you mean?"

"There's a kid in the room behind the coolers. He was bit yesterday and he'll be a vamp soon." I reply.

"You can save him!" Katie exclaims.

I shake my head, "The last time I bit a vampire, I was out cold for an entire night. I can't risk passing out right now."

"Well, you can't let him change into a vamp if he's just a little boy. You have to do something." Katie retorts.

Jason steps forward, pushing his way inside the gas station and says, "I've got an idea that might help. We'll need something sharp and a cup or a bottle for him to drink from."

He goes right to work, searching the gas station for a knife or something sharp enough to break skin. Katie follows him and looks for a cup in the deli part of the station. I take a few steps backward, allowing the rest of them to come inside. They group together by the cash register and stare at the coolers. Ryder closes the glass door and clicks the lock back in place.

"I found a cup." Katie states as she holds a paper cup over her head and walks next to the coolers.

I take Ryder's hand and lead him to the rubber door that is still stuck open. Katie holds onto her find and follows us into the small room. The little boy is pressed against the wall again as he stares at the two people I've brought with me. He's even more frightened than before and I can see a look of hunger building in his eyes. We need to hurry with this or it'll be too late and I'll have to do this the wrong way.

Jason rushes into the room behind us and says, "Found a piece of glass we can use."

He stops moving the second he sees the boy. I guess he wasn't expecting to see someone so young changing into a vampire right before his eyes. It's unfair for this to happen to any child out here, but that is how life has to be in this point in time. The zombie-vampire era is a hellish world to be a part of, but with me around, there just might be an end in sight.

I let go of Ryder's hand and lift the sleeve on my right arm. I take the glass from Jack's grip and turn to Katie. She reads my mind and lowers the cup under my forearm as I take the piece of glass and press it against my skin. I feel the poke as it cuts me and see the blood trickling down my arm. I slice into my flesh, letting as much of my blood pour into the cup as we can get. This is the only time I've ever done it this way and I have no clue how much he'll need to drink in order for it to work. The more, the better in my book.

I drop the shard of glass and the last few drops of blood splash into the cup. We managed to get a little less than half which I hope is enough. Katie hands me the cup and I turn to the boy. My arm is already starting to heal as I approach him as calmly as I can.

"Are you...sure this will work?" he asks.

I nod, "I'm sure. You'll just fall asleep for a little while, but we'll all be here when you wake up."

He nods and reaches for the cup, taking it from my hands. He hesitates before taking a drink and sniffs the red liquid. He closes his eyes and presses the paper cup to his mouth and tilts his head backward so the blood can flow down his throat. Some of it spills out and drifts down his chin and onto his shirt. I can see every swallow he takes as he finishes the drink. It falls from his hands and hits the floor with a quiet thud. He looks at me for a moment and his hands begin to shake. His breathing quickens and his chest moves up and down even faster.

I guess I haven't had the chance to actually see what their bodies do after I bite them. The few I've cured fell out of my arms as I was biting them. This little boy is much younger than the others, he looks no older than ten or eleven. His little body might not be able to take this and could be shutting down completely. I really hope that's not the case, but he is shaking quite a bit and his eyes are rolling back in his head.

"Bridget?" Katie whispers, "Are you sure this is going to work?"

I shrug as the boy's eyes close completely, "No clue."

He lets out a quiet groan and his hands stop shaking and his body stops moving. He goes limp and starts tilting to one side. I bend down and reach out to catch him before he hits the floor. His body is cold and he stinks of death. The only thing we can do, is wait for the cure to have effect on him and pray for the best.

* * *

The sky is dark and the stars are out now. We haven't had encounters of any kind and it's beginning to worry me. Adam should have been here by now. I know they were out-numbered and all, but *someone* could have made their way to the truck stop. I can't help but think something bad happened to them. Trevor had a lot of people with him and they all seemed pretty knowledgeable about using their guns. They could have easily killed everyone back there. I know the others are thinking the same thing. They can't hide the worry on their faces as they try keeping busy.

Katie is responsible for watching over the boy as he lies motionless in the room behind the coolers. She hasn't given us an update if he's alive or not and watching over him is the only thing to keep her mind off the whereabouts of her father. Annah and Rose are trying to catch some sleep on the floor behind the checkout counter. I left Jason and Hank in charge to keep watch over everyone inside. With the one gun they have, they can offer some sort of protection if something finds us.

The moon is high above us and the stars are shining bright. It's beautiful out here as I keep watch on the roof of this old building. I can see for miles and will be the first one to know if someone or something is approaching. I'm not *just* up here to keep watch. I felt the need to be alone for a bit while Ryder is down there dealing with his emotions over Carter. They were good friends and always had each other's back. His death hit Ryder pretty hard and I think it's starting to sink in with me as well.

Carter was a great guy. He saved my life when I thought for sure I was going to die back in Hatfeld. When that gun was held to my head and I closed my eyes, waiting for things to be over, he was the one who stopped that man from pulling the trigger. He was the one who actually understood why I needed to feel important and go on with killing zombies outside the city walls. Most importantly, he was the one who held Ryder back in order to keep him alive right after I was bit. I hate myself for not being able to stop him from getting shot. I wasn't fast enough to stop that bullet. I'll miss Carter like he was a member of my own family. Like the giant, older brother I never had.

I force myself not to cry as I stare at the empty field

below. My shades are hanging over the collar of my shirt and I feel like a human without them on. I don't feel like I'm hiding anymore. My eyes are still different, anyone can see that, but I don't need to be different by wearing the shades at night. No sense in that.

I stare at the night's sky and the stars that go on forever. They twinkle and shine, I've counted two shooting stars since I jumped up here. Out in the open is the best place to spot those things and they are amazing. When I was younger, I'd make wishes on them. Asking for a more exciting life, for something that made my life worth it all. In a way, I got that wish. It might not be in the same sense that I wanted when I was a kid, but my life is definitely more exciting than it was. I don't really have too many things I could wish for anymore. Save for one thing.

An answer to a question I know I'll never get.

Those people in the building below me, they all have a life they can live without anyone questioning it. They could walk into a group of other humans and feel right at home. If some random person were to get a good look at me, they'd scream for help and run for a gun. I might be here to do something wonderful for this planet, but where do I stand when it's all said and done? Where's my cure?

It sounds selfish, I know it does. That's just how people get when someone else gets something so amazing and they can't figure out why they aren't granted the same thing. A rich kid gets a fancy bike while the poor kid gets nothing and they constantly question why. That's similar to my dilemma. A difference being, and it's a pretty important one, I'm the one who's giving the amazing thing to those who need it. I can give the cure to the world, but the world might not be able to give a cure to me.

I guess that's why life is so unfair. This *god* character is toying with me all over again. I've asked him over and over to give me a break with all this nonsense. Sure, I might have gotten that when I was living in the city for the last year.

That's not the answer I was looking for and neither is this. I never wanted to wind up in this situation. I wanted to be happy, living with Ryder for the rest of my life. I still have him, but it will never be the same.

Another shooting star soars through space. No point in wishing on this one. I turn away from the sky and stare at the open field behind the truck stop. The only movement I've seen in the last hour, was a deer jolting through the tall grass. No vampires looking for a snack, which is kind of surprising. I figured we would have had that issue tonight. I also thought Adam would have come here, but I'm obviously wrong about that too.

The metal of the roof creaks behind me as I hear footsteps approaching. I take a deep breath, smelling the air. The human scent fills my nose and I turn my head just enough so I can see who's coming. Ryder, with a bottle of water in his hand and a thin smile across his lips when our eyes meet. He carefully strolls across the roof until he's able to sit next to me with his legs dangling over the edge.

"Thirsty?" he offers me the water.

I shake my head, "No."

He sets the bottle on the roof beside him and says, "I haven't seen you eat or drink anything since last night with the zombies and I don't consider *that* food. Are you okay?"

I shrug, "Food doesn't taste good to me anymore. The last time I ate anything other than zombie meat, I felt like I was going to throw it back up right in front of me." I'm sure he can hear the sadness to my voice.

"I hate that you have to deal with this alone." He says.

"I'm not alone," I reply, "there are thousands of other undead humans out there who are going through similar things."

He takes my hand and gives it a slight squeeze, "You're not one of them. You're still the smart ass, brave chick I fell in love with. You're just a little more badass and crazy now."

I try to smile. Hearing his words makes things better, but

it doesn't make me human again.

"You know, a monster wouldn't have saved that little boy's life earlier. Someone other than you would have killed him or left him there to die on his own. You did a good thing, Bridge."

I try to smile as I nod my head. There's still no saying if that boy is going to make it or not. He wasn't fully changed when we found him and I don't know if it works that way. Believe me, I'm hoping beyond hope that it worked. I don't want to think what I did for that boy was a waste and this cure of mine won't work on certain victims. But, that little boy isn't the thing on my mind right now. I've got issues that go far beyond the hope that he'll wake up human again.

"Why are you up here anyway?" Ryder asks, after a few silent moments.

"Thinking." I say.

"You know that's bad for you, right?" he states. "What are you thinking about?"

"Nothing in particular."

He nudges me with his shoulder and says, "You're upset about something, Bridge, I can hear it in your voice."

"I'm not good at hiding it, am I?"

He shakes his head, "Not really. Why don't you tell me what's wrong?"

There are so many things wrong with me right now, I have no idea where to begin. Good thing he already knows the obvious so I can leave that out. Not being able to kiss or touch him the way that I want to is another obvious and we don't need to go there. I'm sure he's just as upset about that as I am.

"Bridget," he says, "please tell me what's wrong?"

I nod my head and turn my eyes to his, "There is something I've been thinking a lot about lately. Something I probably shouldn't be wondering, but you know how I am."

"What is it?"

"I get that I'm the cure now and I'm supposed to help

save the world. As Rose and the others like to put, I'm a miracle and the best thing to happen to the planet."

"So, what's the problem?"

"It's just," I pause for a moment before going on, "if I'm the cure for all of them, for all the *real* monsters that are out there," another pause and I stare into his eyes, "what's the cure for me?"

His sad eyes stare back at me without an answer. It would be impossible for anyone to have that answer which is why I can't stop thinking about it. I'll be stuck this way forever, not knowing if I'll die with the rest of the humans or if I'll be forced to outlive the few people I really care about. I don't want to be like one of those vampires in the movies who watch the person they love grow old and die right before their eyes. I want to die right along with them.

Ryder squeezes my hand a little tighter and says, "I really wish I knew. I'd want that more than anything. But, you can't dwell on this one little bump in the road. I've seen you wrap your mind around something for so long that it drives you crazy until you get it and you can't do that right now. We need you to be strong in order to get through this."

"But I'm not strong enough. That's why I'm in this situation by myself."

He shakes his head, "You're not in this alone. There is never going to be a moment where you're forced to face this new life of yours without me by your side. I'm always going to be here. I'm always going to love you. Till the world stops spinning, I'm not going anywhere."

Ryder's always the best person to make me feel better about things. He's always there to make the sadness disappear and make me forget how horrible the world is around us. Kissing him would help a lot more right now, but I'll be happy just knowing his hand is in mine. Feeling the warmth of his skin against my own, is enough to help with the bad thoughts roaming through my mind.

I scoot closer so I can rest my head on his shoulder. This

is going to be a tough world to go through. Knowing there's a group of people hunting me, makes it a lot worse. We'll all be lucky if we make it to the city alive and in one piece. At least I'll have Ryder here to go through it with me. That might not seem like the best thing in the world, but if things go wrong, at least I'll die with him.

* * *

Ryder and I sat on the roof watching the stars and glancing to the empty field for another hour. We waited, hoping we'd see someone walking this way. There was still no sign of Adam or George or even any of the bad guys who attacked us. I expected to see someone heading here. Even if it was just Trevor and his men hunting me down so he can take over the world. Seeing anyone would be better than seeing the empty field all night.

We walk across the roof until we get to the ladder on the back part of the building. This was the way Ryder came up and the way he is going down right now. I found a different way when I came out here earlier. Of course, when it's super easy to jump ten feet in the air without a problem, getting to the top of a small building is nothing. Jumping down is pretty easy as well and I get to the ground before Ryder is halfway down the ladder.

"Cheater." He says once his feet hit the concrete.

I smile, brushing my hair out of my face and the two of us walk around to the door. Hank is standing close to the glass and unlocks it when he sees us approaching. Ryder goes inside first and I take another look around before heading in. I focus my eyes, forcing them to see far enough to catch a sign of any movement. The branches on a few trees sway in the wind and a plastic bag floats in the air. No humans or vampires.

We're completely alone out here.

Hank locks the door when we're safely inside. The others are wide awake and staring at us like we have a plan or something. Jason is sitting on top of the counter while the girls are huddled around the small table. These guys were supposed to get some sleep. There's no saying what kind of day we'll have tomorrow and it's best if we're all well rested. I can't have a bunch of tired people wandering the world with me while we're trying to stay safe.

"Did you see anything out there?" Katie asks as she comes out from the room behind the coolers.

I shake my head, "No. Anything different with the boy?."

She shakes her head and says, "Nothing yet."

"What do we do?" Rose asks. "I mean, we can't really just sit here waiting forever."

"Yeah, shouldn't we come up with a plan of our own for figuring out where they are?" Annah chimes in. "Like, shouldn't we go searching for them?"

Coming up with plans has *never* been my strong point. I'm the type of girl who rushes in to save the day without knowing what she's doing at all. I don't really have that option when all of these people are expecting something more from me. We could head back for the village and hope there's not a trap waiting for us. *Waiting for me actually*. I'm the only one they're after and it would only make sense if Trevor has something set up just for me.

"We'll lie low for tonight. Wait till morning and pray they show up." Thank *god* for Ryder stepping in a saying something for me.

"And if they don't show up?" Annah asks.

"Then we'll go back to the village and look for them. We could find out what happened if we go back there and it's best to wait till morning." He states.

Katie leans against the wall and says, "I know my dad is back there, but I agree. There's no saying what we could run into out there and I don't want to risk getting attacked by another vampire or come across a horde of zombies. I was dead once and I am not going back."

"Same here." Jason and Rose say at the same time.

I run my fingers through my hair and wish I had a better solution for all of this. The few people sitting in this small truck stop with me, risked the lives they *just* got back to get to this point. Everyone back at the village risked their lives for a cause they only just started believing in. I can't keep having a bunch of humans die for me. I've lost so many people over the years, all of them close to me in some way, I don't want to lose anyone else. The people here now, are all I've got in this world until we make it to Des Moines. Even then, I might not have anyone if no one wants to believe me. There's a decent chance of getting shot down before they give us the chance to try to explain things.

I wish I could lie and say that I'm not happy about getting bit and discovering the cure for the world's issues. In a strange way, I'm glad it happened. In a worse way, I'm glad it happened to me and no one else. I might not know how to handle things just yet, but I'm learning and it's easy to manage when I get the hang of it. That and I know what the smart thing to do with the cure is. Someone else could use it to their advantage and not share it with the world like they should. I know the human race needs saving and I'll be damned if I don't let that happen.

There's another part of me that wishes for this to never have happened. I mean what normal person wouldn't want a time machine. I could go back and stop myself from leaving the city with Ryder and the guys that day. We could still be happy living in our old house for the rest of our lives with the minimal excitement I get from working in the tower outside the wall. Carter would still be alive and none of us would be in this situation. Of course, there are a few people in this room that wouldn't be alive if it weren't for the cure I gave them.

"Bridge," Ryder's calm voice interrupts my thoughts, "what are you doing?"

I shrug, "Just thinking."

He smiles, "I've told you a million times how dangerous that is for you. When are you going to learn?"

I smile back and say, "Probably never."

I stare into his eyes. Those perfect hazel orbs staring back at me. Those soft lips begging to be kissed. I'll never get to feel those lips against my own again. Never get to feel his gentle touch as we make love in the middle of the night. Out of every human part of me I once had, the intimacies I share with Ryder will always be what I miss the most.

"Guys." Katie calls and I turn my attention to her, "He's moving around back here."

I brush the memories of times spent with Ryder out of my mind and walk through the station. I meet with Katie and the others at the rubber door leading back to where the boy is lying. They let me go in first. If something bad happens, I'll be able to handle it easier then they will. I poke my head around the corner of the room, letting my eyes adjust easily to this darkness.

The boy is on his back next to the wall, right where we left him. I stare at his chest, it's slowly moving up and down. He raises his arms off the floor and I smile as I see the color of his open eyes. They are brown, the same color mine used to be. Katie notices the smile on my face and walks past me. She kneels on the floor next to the little boy and puts her hand to his chest. A big smile crosses her face and I know she's feeling a pulse. The boy pulls himself to a seated position and looks around the room. He stares up at Katie and opens his tiny mouth.

"Am I normal again?" he asks without any force of the words at all.

She nods, "Yes you are. Can you tell us your name?"

"Joshua." He says quietly.

"I'm Katie and the girl who saved you is Bridget. We're going to take care of you."

Joshua smiles and says, "Thank you."

* * *

Morning's here. A foggy morning and I can smell rain in the air. No doubt a storm is coming and we'll get soaked before we find anywhere to hide from it. This is one of the few parts about being a traveler I don't miss. Getting rained on constantly was never a fun thing, although it did help lead to a fun thing once. It won't happen again, but I'll always have that memory.

There's still no sign of Adam or George or *anybody*. I stayed up all night and not a sound came from any creature outside the truck stop. No deer running by or vamp trying to sneak a late night snack. I hated every second of the silence I was hearing. If it weren't for Ryder's quiet snores, I would've gone crazy. It just means that we really have to trek all the way back to that village in hopes of finding someone still alive.

Hank found an old satchel inside the truck stop which he used to load some food and the rest of the water. There isn't much left, but it will help them out in case they have to go without for a little while. The newest member of our small group, Joshua, has already helped himself to a stale bag of cheese puffs and ate it like he's never eaten before. He's a happy kid now that he's human again and he can't wait to find more people to be around.

Speaking of food, I do find myself a little weary from hunger this morning. I haven't ate much of anything since I met all of these people and had a quick meal of their blood. Ryder doesn't count that as a meal, but when you're part of the undead world like I am, anything you eat counts as something. As long as that anything consists of flesh and blood, then you're good.

The fog isn't as thick as it was at dawn. We can see a good thirty feet in front of us as we walk through the tall grass back toward the village. It won't take very long to walk there, about thirty minutes maybe. Five miles is nothing to walk, even on a miserable looking day as this one. However, it feels like a million miles when I have to force my feet to keep moving. I guess I'm hungrier than I thought. I can't focus on anything and my stomach hates me right now for not feeding it. The only thing around that would even remotely cause the hunger pain to go away is the one thing I'm not going to give it. I'm sorry, but I'll let myself starve into a state of not being able to move again before I let that happen.

I can't push the thought out of my head though. Being this hungry and this close to something that can solve my issue, makes them even more desirable. It's hard to describe a feeling that could even relate to this. I guess it would be like a prisoner knowing freedom is right outside the fence but he knows he'll never have it. In a way, I *am* a prisoner and I'll never taste the one thing my mind and body so obviously crave.

There's a rustling up ahead. I open my eyes wide and strain my ears to listen. I don't think anyone else can hear it. No one is paying attention to it or looking for the sign of the noise. They're busy walking and looking for the people we were supposed to meet up with. There's the sound again. Leaves are being kicked around by something and I can hear it perfectly, like it's not more than a few feet away. I take a deep inhale through my nose and smell something that might bring a slight end to the pain in my gut. It's not dead nor is it a human. Definitely not another rabbit or rodent of any kind.

That's a plus in my book.

I hear the sound again, this time I can pinpoint exactly where it's coming from. Off to my left and not far away. I stop walking and stare in the direction of the noise. Another sniff and I can smell the dirty fir on its body. The smell of the skin and meat under that fir is intoxicating. So much so that I bite my lip and take a step toward it without bothering to tell anyone what I'm up to.

"Bridget?" I hear Ryder's voice, but I don't turn to him, "You alright?"

His voice isn't enough to break my concentration. I hear the animal moving even louder now. It's four legs trotting through the grass, getting closer to me and its odor intensifies. The small doe appears from behind a bush. She doesn't notice me or the humans standing behind me. I can feel their eyes on my back. They're probably trying to figure out what I'm doing.

I slowly move my feet toward the creature. Her head is turned the other way and I move so quietly, I can't even hear my footsteps. The smell grows and it's all I can focus on. The blood boiling under that fur coat she's wearing. That luscious flesh, it will be so filling and end the pain in my stomach. My mind is a blur. Nothing else is around me as I close the gap between myself and my meal. The monster inside is consuming me, begging me to end its suffering. Just a few bites and I'll be satisfied. I can gain the strength I need to take on the world. A few feet to go and the doe finally turns her head. Her glasslike eyes are staring at me.

Those eyes, calm and unafraid, are not enough to destroy the building frenzy. I can feel it taking over as I take one, final step before diving through the air to get to her. I wrap my arms around her neck and she struggles against my grip. I bring her to the ground and her hooves dig into my stomach and legs. This deer is no match for my new strength. I hold onto her with my arms wrapped around her tightly. She lets out a frightened wail as she continues to kick at me and the ground in hopes of getting away. I take in another whiff of her scent and close my eyes to get the full effect.

Whatever has been growing, has complete control over everything I'm doing to the deer. Squeezing her neck tighter until I can't hear her breathing anymore. She kicks and struggles, even after I bring my mouth to her neck and bite down hard enough to break the skin. Her warm blood fills my mouth and the frenzy I'm slowly getting used to is building all the more. I claw into her body with my fingers, feeling the skin and fur getting trapped under my nails. I take another bite, letting her flesh and blood flow down my throat, bringing an end to the hunger pains.

Her blood drips down my hands and I can feel it soaking the sleeves of my hoodie. Her body slowly stops moving in my grip. I take another bite, then another, until there's a decent gap on the side of her neck. I hold onto her lifeless form and let my monster win this little battle against me.

Hunger is a horrible thing to ignore, even worse when you're not human anymore. It's like something I can't control and something I don't want to deal with. Whatever happened to me after being bitten is nothing I want to be. This demon that's ripping into the flesh of an innocent animal, is not what I truly am. Yet, it's exactly what I'm giving to the world right now.

"Bridget?" I hear a voice not far behind me.

The world slowly comes back and I let the deer fall to the ground. I open my eyes and see the green grass coming into view. I look at my shaking hands, blood dripping from my fingertips. I can feel the same blood on my chin and lips. I glance down at my handiwork. A gory scene lies before me.

Her eyes are still wide open and terrified.

"Are you alright?" the voice belongs to Ryder and I feel his hand on my shoulder.

How could I have let him see this side of me? It was bad enough he had to see me rip into those few zombies two nights ago. Seeing me covered in the blood of an animal isn't what I want anyone to see. Especially Ryder.

He kneels to the ground next to me and I turn my head toward him. Through the corner of my eye, I can see the others in our group standing there, staring at me. Each one has a look of concern and worry written on their faces. My hands start shaking a little more and I can feel my lips quivering. They've seen what hunger will drive me to do. I can almost guess what's on their minds right now. *The crazy half vampire-half zombie could take us out in a minute.* They could be right, no matter how hard I try to control it. I am a monster, regardless of what Ryder and Jason tell me.

"It's okay." Ryder says quietly.

I look in his eyes. He's not afraid of me or what he just saw me do. I hear footsteps approaching and both of us turn our heads. Joshua is walking toward us. The one person of the group who should fear me the most is calmly walking this way.

"You've got something on your chin." He says with a small smile, revealing his sense of humor.

I quickly wipe the blood from my face with my hands. There isn't a lot of it that dribbled down my chin. Seeing as how my jeans are already bloody and ruined, I wipe my hands on them until they are mostly clean. Ryder reaches for my hand and I hesitantly give it to him. He helps me get to my feet and I stand to face the others. There's not a whole lot I can say to explain myself. I can't expect them to understand. I kind of expect to see them all run away from me.

"I'm sorry all of you had to see that." I say.

My eyes scan each of their faces. None of them look afraid or like they want to run away. They don't want to shoot me for acting like one of the creatures who bit me and them. That's actually a bit surprising.

Jason steps forward and shrugs his shoulders, "Well, if you're not hungry anymore, we really need to keep moving."

He smiles and Annah lets out a quiet laugh. She follows Jason and Hank, heading back toward the small village. Joshua runs back to Katie's side and grips her hand with his tiny fingers. I can feel the relief flow through me and I'm more myself again. Ryder gives my hand a little squeeze and I walk next to him, following the others.

"You see, Bridge," he states, "no one here thinks of you as a monster."

I shrug, "I still feel like one."

He sighs, "I'll get you to stop thinking like that soon enough. Trust me on this one."

I try to smile. I try to let anything other than guilt and shame take over my mind. If I wasn't so hungry, so tired and unable to move like a normal person, I wouldn't have had to tear into the doe like that. These people wouldn't have seen me like another zombie or vamp. I could still hold onto a small piece of my human self. Whenever the monster comes up to play, the only human part of me that's left gets chased down like a dog.

* * *

The rest of our walk back to the village was completely awkward. I wasn't sure what to say to anyone or even what to think when they turned their heads my way. They didn't have much to say to me either. Other than asking if I'm okay or wondering if we're going in the right direction. No one cared to bring up my crazed attack on that poor deer. I'm hoping they know I won't do anything like that to them. Zombies, vampires, and the occasional animal is the only thing on my menu from here on out.

It's a very disgusting menu.

We make it to the village and stand in the middle of the circle drive of the cul-de-sac. I look around, peering at each and every house in the neighborhood. The doors are shut and the windows are boarded up with plywood. Carter's body still lies in the middle of the street, a white sheet is partially draped over him. His feet are sticking out along with his hands.

A few others lie dead in the street, seven to be exact. Michael's body is amongst them, piled with the others from the group of people who are after me. Three more are placed gently in a row next to Carter. There's plenty of blood staining that part of the street and I have to force myself to stay strong. The evil part of me can smell the human blood before me and it definitely wants a taste.

"Dad!" Katie shouts and walks down the street searching for Adam.

Annah and Hank follow her closely, looking for anybody that is still alive. Joshua stays behind with Rose and practically hangs at her side. He's frightened now and being in this place is doing it to him. We told him we'd find people here, others that will help take care of him and now it's like a ghost town. I can only hope that everyone got out alive and found safety elsewhere.

Katie shouts for her father again and her voice carries through the air. I take a few steps away from Ryder and scan the place a little closer. There are bullet holes in the plywood covering the two front windows of a house nearby. The door is ajar and there's something blocking it from shutting all the way. I squint my eyes, focusing on the bottom portion of the doorframe. A foot is sticking out and it's keeping the door from latching. It's not moving and I can guess that person is dead. I look to the house next door and find a few more bullet holes. There's no dead body at that house, but it's a safe bet to think that most of these people didn't get out while they had a chance.

"Where the hell is everybody?" Hank shouts.

He circles the area as his eyes scan everything he sees. This place is empty. Or it appears to be empty only giving me the impression that it's not. If Trevor and his men are after me for a purpose I'll never fully understand, they wouldn't roam too far from the place they found me. I'm sure someone is still here, hiding in a corner so we can't see them. I take a deep breath, sniffing the air. The only humans I can detect are those around me. I'm used to their smell and would be able to tell if someone else is around.

"Dad!" Katie screams at the top of her lungs again.

The echo that follows her isn't her voice coming back. It's not the sound of guns clanking from humans who are ready to attack nor the sound of footsteps walking this way. The response we get from Katie's shriek for her father is a deathly moan coming from behind one of the houses. It's a deep, raspy groan that could only come from one beast on this planet.

I step away from the others, heading toward the sound. Katie rushes back to the group, Annah follows close behind. Joshua hides in the middle of all of them to become the most protected one. I hear the grunting come again along with the quiet shuffling of feet on the grass. I run my fingers through my hair and keep walking as the sound gets louder. This thing smells fresh meat and its song is getting louder.

It appears from behind two-story brick house with a wraparound porch. There's a gash on its forehead and blood staining the shirt its wearing. The zombie is a man and he limps on his left leg while his arms sway carelessly back and forth. His face is dirty and his hair's a mess. Not enough to hide the face I recognize.

"Greg." I say, noticing George's father inching his way to the others in the group.

He doesn't look my way. His black eyes are focused on the dinner standing a few yards away from him. The human smell is enough to get his legs to move a little faster and his groaning to grow louder. I look past him, trying to see further behind the house. Another body is dead on the ground, holes covering the clothes and I can spot a bullet wound in the head. That zombie might be dead, but the five others that are walking my way, are just as undead as Greg.

I don't recognize these other zombies. Two of them are women and the rest are older looking males. One of the men has grey skin and a missing left hand. He looks further gone than the others. His body is more decomposed. I don't know if my cure will work on him and I don't know if I really want to try. It's gross enough that I have to bite the body of the deceased in order for this thing to work. This zombie looks like he just crawled out of the ground after a *long* nap in the dirt.

I glance back to my group just as the five zombies march around the corner of the house and head for them. Katie lets out a loud shriek when she sees just how many there are. Jason raises the gun in his hand while the girls hide behind the three guys. I can't let Jason shoot any of these people. It's going to be hard, but I have to try to cure them. They had a life once and it's the right thing to do to give it back. No matter how disgusting it may be, I have to try.

"Try not to kill them." I say.

Jason nods and keeps the gun held high in case one of them gets too close for comfort. If he has to, he'll pull the trigger, but only to protect himself and the others.

I'll do my best to keep the zombies from reaching them. They're already moving faster than I can think right now, so it's time to get on it.

I rush to Greg, the zombie closest to the humans. He pays no attention to me. I'm dead to him and don't smell appealing. I should feel the same about him. My stomach, however, is telling me otherwise. This zombie would make a decent meal for now and the more I think about it, the more I want to taste his flesh. It's bruised and veiny in places, his eyes are black, and his clothes are bloody. That blood smells pretty damn good too. At least I'll be performing a civil service in the process of ending my hunger.

"Don't worry," I say to the walking corpse, "you'll be back to your old self real soon."

He keeps walking, letting out groans every chance he can get. The five other zombies join in with his song. The maniacal look in his eyes is screaming for a taste of the human flesh standing behind me. I reach out and grab his arm, forcing him to stop moving. *Finally*, he pays attention to me. A growl escapes his throat and he claws at my hand on his arm. His fingernails are sharp, I can feel them breaking the skin on my hand. The pain has no effect on me and I pull him closer.

I feel good about being able to save this one. I guess knowing a person who's been bitten makes this cure of mine a little more meaningful.

I lean in closer, smelling the decay on his skin. The frenzy in my mind takes over and the hunger grows. Greg claws at my arm one more time as I open my mouth for the bite. A sharp blast rips through the air and the world around me seems to stop. My ears ring and I jump back a step. The zombie's arm goes limp and I feel the weight of the body tugging at my grip.

Greg's arm falls out of my hand and I watch him fall dead to the ground at my feet. Blood seeps out from a hole in the back of his head.

"No." I whisper.

Five more shots are fired, each bullet coming from a different direction and I find myself covering my head in case one gets too close. The other zombies fall to the concrete.

Their dead bodies hit with a thud. I lower my hands and look to each of them.

I could have saved them. I could've ended their pitiful lives as zombies and gave them the chance to live again. They didn't need to go out this way, not even the one I'm sure wouldn't have been cured.

I turn to Ryder and the others. Jason shakes his head and lowers the gun when our eyes meet. He's the only one of them with a gun and he's not responsible for this. He believes in this cure and therefore wouldn't jeopardize any part of spreading it to the world.

"I knew you'd come back here." The voice comes from behind me and I slowly turn around.

My nose had failed me this time. I don't know how I missed his scent or how I didn't hear him approaching us. Maybe I was too focused on saving Greg or trying to find the people who were here yesterday. Those aren't good enough excuses for me to not notice Trevor, the man with an evil plan for me. And here he is. Standing a few measly feet away from me, lowering a gun to his side.

After seeing him standing alone with a smile plastered to his devilish face, I know there's something else going on here. I keep my eyes focused on the enemy and my ears strain to listen for other movement. I can hear the nervous breathing and quiet sobs coming from the people behind me. They're afraid and by the other sounds I'm hearing along with them, I know what's frightening them.

* * *

We're surrounded. Trevor had his gang of men and women scattered all throughout this village waiting for us to show up. I still can't figure out how I didn't smell them or hear their breathing when we got here. The hunger pains must have been so strong, they knocked out my super senses for a bit and it's taking a while for them to catch back up. Because of my inability to detect other people around, we are all surrounded with guns aimed at our backs and heads. There's not a gap big enough between the bad guys for us to try an escape attempt.

We are completely screwed.

"You can drop the gun, boy." Trevor shouts.

I turn my head. Jason is still holding the gun tight in his grip. It's the only form of protection they have without me and I know he doesn't want to give it up. I also know what will happen if he refuses to toss the gun to the ground. Trevor will have one of his goons either shoot him or knock him out and take the gun away from him. The best thing for all of us is to do what these people say right now. At least until I have a better plan at getting us the hell out of here.

"Toss the gun, boy, or you will have one hell of a headache." Trevor orders again as one of his men points a gun to Jason's head.

His nervous chest is heaving with every breath he takes. He knows he has no other option if he wants to stay alive. He tosses the gun to the ground and it clanks on the concrete at the feet of the man aiming the gun at him.

I turn back to Trevor. For a man who's a good foot taller than me, he really doesn't seem all that intimidating. Carter scared me more than this guy ever could. Yet, he stands here with a smug look on his face as if he's actually going to win this thing and get away with me in his grasp. I have a newsflash for this guy, I don't go down very easily. It's going to take *a lot* more than a few guns and some pissed off people to get me to give up.

He walks closer with a smile on his face, "You killed a lot of people when you ran off yesterday. Some of them were my own, good men with families to look after that are now my responsibility."

I roll my eyes, "I'm so sorry you have to deal with that. Shame you're little sob story doesn't make me feel bad about it. Maybe it has something to do with how your *precious* guys killed a good friend of mine."

"For someone so valuable, you really have a smart mouth." Trevor replies. "You should watch what you say before something bad happens."

"What are you gonna do? Hurt me? Put a gun to my head and threaten to pull the trigger?" I retort, "Go ahead. If you think I'm afraid to die, try getting bit by a zombie and a vamp and see how you feel."

"I wish I could, but being human is so rewarding. I can do whatever the hell I want and with you, I can accomplish so much more." He says.

"Yeah, well, you can't have me."

He laughs as he steps around me and I follow him with my eyes, turning as he moves. Ryder is not far away from him and his eyes are glued to me. I don't like being separated from him. Even though it's just a few yards, it feels like miles being in a situation like this. If things go wrong, which they most likely will, I can't protect him like I could if I was right next to him.

"I don't understand why you're being so derisive about all of this. Given the powers you now have, you should be standing right here next to me, *wanting* what I want." Trevor turns to face me, "You have the greatest gift this world has ever known and with it you could control it all. You could decide who lives and who fends for themselves against the zombies and vampires. You could decide who you bring back to life and whom you let suffer for all of eternity. Anyone would want that kind of power."

His offer doesn't sound the least bit appealing. If I was a deranged lunatic, I might agree with what he says. I have a little more sense when it comes to dealing with the *great gift* I have to offer. I know how to use it and I know it's the right way.

"I guess I'm a nobody then, because that's not how I would decide the fate of the human race." I reply.

He shakes his head, "You're a naïve young girl. An idiot to be exact. That's why I'm here, so I can make you give me control of the world. So I can decide who lives and who suffers. Without this, the world will continue to go so far through the gates of hell, it'll never come back."

I shrug, "Well, like I said before, you can't have me. You can threaten all you want, but you'll never have the cure."

He takes a deep breath and says, "Think that all you wish, but I always get what I want. I have ways of making you give in to me and soon enough, you will."

"I told you, go ahead threaten me with death all you want, but I really don't care too much if you kill me. You'd be destroying the thing you want most." I say.

He chuckles, "Oh, I don't need to hold a gun to *your* head to get what I want. I do, however, need to find the one thing that will hurt you the most by not having it around." He turns his attention to my small group, "I have a feeling that thing might just be one of these people standing right here."

I watch as he approaches seven very frightened people that are huddled together. Trevor stares at them for a moment, then glances back to me with a smile. He walks around them, staring at each one of them and stopping right in front of Annah, then raises his gun.

"Could it be your own sister that would tear you apart?" he points his gun to Annah's head and looks to me, noticing the look on my face, "Not a sister."

He takes the gun away from her head and scans the other two girls. They are sobbing and holding each other and he decides they don't mean the world to me. He glances down to

Joshua and lingers for a minute. His eyes dart from the boy and over to me before he shakes his head and keeps going. He moves over to Hank and stops walking again. The gun pressed to the older man's right temple and Hank closes his eyes.

"Maybe it's your father who's here with us." Trevor glares back at me.

"My father's dead." I say.

"Good, then we don't need him." he pulls the trigger and Hank falls limp to the ground.

The girls scream and I clench my hands into tight fists. I can feel my fingernails ripping into the palms of my hands and my breathing quickens. I just saved that man's life and now it's completely gone forever.

"You're going to regret that." I say.

Trevor ignores my comment and moves on to Jason, taking aim with the gun, "Maybe it's your brother."

"Stop this." I seethe.

He shakes his head and moves to Ryder, "Or maybe even your boyfriend."

I take a step forward and say, "That's enough!"

A smile comes to his lips and I just gave away the most important thing on the planet. I let it show that Ryder is the one person I care about the most. The only person that would tear me to shreds if I lost him. Trevor can see the look on my face, the anger pouring through my body, and he knows he won this round. He grabs Ryder's arm and pulls him away from the others, the gun pointed at his head.

Why did I have to act like an idiot and let my emotions give everything away? That's not how one survives when life hangs in the balance.

"I guess we found what drives you over the edge, little girl." Trevor says. "This boy will do a fine job getting you to do what I want."

"She'll never give you what you want. She's stronger than anyone else on the planet and better than you'll ever be."

Ryder says with a struggle.

Trevor twists Ryder's arm behind his back and I hear him grunt from the pain. Everything that man does to him is only making the rage rise even more inside me. I can feel it growing, worse than when it's hungry. I guess love is something that drives it crazy just as much as blood. Trevor takes his gun and slams the barrel against Ryder's head.

"You'll keep your damn mouth shut boy or I'll end this before it even begins." Trevor demands, pulling Ryder's arm tighter behind his back.

Through my peripheral vision, I can see Jason taking a few steps closer to Trevor. He gets stopped by two women with guns and he's not able to be the hero I can tell he wants to be. Ryder has a pained look on his face as I stare at him. There's only one other time I've seen his life get threatened like this. I didn't like it then and I hate it even more this time around.

"What's it gonna be?" Trevor shouts to me, "Give me what I want or watch me paint the street with his blood?"

I lock eyes with Ryder, fear floods his face as he stares back at me. I can't believe I let this happen to him all over again. His life hangs in the balance all because of me. Because I had to get out of the city. There's something wrong inside my head that refuses to let me live a normal life without some sort of chaos running amok. I think it might be time to let the chaos die so I won't have to force myself to choose between the one I love and the possibility of an even worse world.

My hands stop clenching and I keep my eyes glued to Ryder. His life would be *much* easier right now if we never came out here. He would be safe and sound back in Des Moines where I know he wants to be. It would be best if he just went back there now and forgot all about these few, long days outside the city.

"Trevor," I say, swallowing whatever pride I have left, "if I give you what you want, Ryder and the others go free.

You let them leave and you promise me you won't go after them."

"Bridget, no!" Ryder shouts.

Trevor keeps the gun pointed to his head and raises his eyebrows at me, "I think that can be arranged."

I nod, "Good, but there's one more thing."

"Oh yeah?" he asks.

"You can't have the cure until I know they're out of here and if I see even one of your asshole goons make the slightest hint at going after them, the deal is done and you can consider yourself dead." I say.

He removes the gun from Ryder's head and replies, "Deal."

Trevor pushes Ryder away from him and motions for his men to let my group leave. They move out of the way, creating a small gap in the wall they surrounded us with. Jason passes me a confused look as he stays close to the girls and Joshua.

I'm not sure what to say to any of them. This is the worst thing my mind could have ever come up with. I know they'll hate me for doing this, for causing the world to spiral further into the fire pit it's dangling over. If I don't do what I have to do, they'll all die and I can't let that happen.

Ryder rushes up to me, a frantic look on his face, "What the hell are you doing? You can't go with them. You can't let them use you for something that is going to destroy the human race."

"Just go with Jason and the others. It's better this way." I reply.

He shakes his head, "No, I'm not leaving you to die again. I'm not going to let you do this. I don't care if they kill me, I can't let you go with them."

"I care if they kill you, Ryder, and I'm not going to stand here and watch you die like Carter or Hank. I love you and if you love me, you'll understand what I'm doing and leave. Just head back to the city and enjoy the rest of your life." I say, then wrap my arms around him for a tight embrace, "Just promise me one thing."

I feel his arms on my back, "What?" he asks.

I keep my voice quiet so only he can hear me, "Make sure you stop at the truck stop one last time before heading to the city. I'd hate for you to get too far and leave something behind."

He leans away from me and passes me a confused look, "What are you talking about?"

I shrug, "Trust me on this one. You don't want to forget something important."

Ryder raises an eyebrow and I smile at him.

* * *

Ryder disappears with the others and Trevor's men stay true to their word. They let them leave and I have to watch them walk away from this village. I follow them with my eyes until I can no longer see them walking on the trail that will take them to the truck stop. I know I confused the hell out of Ryder, but it can sometimes be better not letting him in on my entire plan. Sometimes, just giving off little hints at what's really going on in my head is good enough.

I hear Trevor's footsteps walking closer to me, that evil smile is still plastered to his face. His master plan has finally come to the end he's always desired. He can have a few moments of peace after gaining the one thing he didn't know he wanted until he found out it existed. I just love it when people think like that.

"Oh, little girl, you just made the best decision of your life." Trevor says as he approaches me. "You couldn't possibly understand the depth of everything I want to achieve with you. This world will finally have order again and I'll be the one behind it all."

"I really hope you'll stop calling me 'little girl'. It's doesn't really suit me." I say.

"I guess knowing your name is a good idea. After all, I will be keeping you for a long, *long* time." He states. "Tell me, what do people call you?"

"Bridget." I reply, simply. "People have been calling me that my whole life."

"How long do you think I'll be keeping you? You aren't human anymore, right, so there's no telling how long you'll live." Trevor asks.

"Oh, you won't be having me for very long. Actually, you won't get to have me at all." I reply.

The smile on his face fades away and he glares at me, "You must think you're funny. Take a look around you, Bridget. You're outnumbered, outgunned, you can't possibly get away from us."

I shrug, "Well, you're right about one of those things. I *am* outnumbered. You just have to understand something, I'm not human anymore and the monster deep down inside me would love to come out and play for a while."

"You think I'm afraid of you?" he shouts and the metal of guns starts clanking all around me. "You are a pathetic little girl who let herself get bit and taken down by those beasts who wander the planet like idiots. You are nothing and you belong to me now."

I run my fingers through my hair and shake my head, "Sorry, but I belong to no one."

He comes at me, rage burning in his eyes. I let my hand form into a fist and allow the frenzy to build inside me. I let the world around me disappear and all I can see is Trevor. He seethes at me as he stomps, getting closer and closer until I can hear his angry heart beating in his chest. Close enough for me to get the perfect shot with my fist and I connect it with his jaw, letting him spin around and stammer back a few steps.

That felt good.

That felt great actually. This man is taller, bigger, more intimidating than I ever could be and *I'm* the one who knocked *him* backwards. If only my dad were here to see this. I think he'd be extra proud of this one.

Trevor snaps his head around, blood dripping from the corner of his mouth, "You're gonna pay for that you bitch."

He lunges at me and I take a quick leap into the air, letting him rush right underneath me. He trips over himself until he's able to stand up straight. I land on my feet as a few of his goons come at me, three to my left, one coming up behind me, and four to my right. The first one who approaches me has a machete and he swings it, slicing the air in front of my chest as I take a step backward. He swings it again and I catch his arm before he gets too close.

Okay monster, time to come out and play.

I let my mind wander, taking me to a place so dark and evil, I can only hope I come out of it again. I let myself forget the humans I need to protect, forget all about my oath on never killing a single one of them. These humans standing with me right now, don't deserve my mercy.

I take the man's wrist and squeeze hard enough to get him to drop the blade. Next, I twist his arm in front of him, letting the crack of his forearm fill the air and he screams out in pain. He drops to his knees, cradling his now broken arm and I move on to the next two.

These two guys don't have any weapons, other than the guns strapped around their waists. They are going to rely solely on whatever their fists and feet think they can do. The first one, his hair is greasy and black and he's basically bones wrapped in baggy clothing, rushes me and a scream of anger escapes his throat. He takes a swing and I dodge it right away.

His pal, who is a little bigger and blonder, comes to his aide and grabs my arm before I can move aside. I glare at him, wishing he could see the rage in my own eyes behind the shades. Then, I wrap my fingers around his arm and jump up into the air, landing behind him and dislocating his shoulder along the way. He releases my arm and I lift my right leg, giving him a sharp blow to the middle of his back. The wind escapes him and he crashes forward on top of his little friend.

This is going faster and much smoother than I thought it would.

A woman is coming at me now. She calmly approaches me with her hair in dreadlocks and her dark skin glistening in the sunlight. A spear is in her grip and she twirls it in some choreographed pattern I can't begin to keep track of. She seems pretty proud of her ability to maneuver a stick in a way I'd never want to. It spins over her head and along the side of her body. The blade of the spear sparks against the concrete with every rotation. In one final movement, she swings the spear at my head and is so surprised when I catch it mid swing. She pulls at it, trying to get her toy away from me. I'm just a little stronger.

I pull the thing out of her grip and break the stick in half over my knee, "Oops. You'll have to find a new party trick."

She shrieks at me, then starts clawing her fingers at my face and neck like a deranged zombie or vampire. If it weren't for the whites of her eyes, I'd almost think she *was* one of those things. I back up a few paces, getting away from her, but she still claws at the air. I take one half of the spear, the side with the blade and swing it through the air, ending the clawing and the shrieking.

I hit the side of her head and the blade is stuck in her skull. Blood drips from the wound and her fingers twitch rapidly as her body slowly dies and falls limp to the ground. I stare down at her, the blood pouring on the concrete. The smell of it drifts up my nose and the passion for it grows. The redness of her blood is so inviting, it's begging me to try some. I can't let this go on forever. I can't always shove my hunger aside whenever I feel the need to keep my human self alive. I grab the spear sticking out of her head and yank it from her skull. A cracking sound comes from her head when the blade is freed.

One more man has dared to challenge me. He's older, maybe my dad's age. His hair is grey and so is his beard. For some, unknown reason, this man felt the need to show off his gut by only wearing a denim vest and jeans. His hairy chest isn't very attractive and it completely takes my eyes away from the blood. The knife in his hand is small and unintimidating. He growls at me as he moves closer.

"I think you've had just about enough fun for one day." He says through gritted teeth.

I raise an eyebrow and look to the others in his gang that are standing nearby. A few of them have roamed away from the scene, afraid to die next. I'm not sure why these people thought it was a good idea to get an overweight, old guy to do the grunt of their work, but if he thinks he has a shot at taking me down, who am I to stop him from trying?

I hold onto the spear and let this man take another step toward me. He waves the knife through the air, like he's spreading butter on invisible toast. He licks his lips and winks at me. A sight that is only adding to his disgusting appearance. He takes another step and reaches out with his knifed hand, attempted to stab me or *something*. By his movement, I can't really tell what he's trying to do. He lunges at me again and I latch onto his arm. Another, lower growl escapes his throat and he reaches for me with his free hand.

With every ounce of strength I have wrapped up in this cute form, I grab his other arm, while I still hold onto the spear, and amaze myself with how strong I've become. I heave him into the air and toss him over my head. He screams for help and lands flat on his face a few feet behind me. The screaming stops the second that loud *thud* hits the ground. I don't have to turn around to see that he's not with us anymore. I threw him pretty hard and I'm positive his head cracked the concrete when he landed.

The people around me have stopped moving. Their eyes stay glued to my every twitch. Some of them appear to be frightened of me. I have taken out four of them all by myself now and I left a pretty good dent in their leader's face. I *want* them to be afraid of me. I *want* them to see me as the monster I can feel burning inside of me. There's just one more thing I want to do to add even more fear into their hearts.

I raise the spear and stare at the blood dripping from its blade. The human smell of it still taunts my nose and I want it even more than ever. One taste and my demons will win the fight in my head. I bring it closer to my lips and open my mouth, forgetting the war I'm having with myself on this topic. The blood is much more intoxicating when it's this close to my lips. There's no point in trying to stop myself from trying it.

"God dammit, somebody stop her!" Trevor's voice catches my attention and I stop focusing on the blood.

He stands amid his group, the only one of them who isn't afraid of me. I can smell the anger rising from the pores of his body and it's enough to mask the smell of the blood. He has the blood I *really* want to taste.

There's stomping coming from behind me and I can feel the warmth of the human standing there. His breath blows against the back of my neck. I hear the metal of the gun rising through the air and I can feel it not far from the back of my head. I close my eyes and take a deep, calming breath.

There comes a split second of time where your body is able to do something so amazing, it could never be done again. Even as a person who's not entirely human anymore, I really don't think I could make this move ever again. The man behind me pulls the trigger and in that tiny, iota of a second, I spin out of the way, letting the bullet graze through my hair and I ram the spear right through his chest. The bullet from the gun lands in the shoulder of a young woman standing across from us and she screams out in pain. I twist the spear in the man's chest and watch the life flee from his eyes. He falls to the ground and his head cracks against the concrete when it hits.

I turn back to Trevor and his gang. The girl who was shot is being looked after by a couple of them and the others I managed to disable are still lying on the ground. Trevor stares daggers at me and shoves his way through his men. I let him come close to me. I let him get within an arm's length away. It's more meaningful to me if I let him think he's going to win. I jump up one last time and give him a swift roundhouse kick to the face. He spins around and topples to the ground on top of the woman with dreadlocks.

That feels even better hitting him the second time.

"Anyone else?" I say, staring at the few crowding around me.

They back away. I guess these big guys are afraid of a *little girl* like me. It doesn't seem like I've made much of a dent in their numbers. As long as none of them want a fight, I've won this thing here today. I can run away with that on my mind and let the monster go back into its pit in the darkest corner of my stomach.

I back away from them, stepping over the man with the spear sticking out of his chest, then move a little more quickly. I turn around and let my legs run as fast as they can to get away from this hellhole. The world is blurry as I move, almost like tunnel vision, but I'm still able to see exactly where I'm going.

I push myself to run faster. The sooner I get to my destination, the sooner I can find an end to this day.

Part Three

I can see the truck stop and I'm coming up to it fast. The fields on either side of me are still in tunnel vision mode as I run. I just want to get there quickly so we can finally be on our way to the city. I know we are supposed to find Adam and George and a few others from the village, but I have no idea where they are and we don't have a lot of time to search for them. Trevor and his men will keep coming after me so long as I am out here where they can find me. The faster we get to Des Moines, the faster I can try to convince the city of my *gift*, and the faster I'll be able to breathe again. All this running and constant danger really takes a toll on someone. Even when that someone is me.

I get to the highway and stop running. I think that's about the farthest I've ran with this new body of mine. I didn't even break a sweat. I brush the hair out of my face and approach the building. The grey minivan is still sitting up close to it, not like I expected it to move or anything. I inhale deeply through my nose, taking in the familiar scent of humans. This aroma seems much more appealing to me now. It probably has something to do with all the blood I came in contact with while fighting against those people.

Then again, I could be getting hungry. There was a lot of blood and I was really close to trying some of it.

No.

That monster can't come back right now.

My feet carry me to the middle of the street and I hear a crunching sound echo through the air. It didn't come from me. There's nothing in the street for me to have stepped on. I turn my head to the left and see nothing. No zombies and the sun is too bright for vamps to come out. I look to the right and focus my eyes. There are three figures coming this way. From here I can tell they aren't zombies. One of them is wielding a rifle and the middle one is helping the third one walk. I take a few steps toward them and squint my eyes a little.

"Bridget?" the voice comes from the gas station.

I don't need to turn my head to know that it's Ryder. His smell gives his presence away. I'm glad to know they got here without a problem. He runs to the street, worry and relief cover his face. He stops right in front of me and I can feel his eyes checking me over. Probably making sure I'm not hurt or anything.

I turn to him and smile, "I told you you'd forget something."

He sighs, "Like I'd really go too far without you. You'll have to tell me what happened, you know."

I nod, "I will later on."

The three strangers get closer to us and we turn to them. The one walking alone is a woman. I can see her long, black hair blowing in the wind. The other two are men and their faces are starting to come into view. Katie will be happy to see that her father is still alive and well. He's limping and hanging onto George with all of his might, but he's alive and that's all that matters. They are the only people walking this way and I'm beginning to wonder what happened to the rest from the village. That place was teeming with people and this is all that's left. It can't be possible.

"Dad!" Katie shouts from the doorway of the gas station, then I hear her running toward her father.

I watch her wrap her arms around him and relieve George from carrying him any further. They head for the truck stop with the woman right behind them. George sees me and walks my way instead of going with the others. There's a cut on his forehead and a scratch down the length of his arm. Blood drips from his fingertips and onto the concrete. The smell sends shivers down my spine and I force myself to fight the hunger.

"Are you alright?" Ryder asks as George stops in front of us.

He shakes his head, "Not really."

"What happened?" I ask.

"After you left, that gang stayed behind for hours. They stopped fighting with us but they wouldn't let us leave. Night fell and a few vampires showed up. We took care of them and the noise drew in about a dozen zombies." George wipes his eyes and continues, "Most of us were able to make a run for it and they're scattered all over the place. Not sure if we'll ever see them again. We stayed as long as we could to fight them off, but they just wouldn't go down. They got my dad and he made me leave with Adam and Alix, the girl who is with us. I have no idea what happened to my sister."

I nod and say, "Yeah, we saw your dad back there."

His eyes light up and he says, "You did?"

"I was going to save him. There were five others with him and I was going to cure them all. Trevor and that damn gang of his were there waiting for us. It was a trap and he shot them all down before I had the chance." I glance to my feet, "I'm sorry, George."

He shrugs, "I was ready to accept that he was gone. He was one of them and I was positive I'd never find him if we ever ran into you again. How'd you get away from Trevor?"

I smile, "I kicked his ass a little. Then he tried to kill me, so I killed a few of his guys."

"But he's still alive?" George asks.

I nod, "Unfortunately."

"Then we need to get the hell out of here. He'll be coming for you and he won't let you get away next time."

George walks past us and heads for the glass doors of the truck stop. Ryder and I stay in the middle of the road and he looks at me. He's worried, a look that's been on his face since we found each other after I left him at the overpass. He shouldn't have to wear that look.

I shrug, "I'm sorry."

He shakes his head, "You have nothing to be sorry for, Bridge."

"I do." I say. "I could've told Dwayne to find another group of people to search for that village. Instead, I got you involved and risked your life while destroying my own. Now, there are crazy people after me and I'm just risking your life all over again. There's no saying what would happen if they find us before we make it home."

"They're not going to find us. We're going to make it to Des Moines and you're going to save the world from there." He forces a smile.

I force one as well and take his hand, "I guess we should go inside then, huh?"

He nods and we begin the short walk to the door of the truck stop. Katie is already inside with her dad and that woman, Alix. George is just now walking through the door and we aren't too far behind him. Before we get inside, I stare at the van again. It is in decent shape for sitting in the same spot for a few years. The tires are still aired up and all of the windows are intact. I wonder if it would run or if there's even gas in the tank. It would make a nice getaway vehicle for all of us. It's big enough and it would mean we'd get to the city *much* faster.

I look away from the van and walk inside with Ryder. We let the door close behind us and Jason is there to lock it.

Adam is sitting at the small table with Katie kneeling on the floor beside him. Her head resting against his shoulder with his arm draped around her. Rose is in the middle of giving George a warm embrace, welcoming him back to the our small group. Annah stands alone with Jason, Joshua, and Alix in front of the counter. All of their eyes turn to us as we approach them. I guess they must be waiting for another master plan of mine.

"Glad you made it back okay." Jason states, passing me a smile. "You really are great at making plans."

I nod, "I do my best."

"What's our plan at getting out of here?" Annah asks. "How far is the city?"

"A couple days." Adam answers with a groggy voice. "Longer if we get stopped."

"If that gang comes after us again, we won't make it there at all." George chimes in.

"We'll just have to try. We've lost too many people already and I'm not willing to lose anymore. We *can't* lose anymore." Adam says. "If Trevor finds us, we'll have to fight him off. We'll do whatever it takes to stay alive and make it to the city to spread the word about Bridget. Losing isn't an option anymore."

They have lost too many people because of this. Because of me. I shouldn't have gone with George to his village or even stayed as long as I did. I should have packed it up the second I woke up yesterday morning and hit the road with Ryder and Carter. No one should have died because of me.

I listen to Adam talk some more, explaining to everyone how they need to survive and keep me safe until we get to the city. That's not their responsibility. I don't need to rely on anyone to keep me safe. I think I've done an okay job at it so far. As long as I don't count the whole getting bit by a vamp and a zombie thing. That's beside the point.

I step away from them and walk to the door and stare through the window. Everyone's right. If we stay here, Trevor will find us and kill them just to take me away as his prisoner. It's only a matter of time before I see his men walking through that field to get here. We need a plan. We need a way out of this mess. And I need my dad here to tell me what to do. He's the perfect man to come up with a plan for this sort of thing. He'd know exactly what to do and how to get out in order to stay alive. It would be *really* nice if my brain would shut down for a few minutes, like it has done before, so I can talk to him.

My eyes stay glued to the gas pump across the parking lot. The hose from the nozzle sways back and forth in the breeze and the sun bounces off the chrome frame. The glass where the digital numbers used to be is shattered and a hole has been punched into the machine. Dad could materialize right beside it and that would be great. He could come to me and tell me what I need to do, give me some sort of advice on how to keep all of these people alive. I *need* him to be here.

I focus all of my energy and stare at the gas pump. I try to get my mind to shut down like it did when I saw my brother. I sort of died during those short, few minutes, but my mind still shut down. I was conscious when I saw Maggie, but I was so wrapped up in things, she appeared to me anyway. I thought I was dead when Mom came along and I'm grateful I wasn't. It shouldn't be so hard to get out of my head so my dad can come here and tell me what to do.

That just isn't happening. No matter how long I stare at the gas pump, he's not going to pop out of thin air and stand right next to it. That's not how my life works. I don't get what I want anymore. I don't get help from someone who's been dead for over a year. Instead, I get help from people who shouldn't feel the need to help me at all. They should just go on with their lives and forget about me.

"I don't think walking to the city will be safe. We can't hide in the woods or the vamps will get us and walking on the street in broad daylight will get us caught. If we had some other kind of transportation, we'd be fine." Jason's voice breaks my concentration. "I just don't see us getting to the city at all without some form of cover."

The wind outside picks up and the hose on the gas pump sways a little more in the wind. It hits against the machine, bounces away from it, and makes it looks like it's pointing to something. It stands in the wind for a fraction of a second, but I can still see what it's trying to show me. I press my head against the window and look outside. The grey of the van sticks out and I find myself wondering about it again.

"There's a van outside." I say, turning around to face the others. "We could see if it runs and take it to the city."

Everyone turns their attention to me and George says, "That would be a good idea if there is any gas left and the battery isn't dead."

"Then try it. If what Jason believes scares the hell out of all of you, we need to try this. A running vehicle is the only chance we have at getting to the city faster." I say.

George nods, "Okay, is anyone here a mechanic?"

"I am." Annah's voice takes us all by surprise. "I mean, I used to help out my uncle at his shop in St. Louis. I still remember a few things."

"Great." I say, stepping away from the door. "George and Jason will help you. I'll keep watch and the rest of you just need to prepare for anything."

"Anything?" Katie asks.

I nod, "Just be ready."

* * *

Annah and the guys were able to scrounge up some gas from two of the cars parked in the lot. They didn't get much, about five gallons. I think that should be more than enough to get to the city or at least far enough away from this place so Trevor's gang won't find us. Now, Annah is busy trying to get the battery to turn over. Without a charger or a new battery, it's hard to accomplish. It is nice to hear the sound of an engine trying to turn over though.

After all the cars my dad and I passed when he was alive, we never found one that would actually *try* to start. They were either too banged up, too dead or the tank was empty. This van could be the one vehicle out here that will make my life a little easier. I can use easy right about now.

I've been leaning against the building for close to an hour now. The only thing I can focus my eyes on, is the field across the highway. The quickest path between the truck stop and the village where I left Trevor and his men. I know I should have killed that man. I shouldn't have just stopped when he was unconscious. Finishing the job would have been the only way to ensure the safety of us all. Instead, I left him lying on the ground with his men hovering over him.

I'm such an idiot for not killing him.

There goes the engine trying to crank over again. The motor grinds slowly and the engine rattles under the hood, but no luck with this try. I can hear Annah getting frustrated with it. She said she used to help her uncle work on cars before the *amazing cure* came along. That was also before she was bitten and transformed into a zombie. I'm sure she's forgotten a few things during that horrible experience. Everyone's forgotten how to do things they used to do. The world will never be the same, even with my cure.

She tries one more time then releases the key, "I just don't get why the damn thing won't start!"

I glance over to her and see the annoyed look on her face as she climbs out of the drivers' seat. George stands beside her as they look under the hood. His hands are greasy as well as his shirt and jeans. Annah's been making him do most of the dirty work while she turns the key in the ignition. Joshua stands out of the way, but watches with interest as they work under the hood.

Katie and Rose gathered whatever they thought we could use from inside the station. They found a few things, a couple knives and empty bottles they filled with water from a spigot behind the station. Now, they sit on the sidewalk next to the van, waiting patiently for it to start. Adam, Jason, and the woman, Alix, sit alongside them while Ryder stands against the building with me. He's been giving me worried glances ever since we came outside.

"You still haven't told me what happened after we left you back there." He says, quietly. "Did you kill someone?"

I nod my head, "A few of them and I wasn't sure if I could control myself at the sight and smell of their blood."

"But you didn't taste it, did you?" he asks.

"No, but I really wanted to." I reply.

"Bridget, it's okay if you do. Those people are bad and it won't matter what you do to them." He says, trying to be reassuring.

I shake my head, "I'm afraid if I try even the smallest drop of human blood, I won't be able to send the monster back where it belongs. I can control it enough when I bite a zombie or a vamp, but human blood is much more appealing to me. Every time I smell it, I can feel myself craving it, like my body knows it's still warm and alive. I can't give up what's left of me for a simple drop of human blood."

"I understand." Ryder says. "I think I'd be the same way if I were you."

"I just don't want to kill a human that way. It's bad enough how I killed them back at the village just to get back to you."

He smiles, "You should be used to fighting for me by now."

I shrug, "Yeah, I should."

We hear Annah trying to crank the engine over again. She holds the key down for a few seconds longer, but it still doesn't start. I'm beginning to think that this whole driving to the city idea was a bad one. The van probably needs a new battery, along with several other parts, and even then we'd be lucky if it turned over. We should've started walking and put some distance in while we still had the chance.

Annah lets go of the key and curses to herself. I look back to the empty field and stare at the tall weeds and grass. They sway back and forth in the wind and I glance to the sky. The clouds drift through the blue ocean above my head. The dark grey color of them threatens us with rain, but haven't taken over the sky completely. The sun still manages to shine through and, even with the sunglasses on, looking near it burns my eyes. I blink the pain away and look back to the field.

"I think it might rain soon." I say.

"Looks like it." Ryder adds. "The wind is picking up too."

I let the wind flow through my hair and I take a deep breath letting the smells drift up my nose. These humans around me are so intoxicating. It's painful knowing that a big part of me wants to devour them. As long as I can keep that part locked away in the pit of my stomach, we'll all be okay.

The crank of the engine fills the air one more time. It's not as slow as it was a minute ago and I turn my eyes to the van. Annah has a determined look on her face as she holds the key down.

"Give it some gas!" Adam shouts to her.

She closes her eyes and slams her hand down on the dashboard while still holding the key. In that instant, a squeal comes from the belt in the engine and smoke rises from it. The van roars to life and shakes from side to side for a brief moment until settling into an easy idle. Cheers come from everyone sitting on the concrete and Joshua jumps up and down for joy. Ryder claps his hands next to me and I give a much needed sigh of relief.

"Finally." Annah says, then climbs out of the van.

Katie helps her injured father to his feet while Rose walks over to George. They smile at one another and he slams the hood of the car shut. Smoke still seeps through the seams, but the van stays running.

"I guess this means we can hit the road." Adam says, leaning against his daughter as they walk to the van.

"Time to go, Bridge." Ryder takes my hand and we step away from the building.

I take a second to scope out the field before we get to the van. There's no one there and the only humans I can smell are those around me. Things are going our way and we'll finally be able to get to the city. Katie helps her father into the backseat of the van then climbs inside herself. Alix sits in the very back and Rose sits beside Katie.

"Hey, what's that flying thing?" I hear Katie's voice asking from inside the van.

She's pointing at something she sees and I follow her finger with my eyes. There's a small black object flying through the air. It's too round to be a bird and I don't see any wings on it. I squint my eyes, focusing on the item the best I can. It's small and metallic looking and is headed right for the truck stop.

"Everybody get down!" I shout, thinking the worst.

Those outside the van duck against it while the few inside cover their heads with their hands and arms. Ryder gets to the ground and I kneel next to him. The round object, the grenade, crashes to the ground on the other side of the parking lot. The ground shakes and rumbles as debris and pieces of a shed explode through the air. Fire lights up the air not far away and black smoke billows down on top of us. If I could hear anything other than the explosion, I'd hear the screams and shouts coming from everyone around me.

The smoke has taken over the area. I can't see much

through it, other than the back of the van and a few feet passed it. Squinting my eyes doesn't help at all and the smell masks any other scent around me. The ground stops shaking and debris stops falling. I get to my feet and frantically search for the source of the explosion. I move away from the van and wave the smoke away from my face. It helps clear the air a bit, but I still can't see much.

Fire simmers in the grass and a few branches of a nearby tree. The grenade crashed into a shed about fifty yards from the gas station and fairly close a gas pump. There would have been a much bigger explosion if it landed on that. Pieces of wood and dirt clutter the concrete of the parking lot and small fires are spread all over the place.

The smoke begins to clear and the highway is starting to come into view. I can see the grass and search for signs of other humans. I walk further away from the van, forcing my eyes and ears to focus on everything around me. There are other humans around here and I know exactly who they are. I might not be able to smell them just yet, but I know they're here somewhere.

I can hear twigs breaking under heavy footsteps. They're getting closer and closer and I peer my eyes through the smoke hoping to spot them. The sounds are a bit staggered and seem labored to me. The louder they get, the more I can tell they aren't human footsteps. I strain my ears and hear the first zombie groan fill them. It came from behind me.

Just what we need.

Zombies *and* the threat of a human force surrounding us.

* * *

I spin around on my heels as the groaning gets louder. The wind is doing an okay job clearing the smoke away from this place. I take a second to glance over to the van. Ryder is standing at the back end of it, staring at the field across from us. Jason and George are looking everywhere for the source of the groaning and whoever threw the grenade. I look back ahead of me and see the zombies approaching.

Three of them, all females with blood dripping from their fingernails and mouths. They're like a group of girls in high school trying to claw their way to what they desire. Currently, that's a few humans crowding around a van. The zombies stumble in the grass and trip down the curb leading to the parking lot. Not a single one of them looks my way and they are practically running to the van. They move quicker than most zombies I've seen and there's hunger burning in their eyes.

I take a breath and quickly move across the lot to get between the zombies and the van. The closer I am to them, the more the smell of their blood sends a frenzy through my mind. I want to bite into them, let their flesh and blood flow down my throat. I need that feeling of hunger to go away so I can be stronger again. I need my hunger to end.

The first one, her hair is crusty at the ends where blood has dried. Her eyes are as black as the short dress she's wearing. There's a long scratch down the side of her face going along her neck, stopping just above her chest. That's probably the mark that gave her this life. She claws at me and I grab her arm, tossing her to the ground. She lets out a deep groan and digs her fingers into the concrete.

The next one has a bite taken out of her shoulder. It's rotten around the wound and black bruises cover most of the skin I can see on her. Her hair is knotted, covering part of her face. I lunge at her, wrapping my arms around her waist to tackle her to the ground. She lands with a thud and digs her nails into my back. I hold her still, pinning her to the ground and lean closer to her neck. The scent of her dead blood fills my nose and I can't hold it back any longer. I open my mouth and close my teeth against a small portion of her neck. The skin breaks instantly and blood fills my mouth. I let a lot of it flow down my throat and I can feel myself getting stronger as the seconds tick by. I wish I could keep going, keep letting this magnificently disgusting thing fill my stomach forever, but I can't. I've got humans to look after.

I pull myself away from her unmoving form and get to my feet. I turn around and see the other two zombies chasing something away from the van. The girls inside the vehicle poke their heads out and look through the window. George steps out from where he had taken cover and stares at the zombies walking away from them. Joshua is ducked down on my side of a garbage can with his eyes watching the zombies. I look past the two women stumbling across the parking lot. Jason and Ryder are coaxing them along, pulling them further away from the van so the others can be safe.

"Come on, follow us." Jason shouts and the zombies reluctantly obey.

I shake my head, staring at Ryder as he lets the zombies follow him. They're getting closer, too close for me to be comfortable with any of this. He shouldn't be the one to risk his life for the sake of others. That's my job. I'm the one who's supposed to keep him safe.

I take a few, quick steps, closing the short distance between the zombies and myself and hear a voice calling from behind me.

"Look out!" George screams from the van.

My feet instantly stop moving and I look up to the sky. The smoke has cleared enough for me to see another small, round object falling down on top of us. Another grenade has been launched and I don't have enough time to run for cover. I drop to my knees and cover my head with my hands. The grenade explodes on the ground not far away from me. The force of the blast knocks me over and I roll across the parking lot a few feet closer to the garbage can where Joshua still sits. I can feel the cuts in my skin, the tears in my ruined jeans. I can already feel my skin healing itself as I open my eyes to look around.

The bomb fell next to a gas pump and fires are starting to spread. Chunks of concrete are all over the ground around me, with dirt and debris as well. I push myself up with my hands and get to my knees. I look to the hole in the ground and see the body parts scattered around. An arm here and a leg over there. Bits of clothing fly through the air, floating to the ground. That took care of the two zombies, but I have no idea if it killed anyone else in the process. I look around for Ryder and Jason, but the smoke is too dense for me to see anything.

I pull myself to my feet and look to Joshua. Tears streak his filthy cheeks as he stares at me. I put a hand on his shoulder, checking to make sure he's okay. He's got a cut on his forearm from a small piece of concrete flying through the air and hitting him as his arms covered his head. I glance to the van and the others. This isn't safe for any of them to be here anymore. They've risked their lives too many times for me and they all need to leave. I can't take losing anybody else. I grab Joshua's hand and pull him to his feet. We quickly walk to the van and I see to it that he gets inside safely.

"You guys need to get out of here." I say to George and the others.

He shakes his head and says, "No, we can't leave without you."

"Don't worry about me. You have to get out of here, find the city, and be safe. Take care of Joshua and make sure he lives a long, happy life. I'll be fine." I say, then turn away from the van.

I don't give them the opportunity to protest and I can hear Adam's voice telling George to listen to me. Not a single one of them wants to listen. Keeping the cure out of the hands of a very bad man is what they think is right, which it is. It's just more important to me for them to survive and make it to the city. They can tell the people in charge what's going on and, maybe, I'll have a decent chance of someone coming to my rescue if things go badly today.

"Bridget?" Jason's voice calls to me and I can see him pulling himself to his knees not far ahead of me.

"I'm alright." I say.

I move closer, stepping over objects as I walk. I don't see Ryder. I don't hear him moving or smell his blood at all. The concrete is black as I get closer to where the grenade exploded. My ears are working to the max and I can hear the footsteps of dozens of humans. They aren't labored or forced. There are no moans coming from these people. Just their harsh footsteps and the metal of their guns clanking as they walk. I turn back to the van. Adam has the back door open a bit.

"Get the hell out of here!" I shout to them.

George leans over Adam and slams the door shut. Annah is behind the wheel and I see the reverse lights as she backs away from the building and drives away.

"Ryder?" I call, hoping to get an answer.

There's nothing. The only sound is the ever growing presence of the human threat coming at us. I can't find him. He must have been too close to the blast and got in the way. Those must be *his* body parts scattered in the parking lot. I shake that thought out of my head and move a little faster. Jason is searching the ground as well, aiding in my attempt at finding the one person I care most about.

I step over a large piece of concrete and the smoke clears a little more. I squint my eyes, keeping my gaze close to the ground. Dirt and fire are spread all over the place. The footsteps are only getting louder and I know it won't be long before they have me in their grasp.

I keep searching. I have to find him.

"Ryder!" I shout at the top of my lungs.

He still doesn't answer. I walk away from the blast zone and step around another gas pump. I see a pair of feet pointing up at the sky. I scream his name as I rush to his side. His eyes are closed and the left half of his face is burned and blackened with smoke. Blood seeps from a wound on his head and there's a piece of metal lying on the ground beside him. I put my hand on his chest, feeling for a pulse. I press down harder, grabbing his hand and squeezing it tight.

"Ryder, wake up." I order.

There's a scuffle going on behind me. I hear a struggle between Jason and one of Trevor's men. I take one quick second to turn my head. Two big guys are ganging up on Jason. One has him in a headlock while the other slams his fist against Jason's stomach. A few of Trevor's men spot me and I turn my eyes back to Ryder. My hand stays pressed against his chest, begging the heartbeat to reach it. The sadness is starting to take over my mind as I stare at his seemingly lifeless face. A small trace of blood is under his nose and his cheeks are stained black from the smoke. There are footsteps moving closer to me and harsh voices fill my ears. I keep Ryder's hand in mine and beg him to wake up. I need him to twitch or blink his eyes or just do *something* to let me know he's still alive. Not knowing is the worst part of this.

Two of Trevor's men are right on top of me. I refuse to move away from Ryder. I know I should stand up and fight my way out of this. Rage should be consuming me right now. The monster should be coming out to play and rip into these guys with everything I've got. Sadness is the one human part of me that's left and it's holding me down. It's keeping me from doing anything.

They grab my arms and pull me away from Ryder. I struggle as his hand falls out of mine. I kick at them and elbow one in the gut. That only gets him to clamp his hands down on my arm even tighter. I can't get away from these goons. My mind is so wrapped up in the fact that Ryder is lying on

the ground in front of me and he could very well be gone forever. I could be staring at him right now and remember this
look on his face as the last memory I have of him. Just like
my father, this could be my last image of the one I love.

The two men, each with a tight grasp on my arm, force
me away from the scene. I dig my heels into the ground,
trying to get them to stop. I guess the small amount of blood I
got from that zombie girl isn't enough to give me the strength
I need right now. Trevor walks around the guys and stands
right in front of me. The most devilish smile is plastered on
his face and he knows he won this round.

"You should've joined me when you had the chance.
You don't know the kind of hell you're in for now." He says,
the reaches his right hand to my face, "Let's see those deadly
eyes of yours."

The sun is blinding, even for the short second it catches
my eyes. They burn like fire and I squeeze them shut as tight
as I can. There's no stopping these guys from dragging me
away now. I can't see to defend myself and I'd look like a
fool if I tried. Still, I struggle against their grip. I want to get
away only so I can be by Ryder's side one last time. He's
lying on the ground, not moving. I couldn't feel a heartbeat
and couldn't see his chest moving up and down for air. I have
no idea if he's alive or if I just lost the last person I truly care
about.

Acknowledgements:

I would like to thank my family for always being there to encourage my writing. My niece, Annah, for volunteering to be on the cover of The Fighting Chance and for pushing me to get it finished. I thank my friends for making sure I never give up with things. A special thanks to my husband, Brad, for always listening to my crazy ideas for my books and never allowing me to give up. Lastly, I thank my fans for all the amazing reviews my work receives.

About The Author

Born in 1988, Tahnee Fritz is the youngest of four and grew up in the small city of Burlington, IA where she still resides her husband. She studied creative writing and English before graduating from Southeastern Community College with her Associates degree. *The Human Race*: book one of the trilogy, and *Crazy For Love* are among her works of fiction.

www.trfritz88.wordpress.com

www.ingramcontent.com/pod-product-compliance
Lightning Source LLC
Chambersburg PA
CBHW071125170626
46809CB00002B/499